THE
LIE
OF
YOU

Jane Lythell worked as a television
producer and commissioning editor
before becoming Deputy Director of
the BFI and Chief Executive of BAFTA.
She then worked at the Foreign and
Commonwealth Office before deciding
to write full time.

You can follow Jane on Twitter
@janelythell

'A very credible portrait of obsession to the point of madness... a clever, involving first novel.'
Literary Review

'Fascinating... clever... the author's real skill is her ability to invent memorable original characters. A thrilling read.' Daily Mail

'Pumps up suspense like Gillian Flynn's *Gone Girl*... delivered in a sharp, pragmatic style that is gripping and readable, but behind the adventure the plot hints at bigger, more complex questions about our society.' Scotsman

'A clever psychological thriller... Lythell has a flair for leading the reader into assumptions then pulling away the foundations.' Daily Express

'Great writing and interesting female characters make this an entertaining thriller about rivalry, will and desperation.' Diva

'Secrets, lies and assumptions all blend together to create page-turning momentum.'
We Love This Book

'Brilliantly intense and compelling, exciting and unputdownable!' Victoria Loves Books

THE
LIE

JANE LYTHELL

OF
YOU

HEAD
of ZEUS

First published in the UK in 2013 by Head of Zeus Ltd
This paperback edition published in the UK in 2014
by Head of Zeus Ltd

9 7 5 3 1 2 4 6 8

A CIP catalogue record for this book is available from
the British Library.

ISBN (PB) 9781781855300
ISBN (E) 9781781855270

Typeset by Palimpsest Book Production Limited,
Falkirk, Stirlingshire

Printed and bound by CPI Group (UK) Ltd,
Croydon, CR0 4YY

Head of Zeus Ltd
Clerkenwell House
45–47 Clerkenwell Green
London EC1R 0HT
WWW.HEADOFZEUS.COM

To my heroic mum Margaret Lythell Clarke

HEJA

APRIL

Kathy thinks she has everything: the job; the baby; the friends and him. But she does not have my will. It is all on the surface with her. She has no hidden places. She does not know about her dark side, or about others'. She always believes the best of people.

When I heard that she had got the promotion to editor I called her at home and asked to see her. I said that I needed to discuss my position with her. She was about to agree to meet me. At the last minute she changed her mind.

'Let's meet for lunch in my first week back, OK, Heja? I really need to be at home these last few days.'

Ever since I told her in my interview that my name was pronounced hay-ah, with a soft J, she has tended to overuse it in her speech. It irritates me. I pressed her, saying that it was important that we meet as soon as possible. That offers were being made to me. That if she valued my contribution to the magazine . . .

She struggled. She finds it hard to say no to people. The baby started to whimper and this fortified her.

'I'm sorry, Heja, it really will have to wait till I get back. I must go now. See you soon and thanks for calling.'

On her first day back at work she was wearing an orange silk shirt and a grey pencil skirt with expensive two-tone shoes, black with tan. The skirt was a bit tight over her stomach and her breasts were full. She hasn't completely shed her baby weight. She has thick wavy dark hair and strong dark eyebrows. The team members, Laura, Karen, Tim and Stephanie, all clustered around her. They said how pleased they were that she was back; how well she looked. She is not beautiful. She is not even typically pretty. Her skin is good. It has a glow to it and her eyes are quite fine, almond shaped and hazel. Her face is too full of expression and demands a response. It is wearing to look at her.

She spent that first morning with Philip Parr, the publisher of the magazine, in his large glass box of an office. In the afternoon she called a team meeting. There are six of us in the team, including her assistant Aisha. She explained how she wanted to take the magazine forward. She leaned forward in her chair and asked us all for our views. She believes in communication, you see, in management through praise and encouragement. The others all made comments. I said nothing. At no point did she call me aside and arrange our lunch.

On her second day back she stopped at my desk.

'Now, our lunch. Can you do Friday, Heja?' she said, all brightness and friendliness.

I said Wednesday would be better for me. She could not do Wednesday, so I agreed. I have not had any offers. And I do not plan to leave the magazine. This way I am able to see her every day.

KATHY

APRIL

At lunch today I sat across the table from Heja, savouring a great juicy mound of spaghetti vongole with guilty relish because it had so much garlic in it. I adore garlic but knew it would come through into my breast milk tonight. Heja had chosen grilled sea bream with fennel – the sort of dish you can eat without splattering spaghetti sauce everywhere. Just as well too, as she was dressed in an ice-blue linen shirt and a tailored cream jacket, groomed and immaculate as she always is. She wears her hair in this French plait, scraped back from her forehead, and it makes her look rather untouchable. She has lovely high cheekbones and her hair is ashy blonde and fine and if I were her I would have it cut very short and boyish. She could carry off a cut like that.

We discussed the current issue of the magazine in a desultory way. I knew she was building up to something because she'd asked for this meeting – in fact, she had pressed for it. She seemed rather distracted, though, and as I was talking to her she often rested her eyes over my right shoulder as if she wasn't that interested in what I was saying, and this was mildly disconcerting. Then my coffee arrived and I was thinking, That's good, she won't raise anything major now. Perhaps she had just wanted to reconnect after all these months. She was drinking green tea. I've noticed she's very health conscious, and she swallowed two capsules of evening primrose oil with her tea.

3

Then suddenly she launched into a speech about how I should make her my deputy. She talked in that stilted way she does, always perfect English, but a bit too perfect, so that you know it's a second language.

'While you were away I wrote articles for all the sections,' she said.

Now I was the one who was finding it hard to concentrate on Heja.

There was this couple at the next table who were having a nasty argument. The man had his arms crossed over his chest and he was staring furiously at his empty pudding plate, which was smeared with raspberry sauce. The woman was agitated and colour flooded up her neck and into her face as she twisted a napkin. I saw a waiter approach their table and then he hesitated and I thought he must be used to such scenes, so many unhappy couples. Heja was coming to an end.

'I *have* essentially been working as deputy editor while you were on maternity leave and I would like more responsibility.'

'You've been doing a great job, Heja, and I'm really grateful for all you've done. We're such a small team and the magazine just doesn't need a deputy editor, and Philip simply wouldn't agree.'

Why had I invoked Philip, the big boss, in this way? Why couldn't I have just said no to Heja in a kind but firm voice? She hadn't been at the magazine long and a promotion so soon was just not on.

The unhappy couple had turned their attention to paying their bill. He had thrown his credit card down contemptuously on the table and looked away and she was ostentatiously counting out notes and coins, leaving exactly half the amount of the bill, her face taut and ugly.

Heja leaned forward towards me now and she crackled

with a kind of pent-up energy. 'You have such demands on your time now, I thought you would welcome some extra support.'

I almost snapped at her then. 'That won't be a problem. We're a good team and we all know what we're doing.'

Yet my heart was beating fast as I called for the bill.

During the afternoon I felt slightly sick and anxious, probably prompted by Heja's comment. Why was I sitting in my glass-panelled office with piles of work on my desk, acting the editor? Why had I even gone for the promotion? I just wanted to get home to Billy and hold him close. As the day wore on it was as if the umbilical cord had never been cut and I was being tugged back to his sweet-smelling head and strong-sucking mouth. I was still breastfeeding every evening when I got back from work. I took out his photograph from my bag and looked at his dear little face and my breasts started to tighten and tingle. Then I put it on the side and pulled the production schedule over.

Karen, the production manager, came into my office and sat down at the meeting table. As I walked over to her I noticed she was looking up at me oddly.

Aisha, my assistant, came in at that moment and said, 'What have you spilled on yourself?'

I looked down. Two wet circles had formed on the front of my shirt. My breasts had leaked.

HEJA

APRIL

I have a dark green convertible with pale grey leather seats and I take great pleasure in it. It is one of the ways I have been kind to myself. She left work before me. As I walked towards my car I thought about how she was at our lunch. There had been something coarse about the way she had tucked into that pasta. She likes her food too much. If she is not careful she will run to fat in middle age. Her attention has also fragmented. She used to be more focused.

The car door is heavy but the engineering is so perfect that it glides open and allows me to slide into my seat. I lock the doors and turn on my CD player. I am working my way through every version of Rachmaninov's four piano concertos. I am seeking the perfect recording of each one. For the third it is Martha Argerich's tour de force in Berlin in 1982. She brings out the darkness as well as the wild ecstasy of Rachmaninov.

I drive home over Waterloo Bridge. I like to see the buildings at night with their lights reflected in the river. I admire the brutal bulk of Lasdun's National Theatre. The British are too timid about architecture and they criticized his achievement. They are wrong. His building will outlive its critics. Architecture is the most important thing in the world. We spend our lives in buildings. We are born in them. We grow in them. We make love in them. We work and think in them.

Usually we die in them. Buildings stand after we have died. Buildings can get sick, like us, but only if the architect has been stupid or lazy or greedy. Great buildings live long and noble lives.

My lover, Robert, is coming round this evening. The sex is good and it helps me to sleep. I never let him stay the night with me. He has accepted this as one of my quirks, which he is prepared to humour. Robert is highly sexed. I think he is quite turned on by the idea that he comes to my flat for sex and then has to leave. He never showers afterwards. He just dresses and goes. He told me he likes my smell on him when he gets back to his flat.

He is American and recently qualified as a psychoanalyst. I cannot imagine going to see him as a patient, though. His manner is too sincere. He likes to be liked and I cannot see him having the right level of aloofness to become a great analyst. He has come to analysis late. He tells me that age is an advantage in an analyst. It is a job you get better at as you get older. You can still practise when you are eighty, he said. He had no idea what pain it gave me when he said that. The skin on his face is pockmarked and his lips are fleshy. When you look at him your eyes are drawn to his large dark brown eyes, which are serious and thickly lashed, like a child's. He is always trying to draw me out. He does not do this in an obvious way. He rarely asks me a direct question.

Instead he will say, 'Just now when I mentioned my father's death you looked so sad.' He waits for me to fill the silence that is vibrating between us. He wants a revelation from me and I say nothing. Early in our relationship, frustrated by my reserve, he asked me if I had ever been in analysis.

'No. Why do you ask?'

'Because you have this way with you of listening, and I always think that you're reinterpreting what is being said.'

'We all do that. We filter everything, don't we?'

'It's usually people who have been in a long analysis who acquire a habit of interpretation, as though experience is a code to be cracked.'

'I was never in analysis,' I told him.

This was a lie. When my depression had become unbearable I had sought out the revered psychoanalyst Arvo Talvela. There was a two-year waiting list and no one could get access to him. I wrote to him in confidence, explaining my situation, and he agreed to see me at once. Celebrity has some benefits, it seems. He wrote back to me asking me to come to his consulting rooms in the centre of Helsinki. My early reaction to him was one of profound antagonism. At our first meeting he opened the door and gestured in a courtly manner for me to come into his room. His face was fierce and intelligent. His grey eyes scanned my face.

'Please take a seat, Heja.'

I looked around the room: the large, gracious windows; the books floor to ceiling; an expensive carpet; and the couch placed with a chair at its head.

'You are not going to make me lie on the couch, then?' I asked in a combative tone of voice.

'I let people decide for themselves when they feel ready to lie down,' he replied.

'I will never be ready to lie down!' I snapped at him.

I was now standing in the middle of his room and noticed this perfect blue glass vase that sat on his polished desk. He followed the direction of my eyes and he knew that I wanted to pick up that vase and smash it on the floor so that it would break into a hundred pieces. My rage consumed me.

We battled for months and gradually I fell in love with him. It was not transference; it was love.

Good Friday and Robert had bought us tickets for a performance of Bach's *St Matthew Passion* at St George's Church in Hanover Square. He picked me up at my flat and drove us to the church. We joined the queue. What a middle-class English crowd; they looked like civil servants, librarians and lawyers. We were among the youngest ones there. The doors were pushed open and Robert manoeuvred us to prime seats in a box pew in the gallery.

There were six chairs in each box pew. They did not look comfortable and I knew that the music would last for over three hours. The players were tuning their instruments and then the noise fell away as an elderly white-haired canon walked slowly towards the pulpit. The conductor walked just behind him.

The canon mounted his pulpit and asked us if we would please turn off any mobile phones and not to applaud, as this was both a service and a performance. He sat down in his pulpit and was almost dwarfed by its high, carved sides. He was wearing a heavily embroidered cope, gold on black. It was as if the weight of his robes was pressing down on him. The sun was pouring through the high arched windows of clear glass on either side. I enjoyed watching the shadows of the panes as they worked their way up the stone arches. The man who sang Christus was marvellous, he had a memorable voice. The soprano was a bit shrill, I thought.

After two hours there was an interval and I was grateful to stand up. We walked back to Robert's car and he produced smoked-salmon sandwiches, a half-bottle of champagne and two glasses. He opened the bottle and poured a glass for me.

'You think of everything,' I said. 'Thank you. Do you believe in any of this?'

'What do you mean?'

'The Resurrection, the salvation of souls, the afterlife.'

He chewed on a sandwich. 'No, I don't. I see religion as a check on human vanity.'

'Vanity . . .?'

'We can't understand everything and the absolute certainty of our individual death stops us from being lords of the universe.'

'You mean death as the great leveller . . .'

'The great humbler.'

'I can find no comfort in that,' I said.

'Has someone you loved died?' he asked. His voice was gentle but there was an inquisitive glint in his eyes.

'Only my great-aunt, many years ago.'

'Were you very close?'

'She was a special person, Tanya. She was a great singer. And I did love her.'

He nodded, waiting for more detail. I looked out of his car window.

'She used to sing this piece, she was famous for it. She said I had a good voice too and she would teach me songs. She was always so patient with me.'

'So she died quite young?'

'Yes, too young.'

The second half was longer than I had expected. The canon delivered his Good Friday sermon before the music could start again. I wondered at Robert liking this piece of music and wanting to come on this day. As a child I had been used to sitting through long musical performances. I had heard Tanya sing this oratorio so beautifully once. It was not something I would have expected Robert to like so much. Finally the last words of the *Passion* were sung.

And call to Thee, entombed in death:
Rest thou softly, softly rest.

The canon asked us all to stand and sing a hymn and then it was over. As we turned to leave the church I looped my arm over Robert's. He looked pleased at my gesture and we walked down the stone stairs and out into the early evening coolness.

KATHY

MAY

I've been back at work three weeks now and it's far more difficult than I imagined it would be. My tiredness goes down to my bones and it's as if the world is wrapped in this layer of something soft and fuzzy that cuts me off and I have to work very hard to penetrate the layer. I was reading an article about a high-powered woman in New York who was back at her desk two weeks after the birth of her first child, kicking ass and delivering targets, and I thought how was it possible to do that?

So why did I go for the promotion to editor? Because the magazine is Britain's most prestigious architectural magazine, and because Philip Parr called me at home and said it was as good as mine if I wanted it. He had the old Kathy in mind, I'm sure. I also thought, This is what I've wanted for years and I'd regret it if I didn't take the opportunity. I hadn't reckoned on how exhausting it was to work at full throttle when you have a small baby.

I got through the day at the office. This evening, after Billy was asleep, I was languishing over the soup and salad and Markus said, 'Go to bed, you look worn out. I'll clear up here.'

I stretched out between the sheets of our large bed hugely grateful at the prospect of unconsciousness and must have slept for five and a half hours, which is the longest stretch of uninterrupted sleep I've had for months. I don't know why

I woke up. Markus was lying with his back to me, deeply asleep, and I put my hand over his stomach, which is deliciously soft and hairy on top and firm underneath. He stirred and slept on. I looked at the digital clock: 02.57. I got out of bed and went to check on Billy. We moved him into his own room last weekend and I'm still a bit anxious about it. It's a lovely room, though, one of the lightest in the flat.

We live in this 1930s mansion block off Baker Street. It's an old-fashioned place with a long central corridor and odd angles in the rooms, and although the ceilings are high it is rather a dark flat, some people might even describe it as gloomy. It will never match up to an architect's ideal of modern, bright living. My Aunt Jennie, my dad's sister, lived here for twenty years and when she retired to Cornwall she signed the lease and most of her furniture over to me. She helped me so much by doing that; you could say that she put my life back on track. I needed somewhere to live. It was just after Eddie and I had had our last, hopeless reunion, when he tried to stop drinking again. It ended badly, as it always did, and I needed to get away from him. In spite of the flat's faults I love it because it feels so safe and solid and no sound comes through these substantial walls from the streets below.

Billy had rolled onto his back with his arms outstretched and his sleep blissful. He has the most adorable peachy fat cheeks and I wanted to pick him up and cover him with kisses. When he was born I was filled with this healing love that made me feel I could have a good life after all. When they put him into my arms all my fears that I might not be able to cope with a baby just melted away.

I met Markus at an architectural conference in Newcastle. We were in the same break-out group and were discussing the role of regeneration. Markus was so articulate and emphatic in his views on everything. It was obvious he didn't like the man who was chairing our group, who was the well-known architect behind the successful regeneration of London's East End. This man had made a fortune from the regeneration and he and Markus got into this argument about the social responsibility of architects.

Markus said it was the role of the architect to make living in cities and towns better for the majority of the people, not just the wealthy. We should never create ghettoes of the rich and ghettoes of the poor; communities should always be mixed. I could see that Markus was winning the argument and asserting himself over the rest of the group. Then I was asked by the chair to do the report-back. He'd seen me scribbling away on my pad while the two of them had argued. We all shuffled out then to get coffee, except for Markus who stayed behind in the room, writing something. Fifteen minutes later he came up to me and handed me a sheet of paper with all his arguments listed in perfect logical order.

'For your report-back,' he said, his first direct words to me.

He had a physical presence about him that you couldn't ignore with his handsome, broad face, long, ice-blue eyes and narrow, straight nose. His notes were a test, I think, which I must have passed because at the end of the conference he came up to me and said, 'Can I call you when I get back to London?'

On our first date he took me to The Widow's Son pub in Bow in East London. It was a large, noisy, cheerful place close to where he lived. We sat in a corner by the window and Markus pointed over to the bar.

'Look up there,' he said. 'See all those hot-cross buns?'

14

I looked up and hanging from the rafters above the bar was a collection of hot-cross buns at various stages of age and decay. Some were large and glossy, others small and blackened with age, and there must have been well over a hundred buns hanging there.

'Every year they add another hot-cross bun to that collection,' he said.

'How strange . . .'

'It's a tradition. The first owner of this pub was a poor widow with an only son. He was a sailor and was expected home at Easter, so she kept one of her hot-cross buns for him. But he didn't turn up. She waited and waited, and he never came back from his voyage. She couldn't accept that he was drowned, so every year she baked her buns and put one aside for him. And the collection grew. As long as she kept the buns for him she thought that one day he might come home.'

'That's such a touching story.'

'It is. When she died they found the buns hanging from that beam and they've kept the tradition going. Every Good Friday a sailor comes to the pub and adds a hot-cross bun to the collection.'

'Wouldn't the buns smell? I mean, as they got old and mouldy.'

'Strangely enough, they don't,' he said. 'Something in the spice mixture made them turn brown but not mouldy.'

On our second date he took me on a tour of his favourite buildings in the East End. He liked industrial buildings, those with a clear function: warehouses; printing works; grain stores. Most of these stood by the river and had been turned into expensive riverside flats for city workers. He enjoyed looking at the Victorian brickwork and the original tiles and the elaborate chimneys and he pointed these out to me.

We ended up in another pub after three hours of walking and talking and I was so attracted by his heartfelt enthusiasm for the buildings. I also thought how sexy he looked in his black leather jacket and jeans. We sat next to each other on the banquette in the pub and our thighs touched. You know that moment when you make physical contact for the first time with someone you are attracted to – shy, embarrassed, awkward, happy. The evening slipped away.

Markus seemed to spend a lot of time on his own, working in his stark, barely furnished flat or going for walks along the canal towpath near where he lived. He had grown up in Helsinki and didn't have many friends in London and I think I brought some warmth and colour into his life. He made me feel safe at last after the chaotic ups and downs of my years with Eddie and we started to see each other regularly.

Six months after that first meeting in Newcastle I discovered that I was pregnant. This was entirely unplanned and came as a shock to me. Markus was also stunned by the news of my pregnancy, so much so, in fact, that I did a second pregnancy test at my flat. He arrived on that Saturday morning unshaven, looking like he'd had a bad night. I had bought a more complicated pregnancy test from the chemist, just to be sure. I set the apparatus up in the bathroom and made coffee for us while we waited for the result. After ten minutes I called him through and showed him the tell-tale dark red circle in the bottom of the test-tube. It's always quite chilly in the bathroom. Was that why he shivered as he looked at the result of the test?

'What happens now?' he said finally.

'We need to give ourselves time to think about it. It's come as a shock to us both.'

'You must know what you think, Kathy.'

'I guess I feel relieved that I *can* get pregnant and a bit scared that I *am* pregnant. How do you feel?'

'Overwhelmed, I hadn't expected this to happen.'

We walked back into the kitchen and sat at the kitchen table. I felt obscurely guilty.

'Would you like some more coffee?'

'Yes, please.'

My kitchen is a comforting kind of place. I felt I wanted to sit there all day at my aunt's much-scrubbed and scratched wooden table. I got up and rinsed the coffeepot and then Markus was standing right behind me.

'I'll make it,' he said.

'God, I don't need pampering yet!'

'I just want to make it a bit stronger than the last lot.'

He frowned at the packet of supermarket ground coffee and then spooned a lot of it into the funnel and pressed it down hard.

'So you have decided you want the baby?' he said quietly.

'Why do you say that?' I asked.

'Your remark just now, about being pampered . . .'

'Oh.'

After he'd gone the next morning I walked slowly around the flat and looked into each room with new eyes. It was strange how things worked out. This flat had been my refuge, my safe port in a storm, and now I could see that it would be a good home for a baby too, this solid, roomy, old-fashioned flat. I found that I did want the baby. I didn't want to tell my parents or my friends just yet; I needed to nurse the idea quietly and peacefully for a few weeks while I absorbed what it would mean.

Markus has a strong puritanical streak and he hates waste and conspicuous consumption. In fact, good coffee is one of the few luxuries he allows himself. A few months after we decided to have the baby he moved in with me and I noticed how little he brought with him. He must have lived like a monk in his East End flat. He has an ancient Saab, a good drawing table and a plan chest, boxes and boxes of books, some diving gear and a few very fine, much-washed shirts.

We were happy together during the months of my pregnancy. We rarely went out in the evenings. Markus was working on a project and said we needed to be quiet, and I welcomed this new found domesticity. Eddie would always get claustrophobic if we stayed in two nights in a row. He would talk me into going to his local where his friends would be gathered and where he had a willing audience to listen to his funny stories. Too many nights we had rolled back late and drunk to our flat. Now my life had changed so much. I had given up alcohol during the pregnancy and I got into cooking healthy meals for us and I felt content.

When I was five months pregnant Markus and I spent a long weekend at Portland in Dorset. I think this was our happiest weekend together, even though it is a rather bleak and windswept place. I've noticed that Markus likes these stark coastal landscapes – Portland Bill, Spurn Point, Selsey Bill. He dislikes anything chocolate box or picturesque. So he has taken me, the native, to places all over England that I would never have thought to visit. We were staying in a bed and breakfast in the village of Southwell, and on the first day we walked the coastal path to Portland Bill. It was a glorious June morning with a soft breeze and I felt healthy and hopeful; my pregnancy was going well. As we set off through the village we passed a sweet shop, which had row upon row of those old-style confectionery jars filled with loose sweets.

'Let's go in here,' I said.

I pointed out my favourites to him.

'They look disgusting,' he said.

'They taste of nail-varnish remover. And I'm craving some right now.'

He laughed and asked the woman in the shop for some pear-drops, which she measured out and put into a small paper bag.

'Tell your wife she'll have an easy time giving birth,' she said to him.

'Really?'

'I was a midwife before and your wife has big feet, always a sign of an easy delivery.'

'Thank you.'

We were giggling about her remark as we followed the coastal path towards the main lighthouse, a resplendent white tower with a large red stripe around its middle. The landscape was striking with great ledges of limestone, which are softened in the summer by the grasses and the sea-pinks. There was barely a tree in sight. We sat down on the grass and I sucked contentedly on my pear-drops.

'I love it here,' he said.

'It looks wonderful today in the sun but it would be awfully bleak in the winter. There are no trees!'

'That's what I love about it; just sea and sky and not much evidence of man, except for the quarries.'

He pointed out Pulpit Rock to me.

'That was created by quarrying. And there are steps cut into it so you can climb to the top. The local kids jump off that into the sea.'

'It's a long way to jump! How did you find this place?'

'Through my diving club; there are some good dives here, around the sea caves. We can walk over and look at them in a bit if you feel up to it.'

'I feel great.'

He helped me up and we walked east to look at the caves in the cliffs. Markus was holding on to my arm in a protective way as the ground was a bit uneven and then we reached the cliffs and there were these huge, echoing caverns. There were large piles of seaweed that had collected in the gullies and they gave off a distinctive rotting, salty smell. We sat down again outside the caves and Markus threw pebbles into the sea. He looked as happy as I had seen him.

'One day I want to build a house by the sea,' he said.

That night I told him that my big feet were obviously a mixed blessing and we laughed as we hugged, curled up in the lumpy B & B bed, my bump against his stomach, my big feet keeping warm against his.

The next morning I woke up at six-thirty to see Markus standing naked by the window of our room, which had a sea view. I lay in bed gazing at him, feeling languorous and happy and admiring his broad shoulders and shapely bottom. He was looking out of the window with the kind of intensity that you see in children, as if caught up in the wonder of the moment. I wanted to make love again, as we had the night before. He turned round then and saw me watching him.

'I didn't mean to wake you.'

'You didn't.'

I patted the bed and he sat down next to me and pulled back the covers and started to stroke my bump gently.

'You should sleep a bit more. I think I'll go out for an early morning walk.'

'I was admiring your bum!'

He laughed.

'I bet you have loads of women admirers.'

He bent down and kissed me lightly.

'I'm a one-woman man. Now rest and I'll be back for breakfast.'

As he dressed quickly I mused that even then, when we were at our most happy and relaxed, he did not want to talk about his past, about any attachments he had had. And I already knew that it was best not to push it with Markus.

Later, over a big fried breakfast, I took the plunge and suggested he move in with me, and he agreed.

The woman in the sweet shop was wrong. My labour lasted thirty-six hours because my contractions were ineffectual. Eventually, after many hours, the doctor injected me with something to speed up the birth as the baby was getting distressed. Billy's head was large and I tore badly as he came out and needed many stitches. And childbirth has changed me, more than I would have thought possible. Before Billy came I was very focused on my work and ambitious too. I was determined to become an editor, perhaps one day even to launch my own magazine. And then I split open with Billy and I lost something. Yes, I lost my dedication to getting on and gained the secret sensual world of my beloved boy.

Billy was born in October. On New Year's Eve Markus was keen that we should go and watch the fireworks that would welcome in the year. Billy was only three months old and I was so tired I wondered if I would be able to stay awake until midnight. Markus said it was important that we share this moment together – our first New Year as a family. I bundled Billy up in a woolly hat and fleece jumpsuit and Markus strapped on the baby sling and we put him into it. We went to wait for a bus to take us to Clerkenwell. There was to be a big firework display there, near where he worked.

While we were waiting for our bus at Baker Street an old man standing in the queue in front of us dropped his shopping bag. There was a crack of something breaking and the contents rolled out of the bag. I knelt down and started to pick up his groceries for him. Among them was a half-bottle of whisky and this had smashed when the bag hit the pavement. The old man was tearful when he saw that his bottle of whisky had broken. This was probably his treat for that special night. I salvaged the rest of his shopping for him and put the broken glass into a bin, wrapped in paper.

Markus was watching all this and he saw the old man's evident distress. He took out a twenty-pound note discreetly and handed it to the old man, saying quietly, 'Please, have a New Year's Eve drink on me.'

The old man looked so pleased and he thanked Markus warmly as our bus arrived. We went up to the top of the bus and I sat next to Markus and Billy and was happy he had done that because it was a kind thing to do. Sometimes I had to remind myself that I was building a life with this gorgeous man. I felt blessed; I felt I had so much.

HEJA

MAY

At lunchtime I sometimes drive to the street and sit outside the block where she lives. My colleagues make a big thing of going out to lunch together. They are a close-knit group. I do not like to go with them. They go to a pub on the corner of Primrose Hill, or to a café, which is hot and noisy. When I first joined the magazine Stephanie would invite me to come along. Now they know that I prefer to be on my own at lunchtime.

It takes me less than ten minutes to get to her flat from work. The block she lives in is near Baker Street and it is red brick, four storeys high and well kept. The flats look solid, safe and comfortable, a bit dull. The street is quiet in the middle of the day. There is a private dental practice there and I see people coming and going to their appointments. Sometimes there is a delivery van from Harrods or John Lewis. It took me a while to establish who their childminder was. After watching the building for several weeks I now know who she is. She is a young woman, in her early twenties, I would think. On one or two occasions I have seen her come out of the block with Billy in his buggy. She must take him for a walk somewhere. Or maybe she goes shopping.

Today I had only been sitting in my car for a few minutes when I saw her coming out of the block with Billy. I decided to follow her. I got out of my car and put money in the meter.

I walked behind her. She stopped to put her shoulder bag into the tray under the buggy. She is quite short and big-breasted. She was wearing tight jeans that emphasized her round buttocks, white trainers and a bright blue top with white buttons down its side. She crossed the Marylebone Road and waited on the traffic island in the middle. I caught up with her there. The cars were three deep and the air was heavy with pollution. A rubbish truck drove by, emitting a sour smell from its back. I saw how it brushed against a cherry-blossom tree and unloosed a fall of washed-out petals.

She bent over the buggy. 'Ooh, look at that big truck, Billy.'

Leaving the main road, she headed up a side road away from the shops. Perhaps there was a park around there? I stayed a few feet behind her, keeping quite close. She walked on past a grimy, unloved-looking church. I saw that she was turning into a large housing estate with four tower blocks grouped around a central square. The tower blocks were about ten storeys high and badly maintained. They had balconies on their inner sides looking onto a central patch of dried-up grass. Washing was strung along lines on some of the balconies. On every level black and white satellite dishes were screwed to the walls and pointed skywards. A dog sniffed around the outer perimeter of the square then lifted his leg to urinate.

This was her destination? What could she be doing here? She pushed the buggy confidently into the estate, under some concrete walkways, covered in graffiti, and over to a shabby little play area beyond the square of grass. Here there were two swings, a battered see-saw and a metal bench against the railings. No one else was there. I did not follow her into the play area, as it would have been too obvious. What would I be doing in such a place? So I walked into the estate as far as the walkway and watched her from the shadows. She settled herself on the bench and took her bag out. Then she adjusted the buggy so that it leant back more and arranged a shade over Billy's face. He had fallen asleep.

She sat there for a few minutes, looking around. Then I saw a young man approach her. He must have come out of one of the flats. She stood up and they kissed. He put his hands on her bottom and gave it a squeeze. She pulled away, giggling. Then he sat down next to her. She offered him a cigarette, which he took. He was dark haired, unshaven and had olive skin. He looked as if he had just woken up. I thought he might be Greek Cypriot. They smoked and talked in a desultory way.

So this was how Kathy's childminder spent her days – on trysts with her unemployed boyfriend. I wondered if Kathy knew that Billy was being brought to this estate for his daily walk. Almost certainly not; she would be the over-protective type. There would be all kinds of rules about no smoking in the flat or near the baby; instructions about his diet and sleeping regime. How trusting she was. How little she knew.

It was time to go. I walked back to my car and drove to the office. As I parked in the office car park I saw Philip Parr getting out of his big, flashy Mercedes. He walked over to me and did that thing of looking me up and down, which he always does.

'Hi. How's it going, Heja?'

'Good, thank you. And you?'

'I just went to a press launch at RIBA. They're launching a new website of all the civic buildings of Britain. The photographs were so dull.'

'Who did them?'

'They're getting enthusiasts all over the country to record their local buildings. I think they've been given some kind of style guide because they all looked the same: dreary.'

He pushed the office doors open for me and we walked up the stairs together.

'I guess we'll have to give the website some coverage, however second-rate the material. Need to keep RIBA happy! I'll speak to Kathy.'

At the top of the stairs we parted. I went to my desk and he walked over to Kathy's office. She was standing next to Aisha and I saw that she had seen us walk in together. I have noticed that Philip makes her nervous. She pulled herself up as he approached her and they both went into her room.

Stephanie looked at me as I sat down.

'Lunch with the big boss?' she asked, her curiosity getting the better of her.

'No,' I said. 'Not today.'

That should keep them guessing.

KATHY

MAY

Most mornings I walk to work through Regent's Park. Markus drives me to Great Portland Street and then he heads east to Clerkenwell. I enter the park at the south end and love the formality of this part of it with its unfolding vista of fountains and flowerbeds. It's a serene oasis in the middle of London. From the formal gardens you cross the road onto the Broad Walk with the zoo on the left. Some days you hear these strange, demented squawks coming from the birdhouse.

Our offices are in Primrose Hill and the whole walk takes me less than thirty minutes. Today there was an unseasonal wind stirring the trees into a frenzy. I had no jacket with me and was walking fast to keep warm. A man with a pug dog and a golden Labrador was walking in front of me. The Labrador was pure noble dog, all fine head and loping walk. The pug, in contrast, was comical and looked as if he was hopping along the path, his short legs working very hard with never more than two feet on the ground at the same time. He made me smile. I suppose some of us are lucky to be born Labradors and some of us have to be pugs and make more of an effort to keep up.

Halfway down the Broad Walk I felt a sensation of definite wetness between my legs. I stopped at one of the benches and sat down, looked down, surreptitiously opening my thighs, and to my horror saw a spreading circle of watery

27

red staining my pale yellow trousers. I'm still breastfeeding Billy so my periods hadn't come back – until today. The trousers were fine cotton and absorbent and I could imagine the blood seeping up at the back. I didn't know what to do.

Either I had to run back to the ladies toilet in the park or carry on to work as fast as I could and sort it out there. I decided to carry on, trying to hold my bag in front of me to hide the stain. In fact, my bag is bright red leather, so it seemed like it was a bit of a beacon and I felt embarrassed and ashamed of my poor leaking body. There was the usual contingent of dog-walkers in the park shouting confident greetings to each other and I imagined their eyes boring into my back as a great red stain spread across my bottom. The last few yards to the office seemed much further away than usual.

I reached the glass doors of our building, rushed past the receptionist, up the stairs and straight into the Ladies. I put on a towel from the machine. There was no one in there so I took my trousers off and tried to sponge the blood out with cold water. This just seemed to make it spread further and the trousers were wet now as well as stained. I was close to weeping as I felt like a child again, confronted by an adult world that was too much for me to master. I wanted to stay locked in the toilet cubicle, hiding from my team.

Finally I got a grip of myself, came out and headed for my office fast. I saw that Aisha was wearing a long black cardigan. I asked her if I could borrow it and I felt better the moment I had it on. I was an adult again. I decided to go up the hill to Hampstead to buy a new pair of trousers and then I would drop in at my gym for a shower and change. Aisha and I had to reschedule the whole morning of meetings.

I tried to tell Markus about it this evening. We were sitting at the kitchen table and I was making stuffed red peppers for dinner. I was pulling out the pithy white skin and chasing that last tenacious seed that always gets caught under the dome of the pepper.

'I don't understand why you got into such a state,' he said.

I put the red pepper down on the cutting board and tried to explain why it had made me feel so uncomfortable.

'It was a bit like the shame a child feels when they wet their knickers at school. You know, you've drawn attention to a private bodily function.'

'Even if someone had noticed, all they would think is that you'd had an unexpected period.'

'Can't you see that it was embarrassing?'

What did I want from him? Empathy, I suppose. He has extraordinary eyes, long and narrow and slightly tilted up at the edges, and the clearest, iciest blue, like arctic waters. He was sharpening the kitchen knives on the sharpening rod, moving the blade back and forth with grace and precision. He always looked as if he was in control of his environment and I admired his expertise as he sharpened the knives. I started to peel and crush some cloves of garlic.

'Someone told me today that Heja in my team used to be one of Finland's top news presenters. Heja Vanheinen. Have you heard of her?' I asked.

He tested the sharpness of the blade against his thumb. 'Yes, she was the anchor for the main channel.'

'You never said. Why on earth would she give that up? I mean, something like that to work on the magazine?'

He shrugged, absorbed with the knife's blade. 'Helsinki is a small city, it doesn't satisfy everyone.'

'She just doesn't strike me as someone who would be a television presenter, though. She's a bit too much of an ice queen for British TV.'

'She was much admired in Finland,' he said.

I'd peeled far too much garlic and would have to throw some of it away.

'So it's odd she left that job. I don't get it, do you?'

He opened the kitchen drawer and put the sharpening rod and the knives away, each in its allotted place.

And then he said rather coldly, 'Why should you care?'

I felt rebuked by him and was instantly defensive. 'Why shouldn't I be interested? I work with her every day.'

Something has changed with Markus since I went back to work. We aren't easy with each other as we were during my pregnancy and I wonder if he thinks I should have stayed at home with Billy. We talked about it and I felt sure he supported me going back to work. He's become more withdrawn these days and our silences are getting longer and more difficult to bridge. We don't giggle together any more. So I chatter on in my nervousness to try to fill the silences and I know this irritates him even more. And he has created taboos around certain subjects. He will never talk about his life in Finland and I know very little about how he spent the first thirty-six years of his life. I wish he would tell me more but I can't push it. I think there must have been a major rift with his family as none of them came to our wedding.

Why did we marry? I did not expect it and, in fact, it was Markus who said that for the baby's sake we should marry before the birth. He said that in order to be free you needed to know which of society's rules you could break and which rules you had better observe. Hardly a romantic reason to get married. We had this low-key registry office affair, which upset my mum, who would have liked us to marry in a Catholic church with the full service. There no way

Markus would have agreed to that. I was heavily pregnant at the time and only close friends and family were invited.

My parents came over from Lisbon and my aunt Jennie was there and I was sure someone would come from his side, one of his brothers if not his parents. His only guest was his partner from the diving club, someone he has met since moving to London. Did he even tell his parents in Helsinki that he was getting married? There has never been any word from them, not even a card. When I asked him about it he was cagey and changed the subject.

We hardly spoke over dinner that night. The stuffed peppers were OK, but it was not one of my best dishes and tears were pricking behind my eyes after his earlier rebuff. I knew I was being over-sensitive. It had been a difficult day and he'd made me feel foolish. I wanted to tell him that Billy had pulled himself up into a standing position just before dinner. Now I couldn't bring myself to talk about it. His face had its familiar closed-off look.

Straight after dinner Markus went into his workroom. It used to be Aunt Jennie's dining room. She never used it much and when Markus moved in with me he made it his own. He took out all the old furniture, ripped out the ancient carpet and sanded the floor. He painted the walls white. Then he built new shelves for his books and installed his drawing table and plan chest. He has hundreds of books and each one is lined up exactly at the front edge of the shelf in the most precise way. He has turned it into a very attractive if rather minimalist workroom. There's his brown leather armchair by the door and I sometimes sit there and read while he works.

Tonight he was sitting as usual on his high stool in the arc of light thrown by the lamp onto the sloping plane of his drawing table. I joined him in there after Billy was asleep because I do love to watch him draw. He is such a perfectionist in his work. I've learned not to talk to him while he works. So I sat there correcting proofs, looking up from time to time to watch and admire him. His concentration is so intense that he creates a kind of force field around him that cannot be crossed.

HEJA

MAY

Kathy is a creature of habit. Every day she arrives at work with a small polystyrene cup of cappuccino. She carries a soft red leather pouch bag worn across her body. I have watched her take out her office keys. The bag has zipped pockets on either side and she keeps all her keys in the left pocket. As soon as she has unlocked her glass-panelled office she lifts her bag over her head and places it on the lower bookshelf at the side of her desk. Then she comes out with her coffee and talks to Aisha, who sits outside her office. They consult the diary and then, usually, Kathy walks over to our section. We are herded together in a group of five desks with our terminals emitting faint radiation over our breasts. She is always friendly in the mornings, chirpy I think is the right word. She asks us how we are getting on and makes encouraging comments.

The more I watch her the more I learn.

Today something had happened to throw her routine. As she came up the stairs she did not have her little white cup with her. She rushed into the ladies toilet. She came out some minutes later. Her trousers were wet and stained. It looked as if she had bled onto them. She walked awkwardly to her office and fumbled to open the door. I walked over to get a better view. I saw Aisha go through to her and close the door behind her. They had an animated conversation for a minute or two, Kathy gesticulating. Then Aisha took off her

33

long black cardigan and gave it to Kathy. She put it on and buttoned it up carefully. She rummaged through her bag, pulled out her wallet and then dropped the bag in its usual place by the side of her desk.

I was walking back to my desk as I heard her say to Aisha, 'I'll be as quick as I can. Thanks so much, Aish.'

She hurried down the stairs to the exit with barely a nod in our direction.

I knew this was my chance. I walked up to Aisha's desk, waiting until she was on the phone.

'I need to borrow the *Who's Who.*'

'Sure,' said Aisha, putting her hand over the receiver. 'You know where Kathy keeps it?'

I nodded. The *Who's Who* sits with the other reference books in the bookshelves by the side of her desk. I walked over slowly and bent down to pick up the book. My back shielded my hands from Aisha's view. As I bent down I reached over to her red bag, unzipped the left pocket, took out the keys, zipped it up again, stood up and slipped her bunch of keys into my jacket pocket. I walked out of her office holding the *Who's Who.* Aisha was still talking on the phone.

I had very little time. I flipped through the *Who's Who* for a few minutes. Then I got up and walked down the stairs and out of the building. Our offices are in Primrose Hill. We are close to a parade of shops. I did not want to use the first place I came to, a shoe-repair bar. I walked further down the road to the hardware shop. I waited while an Italian woman spoke at length to the man behind the counter. I could feel the tension mounting in me so I started to do my breathing exercises to keep calm. Finally he turned to me.

I took her keys from my pocket and said, 'I need a set of these, please. Can you do them straight away?'

He fingered the bunch and said it would take half an hour. I hesitated. She might be back before I had them. I would have to replace them later in the day. I could do it as long as she did not leave for meetings all day, as she sometimes did. And then it came to me. Even if I did not replace the keys it would not matter. She would think she had misplaced them. She had been in a state when she arrived at the office this morning and she would blame herself. I handed the keys to the man, left the shop and crossed the road. I decided to sit on Primrose Hill while I waited.

It was a windy day and the trees surged and dipped. I fastened the buttons on my jacket. My fingers were cold and stiff. A young mother hurried by with a wailing child kicking and struggling in his buggy. The child wanted to get out and arched his back in fury. The mother's face was tense. The child's cries reached a crescendo and she looked as if she wanted to slap him. Instead she pushed faster, her face contorted.

An elegant older woman walked by with her dog. The woman was probably in her mid-sixties and dressed all in soft grey. In contrast her dog was a scruffy-looking piebald mongrel and I wondered at her choice. She must be an animal lover. She would have gone to the rescue dogs' home and asked for the plainest dog, the dog that had suffered the most, the dog that no one else would choose. Certainly the dog looked back at her with adoring eyes, not quite believing his good fortune. I looked at my watch. Give it fifteen minutes more then go back to the shop.

Toiling up the hill to my right, a middle-aged man was pushing his wife in a wheelchair. He stopped at the summit and tucked a tartan blanket more securely over her knees. They talked briefly. Her face was lined but not unhappy. He started on his way again, holding the wheelchair steady

35

against the downward incline of the hill and the suck of the wind.

When I was nine years old my great-aunt Tanya died at the age of forty-seven. She was my grandfather's younger sister and he adored her. She was a famous singer until she was paralysed by her illness, a muscle-wasting disease. She had been forced to stop performing at the height of her fame. It was a rare genetic disorder. My ancestors had a very high opinion of themselves, of the purity of their bloodline. They rarely married outsiders as no one in their small community was good enough for the Vanheinens. Usually they married their first cousins. And Tanya paid the price for their pride.

She had an exquisite voice and would sing hymns and carols for us at Christmas. When she became weaker she moved into my grandfather's house and I remember her sitting in her wheelchair in his garden, always with a book on her lap.

My parents decided I should go to her funeral. On the morning of the burial my father came into the breakfast room at my grandfather's house. He sat down next to me and stroked the hair back from my face.

'Heja, my sweet, Tanya was such a special person and Granddad loved her so much. He is very sad and I want you to sit still and be quiet in the church today.'

'Why did she die?'

'She'd been ill for many years.'

'Why didn't the doctor make her better?'

'He tried. They all tried. Granddad even arranged for her to go to New York, but they couldn't help her.'

'Why not?'

'Some illnesses can't be made better, sweetheart.'

'I liked it when she sang to us.'

My grandfather walked in just then. He bent over and

kissed me on my cheek. There were tears caught in the swollen pouches of his lower lids that looked as if they were about to spill over.

'Yes, my darling, Tanya sang like an angel.'

The funeral frightened me. The coffin was highly polished and set up on a table at the top of the church. I knew that my great-aunt Tanya was lying in there. I remembered an incident with her one summer when we were staying at Grandfather's house. It was a dazzling day. I was lying on my stomach with my book in the long feathery grasses beyond the vegetable garden. It was so bright. The sunlight was bouncing off the pages and the black print crawled in front of my eyes like a procession of ants. I could smell the life in the earth and hear tiny scratchings and scurryings going on around me. I took my glazed pottery mouse out of my pocket and stroked its curved back. I decided to make a home for my mouse in a cave of the shimmering grasses. I would leave my mouse there overnight. I knew that after I was gone it would uncurl and skitter off through the stalks.

Just then I heard the whisper of wheels on the path that ran down the centre of the vegetable garden. It was Great-Aunt Tanya wheeling her chair towards where I was hidden. Then the wheels stopped at the end of the path, by the strawberry beds, and I heard her crying. I lay flat in the grass, my heart throbbing against the warm earth, thinking, She's a grown-up; she won't want me to see her crying, she will see me and be angry. I lay there unmoving as long as I could. Still she cried. Then I had to sit up to breathe deeply and she saw my head bob up above the grasses. She looked startled for a moment. Then she smiled tremulously and beckoned me over to her. I picked up my book and my pottery mouse and walked slowly towards her wheelchair.

She took my free hand in her cool hands that always shook slightly and said, 'Don't be afraid, darling Heja. Sometimes tears are good. They make new life grow.'

After the hymns and the speeches four men, including my father, carried Tanya's coffin on their shoulders out of the church. They walked slowly and stiffly down the aisle. Why were they carrying her coffin on their shoulders? It looked so uncomfortable. Why didn't they carry it with their hands? We followed them out of the church across the graveyard to the hole in the ground. The mound of freshly dug earth next to the hole was like a blanketed body. I watched as my grandfather threw a clump of earth on to Tanya's coffin. Tears were running down his face.

I walked back to the hardware shop and picked up my new set of keys and felt that my power had grown. In the event it was as easy to put her keys back as it had been to take them. Aisha is the same kind of trusting fool as Kathy.

Tonight Robert came over. He has been in New York, visiting his mother and sister. When he arrived he handed me a black box sumptuously gift-wrapped with yards of silver ribbon.

'I saw this and had to get it for you,' he said.

I opened it carefully. Inside the box there was thick white tissue paper folded around a full-length, black silk crêpe kimono. I lifted the kimono free of the paper.

'It's lovely.'

'I bought it at a vintage shop. It's eighty years old. Put it on and see if it looks OK.'

He held it up for me and I put it on over my clothes and pulled it around me. It had a thick sash belt and wide sleeve cuffs.

'The material is so fine,' I said, stroking the sleeves.

'It does suit you.'

'It is perfect, Robert. Thank you so much.'

'My pleasure.'

He embraced me and stroked my bottom through the material of the kimono. Then he put his hands beneath the kimono. He pulled my skirt up and stroked the backs of my thighs. He pushed my mouth open with his tongue and his hand moved round between my legs. Then he put his third finger right up me. His face got very hot and he pulled his mouth from mine, then took his finger out of me and put it in his mouth. His thick fleshy lips closed around his finger, right up to the knuckle, and he slowly pulled his finger out, watching me closely all the time. He repels me when he does this. I have never said anything about it to him. I do not let him see my repulsion.

I often think that Robert has a transactional attitude to our sex life. He gives me an expensive gift and he expects good sex in return. I am using him too. He has a large, sturdy penis and sex with him helps me to sleep. It stills my mind for a few hours. It never moves me, as it did with my true love.

The next day, and the day after, I waited in my car in her street during my lunch hour. I watched the building closely. I was anxious to try out the keys to see if they worked and to get into her flat at last. On the third day the childminder came out of the block with Billy in the buggy. She set off in the direction she had gone before, no doubt off to that housing estate again to meet her boyfriend.

I know the precise position of their apartment in the block. They are on the third floor, the left-hand corner. The first key into the entrance hall worked perfectly. It slid into the keyhole and turned with a satisfying click. I pushed open the heavy wooden door into an entrance hall that was larger than I expected and that had a decayed grandeur about it. It was high ceilinged and painted a dull cream. There was a long marble-topped table along one wall with letters stacked on it. The letters had an abandoned look, creased and curling up at the edges: to tenants who had gone away or who had died. On one wall a huge, slightly spotted mirror gave me back my reflection. As I looked at myself I saw again how my descent into depression and my sessions with Arvo Talvela have somehow changed me permanently. This was not the face that Markus loved.

The lift has a metal grille door that clanks as it concertinas open and closed. I must remember this. I took the lift to the third floor. The second key worked as well as the first. You had to turn the handle too. I opened the door slowly on to a long corridor. There was a russet-coloured carpet that ran along the centre of the hall, with polished wood on either side. A small round table held a lamp with a dark red shade. Off this long corridor was a series of doors. I walked into what must be their sitting room. I was surprised at the heavy old-fashioned furniture. There was so much inlaid walnut, a patterned sofa and a standard lamp with a dull gold shade with a fringe. The flat was a puzzle.

There seemed to be no trace of Markus. Then I found the room that had to be his workroom. It was opposite the sitting room and it was white and uncluttered and functional. There were well-made bookshelves with his books arranged in immaculate order. I looked along the shelves. I had given him some of these books. I recognized one on an upper shelf, the first book I had ever given him: a collection of photographs from The Hermitage. I reached up and took it down and opened the book. I read my loving inscription to him, written with a flourish on the flyleaf. The book had cost me a lot at the time. Then I pushed it back carefully into position. Markus would notice if it was at all out of place.

In the centre of the room there was his drawing table with an Anglepoise lamp clamped to its side. I touched the high stool that stood by the table. It was made of wood and smooth to my hand. His plan chest stood by the wall. I wondered if I would find the plans to our house in there, the house we had wanted to build.

I got down on my knees in front of the plan chest and pulled the bottom drawer open. I know him so well. Of course he would arrange his drawings chronologically – the oldest at the bottom, the most recent in the top drawer. The large sheets had been laid out meticulously. There must have been over twenty in the bottom drawer. I took them out carefully. I remembered the obsessive care with which he treated his work. I found the plan of our house near the bottom of the pile. I had not looked at this for many years. There were deep crease marks on the sheet. I lifted the plan onto his drawing desk and looked at the outline of the house: the house he was going to build for us by the sea. It was the work of a young and passionate architect.

I went into the large old-fashioned kitchen. It was messy and had all kinds of nooks and crannies and much-used appliances. There were a lot of recipe books on the shelf by the cooker. On the windowsill by the sink a large earthenware pot was filled with stained wooden spoons of various sizes and shapes. There were two aprons hanging on the kitchen door. So she must cook a lot.

Next to the kitchen there was a small room, which I assumed was her study. Markus would never leave any room of his in such a state. There was a small desk with a laptop on it and a mess of pens and paper lying next to it. And in front of the desk there were shelves with books and manuals and sheaves of paper stuffed together, looking as if they might fall out at any moment. A wastebasket, full to brimming, stood at the side of the desk. The room was very small. Only enough space for one person to sit in there. I did not have the time or the energy to go through her papers. That would have to wait.

As I was leaving her study I saw a notice board on the back of the door covered with photos of Billy. I looked at them closely. She has charted his development from a few days old. One was a hospital shot. Billy was lying in a plastic see-through cot and had one of those identity bracelets around his wrist. There are several shots of Billy in the bath and one of her breastfeeding him. Her shirt was open and she looked sleepily self-satisfied as Billy sucked at her breast. Markus must have taken that one.

There was only one photograph of him. He was lying on a carpet with Billy resting on his stomach. Billy was naked except for his nappy. His chubby back had little pleats of fat as he strained his head up to look at Markus, who rested his hand protectively on Billy's bare back. Markus's eyes were crinkled with laughter. I took out the drawing pin and put this photograph in my pocket.

My time was nearly up so I took a quick look around to establish the layout of the other rooms for my next visit. I looked into their bedroom; more heavy furniture. Billy has his own room with a white wooden cot and orange curtains.

I found it hard to imagine Markus living in that flat. It was not what I had expected. He has had to compromise to live there with her. I will go back there again soon.

KATHY

JUNE

I'm beginning to think that childbirth sends us all a bit crazy. One day last week I was sitting at the kitchen table trying to work and had fallen asleep with my head scrunched up against my laptop. Markus had tried to help me by putting the clothes into the washing machine. When I woke up some time later and with a stiff neck, I emptied the machine.

'*Oh, no!*'

'What is it?' Markus asked, coming into the kitchen and sounding alarmed.

He had put his black socks in with Billy's pristine white vests and Babygros and the colour had run and all Billy's things now had an ugly grey tinge to them.

'You've ruined his clothes. You've ruined them,' I said.

I was filled with a completely disproportionate anguish as I pulled out the grey baby clothes. Then I sat at the kitchen table and cried over the soggy little pile of spoiled clothes. Markus looked at me as if I was demented.

'I'm sorry! Those black socks must have got caught up with the towels somehow.'

Markus was in Durham for a couple of days. The company he works for is competing for a major project there and he's leading the team. The city of Durham has got together lottery and sponsorship funds to build a big arts centre with a cinema, café, gallery and bookshop and Markus really wants this job.

I thought I'd welcome a few days alone with Billy. In fact I felt edgy and lonely as the flat settled around me with its odd creaks and sighs. Perhaps I could call Fiona. She's my best friend, but Fiona is in Glasgow and the distance felt too far to bridge tonight. I've started to realize that it can feel lonely, being the editor. I guess you cross the tracks somehow and your relationships with the team are changed, you have to hold yourself a bit aloof. It would probably suit Heja better than it suits me because she seems such a solitary person and I know nothing about her life outside work. I've never seen her leave with the others for a drink and she usually lunches alone. Yet how intriguing that she was a famous presenter in Finland, and it *is* odd that she left all that behind. Markus doesn't get it, why I'm interested, that's because he's contemptuous of celebrity and would think it unimportant.

Billy woke up and he wanted a feed. It was always the most marvellous feeling to have him grow heavy and sleepy in my arms as he sucked on my breast. At first his little face was all concentration and then, gradually, his cheeks and forehead softened, his face became blissful and his limbs were abandoned voluptuously against my stomach.

When he was deeply asleep I put him down in his cot carefully, walked into my office, looked at the pile of papers on my desk that I had planned to sort through, lost heart immediately and went and sat in Markus's room, which he always leaves so tidy and immaculate. I found the book on Lisbon, which I'd bought on impulse last week when I was missing my parents. As I was flipping through the pages I came to a spread on the Torre de Belem, which I think is one of the world's most beautiful examples of military architecture. How lovely and how un-British it looked in the brilliant sunshine of Lisbon. I read that UNESCO had named it a World Heritage Site in 1983. Then I came to the spread on my favourite building in the world, the Mosteiro Dos Jeronimos, also a World Heritage Site.

And it suddenly occurred to me that maybe we could run a series on these magnificent buildings in the magazine. I had no idea how many there were. I went back to my study, turned on the laptop and looked up World Heritage Sites. I found a list of all the locations and there are over nine hundred and sixty sites worldwide. Some of the sites are natural phenomena – caves and gorges, volcanoes, forests and barrier reefs. Then there are the world-famous architectural sites: Chartres Cathedral; the Acropolis and the historic centre of Siena. I got excited as I read through the list. If we concentrated just on the cultural sites in Europe we would have enough material to fill a pull-out survey for a year; a popular guide to the sites.

I'm sure I can sell the idea to Philip. It will be expensive to produce, as some of the sites will need to be visited and photographed, and he always puts up a fight when we want to spend money. He'll want a business plan of course. A guide like this would attract lots of advertisers. I felt inspired and I started to type up a first draft of my idea.

The phone rang in the kitchen. It was Markus and he sounded really cheerful.

'It went very well. We're through to the last two,' he said.

'That's brilliant! Congratulations.'

'The other team is strong, though. We're going to have to work hard to win it.'

'You can do it.'

I was so pleased for him. I didn't mention my idea because this was his moment. I wanted to tell him that I was missing him, until I remembered he would be standing in the hotel with his colleagues close by.

'What are you going to do now?'

'We'll have dinner and plan our campaign.'

'In the hotel?'

'No, I saw an Indian restaurant on the way here. It's called Curry Paradise.'

I laughed.

'Tomorrow I'm going to spend time walking round Durham. I need to take a lot of photos so I think it best if I do one more night here.'

'Of course; I'm so pleased for you, Markus.'

I returned to my study and to my list. The United Kingdom has twenty-eight World Heritage Sites. Some you would expect, like Stonehenge and Hadrian's Wall, Canterbury Cathedral and the city of Bath. And then there are more unusual places, like the Blaenavon Industrial Landscape. I saw that Durham Castle and Cathedral were on the list and I took this as a good omen: perhaps everything was going to be all right.

Markus and I were still adjusting to being new parents and to living together. It was bound to be difficult at first. I just needed to stay calm and cheerful about it and not panic, which I have a tendency to do. I was tapping away on my laptop when the buzzer from the front door sounded. I looked at my watch; it was nearly ten, so who could that be?

I checked Billy quickly and he slept on peacefully; the buzzer had not woken him. I walked down our hall and buzzed the front door open and waited as I heard the lift coming up slowly. Then the lift door clanked open and Eddie stepped out.

'Eddie!'

'Hello, K.'

He walked over to me quickly, slipped his hands around my waist and kissed me on the lips.

'I was just round the corner. Can I have a coffee?'

'You can't just show up like this! What if Markus had been here?'

'So he's away?'

I looked at him hard. He wasn't drunk and he didn't smell of drink. His green eyes crinkled as he grinned at me and said, 'It's so good to see you.'

'One coffee, then, I'm knackered and I don't do late nights any more.'

He followed me into the flat and into the kitchen and sat down at the table. I busied myself making the coffee and was finding it disconcerting just how attractive I still found him; his brown hair was all curly and unkempt as it always was. He was wearing his work clothes and his face was tanned and freckled from working in the sun.

'How are you? Really?' he asked.

'I'm exhausted. I never knew tiredness like this before and I'm finding it tough doing the job as well as Billy . . .'

'Ahh, get a grip. My mum had five of us.'

'I'm sure she was Super-Mum. I doubt she was also editing a magazine!' I said crossly.

'True.'

He beamed his disarming smile at me and I stopped feeling cross. He was teasing me, as he always used to do.

'So married life is not all it's cracked up to be?'

I placed a mug of coffee in front of him. 'Stop being provocative and tell me about you. How are things?'

His smile faded and he leaned towards me over the kitchen table.

'I miss you.'

'Oh, Eddie . . .'

'I'm not drinking. It's been three months. I know what a bloody nightmare I was.'

'I couldn't do the chaos any more. It made me so unhappy.'

'I know.'

'You'll always matter to me. *Always* . . . But I've got Billy now.'

He grimaced at my words.

'I'm a bloody fool,' he said, 'a hopeless case.'

He always could disarm me with his charm and his self-deprecation. We had played this scene too many times before and I had to harden my heart against him.

'How's the work going?'

'OK; keeps me busy. I've got a junior working with me now. I'm training him up.'

'That's great; you'd be a brilliant teacher,' I said warmly.

Eddie was an inspired gardener and he could transform an ordinary London back garden into a place of beauty and enchantment. Unfortunately his work had always been erratic. He took a gulp of his coffee.

'This is stronger than you used to make it. I'm doing more garden design now too.'

'Good. You always liked that best.'

'But I'm miserable,' he said, hunched over his mug.

I didn't reply as there was nothing I could say.

'I hope this Finnish bloke is treating you OK?'

He looked at me searchingly. I found my eyes moving away from that direct green-eyed gaze. I felt confused and I really didn't want to talk to Eddie about Markus.

'Do you want to see Billy?' I said, standing up.

He followed me into Billy's room and we both stood looking down at my baby son.

'What a great little lad and don't take this the wrong way, I can't see a trace of you, K.'

'You're right. He is a hundred per cent Markus.'

Billy stirred, his eyelids fluttered and he opened his eyes. He saw me and put his arms up to me. I bent over the cot and picked him up. He was all warm and sleepy and then he started to grizzle a bit against my shoulder.

'Let me,' he said.

I handed Billy to Eddie and he walked around the room and rocked him gently until Billy fell back to sleep in his arms. He was looking down at Billy and as I watched them I felt this ache, thinking that if things had been different we could have had this, a beautiful child together. He placed him carefully back into the cot and put the blanket over him.

'Where did you learn to do that?'

'I looked after the younger ones a lot,' he said quietly.

He looked sad now. He may have been thinking what I was thinking. He hugged me tightly then, kissed me on the neck and left the flat in a rush.

I stood there in the hall after he had gone, thinking all these warm thoughts about him. I adored him once; I adored him for years. We'd had some very good times together. I remembered that day years before when I had gone off for my first day working at a magazine as a junior features writer. I'd been so excited to have my start in journalism at last. When I got home that night Eddie had filled our flat with flowers and made Irish stew for us to eat. He said how proud he was of me and that he knew I would make it in magazines.

I pulled myself up and told myself to stop romanticizing the past. Three months without booze, but he would turn to it again. Unfortunately his periods of abstinence never lasted.

HEJA

JUNE

I heard her tell Aisha that Markus was away in Durham. So she would be alone with Billy. It was late when I drove to Baker Street and parked in her street.

I got out of my car and walked to a good position where I could watch the building. I had the keys to her flat in my pocket. I could see several lights were on in the rooms. I worked out that the lights were from Billy's room and Markus's room and the kitchen. I saw her moving in the kitchen at one point. And then, some time later, I saw a man approach the window in Billy's room and he was holding Billy in his arms!

Markus was away for a couple of nights and she had a man in the flat with her. And that man was holding the baby. I felt outraged on behalf of Markus. It was late, nearly eleven. Who was this man? Why was she letting him hold Billy? He walked away from the window. I was transfixed to the spot, watching the window intently.

Some minutes later, I do not know how many, I saw the large entrance door to the block being pushed open and the man walked out. I followed him down the road. I wanted to see who he was more clearly. He was walking rapidly with his head down. He had curly hair and was dressed in jeans and a rough checked shirt. He wore work boots too. He hurried to Baker Street tube station and I saw his face as he stopped to buy a ticket. Mid-thirties, tanned face, who was he? He went through the barriers and I walked slowly back to my car.

The next evening I dressed warmly even though it had been mild that afternoon. I feel the cold. I put on my soft white leather lace-ups, which make no noise. I locked my flat at around eleven p.m. and decided I would go there by taxi tonight. I walked along the path by the river until I reached Blackfriars Bridge. The river is low this year. You can see the chalky green watermark on the rusty struts of the bridge. The water is well below that line and a whole strip of shingle has been exposed that for many years lay underneath the Thames. I have stood at my window on long Sunday afternoons and watched children with their parents scouring this newly revealed shingle beach, heard their cries of excitement as they found a piece of clay pipe or an old ship's nail.

I told the taxi to drop me one street from her flat. There has been a strong dry wind blowing for the last two weeks. It has blown without respite, so that it has come to seem quite sinister. The trees have been partially stripped of their early summer fullness. Tonight the wind had stilled. The streets carried the debris from the trees. Withered brown leaves, dead before their time, lay in my path. It was all wrong. Dead leaves belong in November, not in June.

I had left it later tonight. I reached her street and scanned the windows. Two lights were on. One light, shining through pale orange curtains, was Billy's room. The other light was her bedroom. After a few minutes the light in her bedroom went off. I would need to wait at least thirty minutes to be sure she was asleep. I walked to a pub on the corner of Baker Street and bought an orange juice. I did not drink it.

The minutes ticked away. This would be a major test of my strength and my willpower.

I walked back to her apartment block. All was in darkness except for Billy's room. This time I walked up the stairs, remembering the clanking lift door. No sound came through the doors of the apartments I passed. This is a well-made block with thick walls and doors. I reached her flat. I could open the door and she could be standing there in front of me. Her bedroom light was off and I had to assume she was asleep by now. I opened the front door very carefully and stood in the hall and listened intently. All was silent. There was warm light spilling out of Billy's room. This was the light I had seen from the street, a night-light in the shape of a great yellow flower. He was lying on his back in his white wooden cot. Above the cot a mobile of grey papier-mâché seagulls with orange beaks stirred gently. I leaned over the side of the cot and examined him closely for many minutes. His hair is fine and white. He is a little Markus. He is a true northern baby.

Then I walked silently into their bedroom. It took a few minutes for my eyes to become accustomed to the dark. As I stood there in the darkness I could smell her perfume, faint yet persistent. Slowly my eyes adjusted to the lack of light. Shapes became apparent with a kind of grainy texture. There was a large, high chest of drawers just inside the door and a wooden bowl with a clutter of bottles and jewellery in it. Their bed was large, king-size.

She was lying on her stomach on the left-hand side of the bed. An open book lay on the bedside table next to a digital radio clock with ugly red digits. I wanted to take in all the details and store them for later, so I can visualize their life in this flat when I am lying in my bed five miles away. I think about him being with her in the dark wastes of the night when I feel very low. It makes me even more determined. I can work, I can plan. My mind is on patrol. My will is strong and getting stronger.

I moved into the room and stood closer to her at the foot of the bed. Her head was turned on the pillow towards the clock. One arm lay above the dark quilt, which covered the bed. She was wearing a white cotton nightdress. The sort with lace around the neck and sleeves, modelled on Victorian nightdresses. He would not have given that to her. He hates reproductions of any kind. A chair at the bottom of her bed had clothes piled on it and a mess of shoes beneath it. There were a couple of those gauze cloths that mothers wipe their babies' faces with lying on the bed. I took one of them.

I was eighteen when I met Markus. He was nineteen. We were both in our first year at university in Helsinki. I was studying history of art. Markus was in the school of architecture. We had both gone to a film-club screening of *Bride of Frankenstein*. The film club held screenings once a week in the university's biology lecture theatre. It was an uncomfortable place to watch films. We sat in long, hard rows with a narrow wooden shelf in front us. The seats were steeply raked. At the front of the room there was a large screen. Every Thursday night some enthusiast from the film club would project a classic film onto that screen, usually a 16 mm copy that was scratched and jerky.

Bride of Frankenstein had just started with a crash of music and the opening shot showed a violent storm breaking over a sinister-looking house perched on a cliff-top. A young man in Romantic dress was standing at the window, looking out at the storm. As he turned towards his companions I felt someone join the end of the row where I was sitting. I liked to have the aisle seat so I moved along for the newcomer rather grudgingly. He whispered his thanks, balanced a big folder of papers on the shelf in front of him and sat back. During the film most of the students laughed at certain scenes. I could not understand why they were laughing. There was so much cruelty in the film and the monster had more dignity than any of his persecutors. The film came to an end and the credits rolled and the harsh fluorescent lights of the biology theatre flickered on.

I bent down to pick up my bag and the man next to me said, 'Rather an apt place to show that film, don't you think?'

I must have looked puzzled.

'Doctor Frankenstein could do his experiments here . . .'

He nodded his head towards the examination table that stood in front of the screen and the scrubbing sink at the side by the door.

'Ah, yes, I see . . .'

'I'm Markus. Can I buy you a coffee?'

'I'm Heja.' We shook gloved hands.

'Do you know somewhere round here?'

We walked through the cold night air to a coffee shop and found a table near the back. I took my gloves off. My hands were numb in spite of them. He brought two coffees and a ham sandwich to our table and sat back in his chair, his eyes full on me. I looked down at my purple and blue tweed skirt, smoothing it over my knees. His eyes were extraordinary.

'It will snow tonight,' I said, feeling foolish as I stirred sugar into my coffee and held the cup to warm my hands.

He said, 'Did you enjoy the film?'

'Yes, I did. It was sad, though. Why did everyone laugh? I didn't think it was funny at all.'

'It had its moments.'

'I liked the monster and I hated his persecutors. Even the bride they made for him rejects him. His last hope of contact with another . . .'

'So he destroys them both, saying, "We belong to the dead." By the way, did you want any of this sandwich?'

'No, thanks.'

'If you like them, they're showing classic movies late on Friday nights on the main channel,' he said.

'I don't like watching films on television. I think they should be projected.'

'I thought you might be a purist.'

'Why do you say that?'

'Because you plait your hair so perfectly . . .'

And we were together from that night for the next nine years.

I looked into her chaotic study again. This was the room I needed time to go through, not tonight. I could feel my power growing as I walked silently around her flat, unknown to her. I am so much stronger than she is. I had to go into her room once more before I left. Still she slept and was oblivious as I walked to the side of the bed so that I stood inches from her. I could see the rise and fall of her chest and the puffy, almost childlike quality of her sleeping face.

KATHY

JUNE

This morning I had to present my proposal on the World Heritage Sites guide to Philip Parr and to Victoria. She is our head of PR and Marketing and wears these sexy little suits, has a flirty style with Philip and I'm never sure quite how much influence she wields with him. He's a known womanizer. She's friendly enough towards me, though. I was well prepared and arrived early. He kept us both waiting outside his office for ten minutes, so I took the time to show Victoria the board I had made up. It was a picture and text layout on Siena as a sample article.

I was fine while explaining my ideas to Victoria. The moment Philip called us into his office my stomach went into spasm and my mouth went dry. He stood up behind his desk and indicated that we should sit on the stylish, uncomfortable chairs in front of his desk. He leaned back in his executive swivel chair and said I had ten minutes to make my pitch.

I had spent hours making that display board on Siena and I handed it to him now.

'There are three hundred and eighty plus World Heritage Sites in Europe and they include some of the greatest architectural masterpieces. These are the buildings people want to see when they go abroad. They like to come home and say they saw that important building. So we will produce an accessible guide that gives our readers all the information they need to understand and appreciate these sites.

'The guide will be visually strong with stunning pictures. Some pictures can be commissioned and we'll get the rest from existing sources. We'll put in key information on the history of the sites and the style of architecture. The guides can run as pull-outs in the magazine for a year. I would like them to have a reference quality to them, so that people will want to collect them and keep them.'

He looked at my display board for several minutes.

'Nice idea, Kathy, but this would cost a lot. Think of the travel and hotel bills,' he said. 'We'd have to pay a photographer and a writer to go to all these sites.'

I had known he would raise the subject of cost.

'Yes, there are costs entailed. We can use local photographers. I have contacts all over Europe, some very good names. The team here would do all the writing as part of their core work. I've done a draft budget and I think the advertising sales will exceed the costs.'

I handed him a spreadsheet with my calculations and I gave a copy to Victoria too, as I wanted to keep her onside. Philip examined the sheet for several long minutes. When he's thinking his whole face tightens and he purses his mouth in an unpleasant way. I've never really liked him. He's one of those men that people describe as 'political', and by political they mean devious and into power. As the silence stretched out I started to feel angry with myself. I try too hard; I know I try too hard. I wished I didn't care so much. I wished I could be cooler about things.

Finally, he put the spreadsheet down on his desk and he kept me waiting while he said, 'What do you think, Victoria?'

'I think it's got a lot of potential. There are some very

glamorous sites on the list. I'm sure we could sell a lot of travel advertising. And it will have a long shelf life too. I might be able to do a tie-in with one of the Sunday supplements, a competition – you know, win a trip to the historic city of Siena.'

'We wouldn't need to send writers to every site,' I said, hoping to clinch the deal. 'We could get a lot of material from other sources.'

'OK; I like the idea. I want to check these figures. In principle, it's a yes. I'll need you to do a presentation to the board. They like to be kept informed and they'll need persuading on the costs.'

'Of course; delighted to do that. Thank you, Philip.'

He's famously hard-headed so this was quite a victory. Victoria and I left the office together.

'Well done!' she said. 'Your team just lucked out.'

'We all did, and there are more than enough great sites to keep everyone happy. Thanks for your support today, I really appreciate it.'

My euphoria lasted all afternoon. I couldn't tell the team about it just yet because Philip had said 'in principle' and I didn't want any idle chatter about it to derail the project. I was feeling so cheerful, though, so I treated them all to coffees and a box of home-made cupcakes from the local patisserie. I chose vanilla and strawberry cakes and bought one for Victoria too. Aisha and I sat in my office and we ate the deliciously soft cakes, which were topped with sweet butter-cream. I told Aisha in confidence about what Philip had said.

Then I sat and wrote notes for most of the afternoon. Ideas for what should be included in the guide came thick and fast. I planned to cover the Portuguese sites myself. It would mean that Markus and I could make that long-promised trip to my parents in Lisbon and I could show him all my special places there.

I was home before Markus and as soon as I heard his key in the lock I rushed up to him in the hall. I'd been looking forward to telling him my news.

'Philip agreed,' I said. 'It's on.'

'That's really good news.'

I wanted a hug and stood in front of him. He didn't reach for me so I initiated the hug and we stood in the hall holding each other.

'Do you want some wine?' I said. 'To celebrate . . .'

'Better not, I've got to work tonight.'

'Well, I think I will.'

I walked into the kitchen and poured myself a glass of wine, talking all the time.

'He only agreed to us doing the really important sites from scratch. I had to tell him we would use archive sources for a lot of places, so it's not a complete triumph. If it takes off, who knows?'

'You've come up with a good formula.'

'Thanks, I'm so relieved. I was worried my ideas had stopped coming. I can start on the Portuguese sites soon. We can have that week in Lisbon. What bliss . . .'

Now he put his hands on my shoulders and looked into my face. 'You know I can't come with you.'

'Why not?'

'You know why not. I've got a mountain of work to do on the Durham project.'

'It would only be five days away. I could show you all my favourite places. *Please* come.'

'I can't, Kathy. I wouldn't relax for a minute. You'll have

a great time and your parents can spend time with Billy.'

'They want to get to know you too, they really do.'

'Sorry, that will just have to wait. I've got to work on the project flat out for the next two months.'

It all sounded so reasonable. After all, he has his career and I have mine. Yet like a small child denied a longed-for treat I started to cry. I couldn't stop myself. I stood in front of him with tears pouring down my cheeks and I felt foolish and useless and knew my tears would alienate him.

'This is silly, Kathy. You're tired and overwrought. The visit will do you good. I wish I could come but I can't. Now I *must* get on with my drawings.'

He walked into his workroom. I sat at the kitchen table and cried for a long time. In my agitation, reaching for the box of tissues, I knocked over and broke a lovely little glazed apple green jug, which had been a present from Aunt Jennie when I moved into the flat. I wasn't just crying about Markus not coming to Lisbon with me, I was crying for my lost self. Too much had happened to me too quickly: the final break with Eddie; meeting Markus; getting pregnant and the birth of my precious boy. I was tired, of course, yet it was the lack of warmth from Markus that was starting to hurt me. I loved him and I wanted him to be kinder towards me, as he had been when I was pregnant. We'd had a special feeling between us then and it couldn't have gone for good.

He had said 'a good formula' about my idea for the guide. 'Formula' was such a cold word somehow. He hadn't hugged me properly or wanted to celebrate. Eddie would have reacted differently. He would have hugged me tightly and insisted we go to the pub at once to toast my success. Then we would both have drunk far too much, and I couldn't cope with that either, could I?

I had this sudden memory of Eddie. I'd just got back from work and could hear loud music on the radio from our sitting room in our old flat. I walked in there to find him lying on the sofa, singing along with the radio at the top of his voice. He grinned at me and I knew at once that he was drunk. I saw that his right hand was bleeding. I turned the radio down.

'What happened?'

'This guy was being a cunt to his girlfriend, pushing her around, so I smacked him.'

'Your hand . . .!'

I went into the kitchen and found a packet of frozen peas in the freezer. I sat down next to him on the sofa and held the packet against his bleeding knuckles. He winced as I touched his hand and went on singing. I felt such a mixture of emotions as I sat there looking at him. I was angry with him for drinking and getting into another fight, yet I found myself also loving him for defending the woman who was being abused. When Eddie got drunk he could get aggressive with other men. He had a real old-fashioned thing about how women should be treated and he would never have laid a finger on a woman. He despised men who hurt women.

The phone rang and it was Heja. I tried to pull myself together quickly and blew my nose on a tissue

'I am sorry to phone you at home. Could I have tomorrow off? I am sorry the notice is so short.'

She gave no further explanation, which was very like Heja. I didn't mind as I didn't want to prolong the conversation.

'It's fine to call me at home, Heja. Will you have all your stuff in by Friday?'

'Yes, I will.'

'Then certainly take tomorrow off and I'll see you on Friday.'

I put the phone down and looked up, and Markus was standing in the doorway. Why did he look at me so intently? Was he trying to work out if my emotional outburst had spent itself so that it was now safe to come back into the kitchen? He walked over to the table and picked up the three broken pieces of the little green jug.

'I can mend this for you,' he said. 'I know how much you like it.'

'Can you?' I sniffed back a tear.

'Yes, look, the breaks are clean. I can glue it and it will be as good as new.'

'Thank you.'

He wrapped the pieces carefully in kitchen roll.

'We ought to eat something,' he said.

Billy started to cry and I got up to get him. 'Would pizza be OK? I'm bushed,' I said.

When I came back into the kitchen, carrying Billy, Markus was taking two fillets of plaice out of the freezer.

'We both need to eat properly,' he said.

'I'll do that. Just let me change Billy and then I'll put them in the oven. You get back to work.'

When I first met Markus I thought he was so strong and sure of himself. I had seen how he dominated that conference discussion in Newcastle. And he had so much integrity too. Here was a man I could feel safe with at last. He had good values, he was practical and he didn't let people push him around. There is a down side to his strength. It's an inflexible strength that he maintains by shutting people out. He has started to shut me out too, and yet I know that something in his life has made him unhappy. If only he would let me approach this sore patch, whatever it is, I know we could get close and tender again as we were in the early months of my pregnancy.

I carried Billy into the bathroom. I can never get it warm in here because it has tiles that run halfway up the walls and a polished wood floor as I can't bear carpets in bathrooms. I took Billy's changing mat and all the paraphernalia into the kitchen and changed him on the rug by the dresser. His latest discovery is that he can suck his toes and he put his left big toe into his mouth and it made me laugh. I left him lying there and washed my hands. The oven takes an age to heat up because it's old. Dinner would be late again. I collected the laundry basket from the bathroom and started to fill the washing machine. The phone rang again and it was Fran, my childminder.

'I'm so sorry, Kathy. I can't come in tomorrow. I felt ropey all day. Tonight I'm just terrible. I've got some kind of bug.'

'Oh, dear, poor you . . .'

'I am sorry. I've got a friend Lisa; she nannies part time. Would you like her number? Maybe she can help out.'

I spent the next two hours trying to get through to Lisa, in between cooking the fish and eating with Markus. I gave up at ten-thirty p.m.

'That's it,' I said to him. 'I'll just have to work from home tomorrow. Philip isn't going to like it but what can I do? It's the first time I've missed a day in the office. I'll get Aisha to come over with the mail.'

This morning I got a card from my aunt Jennie in Cornwall, which made me smile. I opened the envelope and inside was a black and white photograph of a couple seated in a 1950s open-top sports car. The woman was glamorous with one of those headscarves tied around her head and neck in a fifties film-star way. She was looking over at her male companion with adoring admiration. He was sitting at the steering wheel, staring ahead with manly concentration. On the back Jennie had written:

> *I was thinking about what you said to me about Markus being reserved. Well, it is a fact that on average a woman will speak 7,000 words over the course of a day, while a man will only speak 2,000 words. Stop worrying. You have a gorgeous husband and son. Be happy and all will be well.*
>   *Much love, Jennie xx*

Jennie is such a warm and grounded person and when my parents retired to Lisbon she started to keep a protective eye on me. It's a good feeling to know she is there, rooting for me.

It was lovely, being at home with Billy all day, although hard to focus on the proofreading I'd set for myself. We sat on the rug in the kitchen and I went through picture books with him, pointing at the animals and making their noises, and he loved this. Then Aisha came over for three hours and we did get some work done. I have worked with Aisha for years, although it's only since I became editor that she has worked exclusively for me. She's the person I most trust at work. We went through my mail and recent invoices. I told her I would need her help on my forthcoming board presentation on the guide. I wanted to present facts and figures about where our readers travelled in Europe. Aisha is really good with figures, which are not my strong point.

'Was Philip OK about my working from home?'

'He didn't say much. You know him. I'm sure it's OK. He asked where Heja was.'

'Did you tell him she's got a day's leave?'

'Yeah, I think he fancies her.'

'Really? I thought he fancied Victoria?'

'He's a letch! He often lurks around Heja's desk. She's got a boyfriend; I've seen him.'

'What's he like?'

'Tall, dark, smartly dressed, looks like a doctor or lawyer or something. I saw them walking in the Barbican last Sunday.'

After Aisha had gone Billy and I both had a nap curled up together in our big bed. I got up an hour later and decided to make roast chicken and ratatouille. While it was roasting and the kitchen was filling with lovely fragrant smells, I ran a bath and poured some bubble bath in. Then I carried Billy in and we sat in the bath, with Billy between my legs. He has this yellow bucket that has a hole in its side and the water spurts out in a stream. Billy finds this very entertaining so I had to fill the bucket again and again and hold it up while he tried to catch the water in his hands. I heard footsteps in the hall and Markus walked in.

'That looks like fun.'

'It is.'

He knelt down by the side of the bath and kissed the top of Billy's moist head. Then he rolled up his sleeves and said, 'I'm going to wash you Mrs. Hartman.'

He squeezed some bath gel onto his palms and started to caress my breasts with his soapy hands. My breasts are larger than they used to be because of the breastfeeding and I rather like them being bigger. I leant my head back against the edge of the bath, still balancing Billy between my knees, and closed my eyes for a few moments. Markus moved his fingers over and under my breasts with a firm, massaging movement. My skin felt nice and slippery and my breasts started to tingle. Then he burst out laughing. I opened my eyes.

'You're squirting milk,' he said.

He leant over the bath, put my right breast into his mouth and licked around my nipple.

HEJA

JUNE

Yesterday I went for a consultation with a Mr Banerjee in Kentish Town. He practises Ayurvedic medicine and was recommended to me as an extraordinary physician and healer. He was a small wrinkled man with large sympathetic eyes and he spoke with a bit of a lisp. He did not carry out any formal examination as such. He looked into my eyes, felt my pulse, examined my hands and told me to stick my tongue out. He asked me about my eating habits.

Then he said that he believed that Panchakarma therapy could help me. It is a form of detoxification, which has been practised in India for centuries. It involves steam baths, herbal-oil enemas and herbal inhalation. The Panchakarma system cleanses the body. He has put me onto a rigorous regime. The plan is for me to see him every two weeks.

Tonight I parked my car and walked along a street of expensive houses and shops in an area of London I do not know until I found the restaurant Robert had described. He said it was a recent discovery of his and that the food was outstanding. It had a discreetly opulent entrance hall. The walls were panelled throughout with dark wood. A man in a footman's outfit took my jacket and handed it to the cloakroom assistant. Then he led me into a room with leather armchairs grouped around low polished tables. Robert was sitting at one of these with our menus. He was wearing a dark grey suit and white shirt. He dresses formally for a man in his thirties. I think he tries to look and behave older than he is, perhaps for the benefit of his patients.

He stood up, kissed me softly on my lips as his greeting, then stood back and looked at me appreciatively.

'Love the dress.'

'Thank you. I had time to go home first. Have you come straight from work?'

'Yes, another busy day.'

'I never know how much I should ask you about your work,' I said.

'Do I seem secretive?'

'No, just professionally discreet.'

Robert had ordered some red wine and the waiter placed a very large glass in front of me, showed the bottle to Robert and then poured the wine reverentially into the bowl of my glass. I swirled the plum-red liquid and sipped it.

'This is so good. Are we celebrating something?'

'Just wanted the best for you,' he said, toasting me. 'Now, there are some wonderful things on this menu.'

I looked and the menu listed rich and expensive dishes – lobster mousse, Norfolk wild duck with peach and bigarade sauce, truffle sausages and roast venison. Nothing simple like grilled fish and steamed vegetables, which I prefer. After we had made our selection we were shown to our table.

The dining room had the same feel and atmosphere as the other room, that of an exclusive gentlemen's club. There was a high, ornately plastered ceiling and white-linen covered tables with plenty of space between them. The diners spoke in tranquil tones.

'What are you working on at the moment?'

'Our editor has this idea to do a series on World Heritage Sites in Europe.'

'Sounds interesting.'

'I am not so sure. A reference work on historical buildings . . . I prefer to write about new buildings.'

'I think your editor knows her audience. The British love to look back.'

'All the more reason we should be educating them about modern architecture.'

'I think I should subscribe to your magazine. I need some educating.'

'Yes, I think you like to look back too,' I said as I glanced meaningfully around the room.

'Don't you like it?'

'It is delightful, for a change. I couldn't live in such a traditional space, though.'

'I find it very restful,' he said.

'You are a bit of a traditionalist,' I said in a teasing tone.

His dark brown eyes gazed at me seriously. 'I appreciate very fine things. Are you free on Saturday? There's a Bette Davis classic showing in Hampstead.'

'Which one?'

'*Dark Victory.*'

'I don't know it.'

'Bette Davis is a rich, spoiled heiress who falls for her doctor. He discovers she has an incurable brain tumour.'

'Sounds cheerful! I thought doctors were not supposed to date their patients?' I said.

'Suspension of disbelief, if you please . . . They get engaged and she goes to meet him at the surgery. He's already gone ahead to the restaurant. She takes a peek at her file and sees the words "Prognosis negative" written there.'

I wondered whether to tip my glass of wine on to the tablecloth. It would be nice to see the plum red seep into the thick white linen and the other diners would look over surreptitiously and then look away. Robert would be all solicitude.

'So she meets him at the restaurant. And when the waiter asks her what she'd like to drink she spits out at him: "*I'll have a prognosis negative!*" then she does this great thing with her eyes and rushes out of the restaurant.'

'No need to see it now. You've done such a brilliant job describing it,' I said.

'That's only the first act. It gets better. Don't you like old movies?'

'Sometimes . . .'

I knew I was sounding unenthusiastic. He looked crest-fallen. He was not trying to upset me. He knows nothing about my depression or how much I had loved my analyst. It was not my task to comfort him. There was an awkward silence as the waiter walked over and took our plates away. I ran my finger around the rim of my glass.

'I think I've upset you,' he said.

'No, Robert, you have done everything to make it a lovely evening. Don't mind my northern glooms.'

He reached for my hand. 'Heja, I wish you felt able to open up to me more. What brought on the glooms?'

'It's too difficult,' I said, my eyes on the tablecloth. 'Not like it is in the movies.'

He left it then. He does not push it if I give the signal so far and no further. He expected us to take a taxi back to his flat. He was expecting sex after that expensive meal. I told him I really could not. I had brought my car and needed to go back to my flat. I had a demanding day ahead of me tomorrow.

He insisted on walking me to my car. We stood under the lamp-post and he put his arms around my waist and looked down at me a bit mournfully with his large brown eyes.

'Are you sure you want to drive?'

'I'll be fine. I only drank one glass of wine.'

'Did I drink all the rest?'

'When wine is that good it slips down. Thank you for taking me there.'

'Can we meet up this weekend?'

I agreed to meet him on Saturday. It is getting more difficult with him. He has started to want more than physical intimacy. As I drove home I wondered when I would have to end the relationship.

I parked and took the lift up to my apartment. Then I poured myself a small glass of wine and sat at my great window, looking out at the river. These were my special moments when I could be alone and at peace. I could see lights from a few craft twinkling on the river. Markus was strongly in my thoughts again. How he would love this flat and this view.

The first time my mother met Markus she set out to insult him. We had been together throughout our time at university. My parents found out about him when he was filmed leading the occupation at the university. He was all over the evening news. A friend of my mother's, whom I had never liked, told her that she had seen me with Markus on several occasions; that I was clearly involved with the student revolutionary!

So finally, after I had graduated, Markus was invited to dinner at my parents' house. I had my first junior job in television then and he was still studying for his architecture qualification. I was apprehensive about this meeting. My mother could be so cold and critical and would let people know if she did not approve of them. I travelled home the night before. I wanted everything to be just right for him. My mother had bought a large tray of takeaway moussaka from the delicatessen, which she planned to serve up with a salad. The next evening she laid the table with earthenware plates and goblets for the wine.

'Rather fun to be a bit rustic, don't you think, Heja?' she said.

I was beside myself. Had Markus been someone she approved of she would have cooked an elaborate meal for him. Her finest porcelain and silver would have been brought out. She was making a point. He was a socialist, so let him eat takeaway.

The beauty of it was that Markus preferred it that way. I was standing next to her as she opened the door to him and I felt her shock of recognition when she saw him standing there. His eyes were more dazzling than any TV camera could ever capture. He followed her into the sitting room and my dad got up and shook hands with him.

My mother said, 'We're going to be informal tonight. I hope that's all right with you, Markus?'

He turned his eyes on her and smiled. 'Sounds good to me . . .'

I was standing by the fireplace, watching this exchange, and my love for him was so overwhelming that I felt like that paper ballerina who leaps into the fire to join her tin soldier and as he melts she is consumed in an incandescent flame with him.

At dinner Markus and my father spoke easily and comfortably together. They were discussing a recent performance of *The Caucasian Chalk Circle*, which was part of a Brecht revival that had just finished in Helsinki. My mother, who had said very little all evening, broke into their discussion to insist that we take our coffee in the sitting room. We all stood up and trooped through to the other room. Then Markus reached into his rucksack and pulled out a book, which he handed to her.

'Thank you both so much for tonight. I've really enjoyed it. I found this in a bookshop and thought you might like it.'

He handed her a large old book with a brown leather cover, the title embossed in gold. It was a collection of photographs of Helsinki. My mother rested the book on her lap and turned the pages delicately with her manicured fingers. The photographs were all black and white and very beautiful.

'This is most kind,' she said in a tight voice. My dad walked over and sat next to her on the sofa. She turned the book towards him.

'Ah, I know that building – look how the street has changed. May I?' he asked, taking the book from my mother.

He turned to the frontispiece. 'Published in 1932. Where did you find this, Markus?'

'There's an antiquarian bookshop quite near the university. I've been going there for years, looking for textbooks on the cheap. I like to collect photographs of buildings, and the owner knows me now and keeps certain books back for me.'

'This is really very fine. Thank you, Markus.'

After he had gone I helped my mother clear away. She said nothing about Markus and I did not thank her for serving us a takeaway meal. Then we both went back to the sitting room. My dad was still looking at the book. He looked up and saw me watching him and said, 'I liked your Markus very much. He has good taste and lovely manners.'

KATHY

JUNE

Aisha and I were working late. She was typing up my notes for my board presentation, which I was to do the following day. I nipped out to get us both a coffee and saw that Heja was still at her desk and Philip was in his office. He would be preparing for the board meeting too. These were always highly stage-managed affairs and Philip was expert at working his board members.

I asked Heja how she was and she said she was fine, thanks. She didn't say what she was working on. She rarely volunteered information so I asked her directly and she said she was clearing her backlog. I told her I was going to the café down the road and did she want anything to keep her going? She thanked me politely and said she had her water with her. I can never seem to get beyond polite exchanges with Heja.

I hurried back with our coffees and stood at Aisha's side as she typed up my notes and also inserted a table of figures she'd put together. These outlined the demographics of our readers, where they travelled on their holidays and which potential advertisers might want to reach them. It was an excellent piece of research.

'That's brilliant, Aish, just brilliant.'

'You sure that's everything you need?'

'Absolutely. Go! You have packing to do. I can't thank you enough for staying late tonight.'

She printed off my presentation and placed it in a folder with other papers.

'Good luck tomorrow. You'll be great. And I've left some detailed handover notes for the temp and some other stuff that needs your attention.'

She handed me the folder. I kissed her on the cheek.

'What would I do without you? Have a great holiday.'

She was off to Crete for two weeks the next morning and had organized a temp to come in and support me. I sat at my desk for a few more minutes, reading through the presentation notes. They were good. It was nearly seven-thirty and I needed to go. I went to the Ladies and then back to my office; turned everything off; picked up my bag and folder and locked the office. As I walked past Philip's room I saw that Heja was now sitting in there with him. He was sitting back with a glass in his hand, chatting with her, and she was holding a glass too. He looked up and I waved goodbye.

Why did it make me uneasy, seeing Heja sitting in there with him? She was having a drink with him. What was niggling me was the memory of our lunchtime conversation when she'd asked to be made my deputy. I'd said no, that Philip would never allow it, but I hadn't actually asked him. Could she possibly be suggesting it to him now? Was that why she'd been working late – to catch Philip in his office? The idea of her going behind my back made me feel queasy. I hailed a taxi as there was no time to walk home tonight.

Then again he might just have seen her sitting there and asked her into his office to flirt with her. Aisha reckoned he fancied her. He had had affairs with colleagues before. I remembered the whole Andrea business, which had happened about two years ago, and what bad feelings that had caused in the team. Could Heja be getting involved with Philip? It was possible. That thought made me feel uneasy too.

I got home at ten to eight, later than I'd arranged with Fran. I'd just unlocked the door and Fran came out of Billy's room, holding him. She looked flustered and Billy's cheeks were very red and he was crying.

'He's been teething all day. I was about to give him some Calpol.'

'Poor baby; let me feed him first.'

I took Billy from her and sat straight down in his room and unbuttoned my blouse. Billy fastened on to my right breast and started to suck. I looked up and Fran was standing in the doorway.

'Sorry I'm late back. Thanks so much for staying on tonight, you really helped me out.'

She didn't move. She just stood there and her lips began to tremble and then she burst into tears, great gulping sobs that shook her body.

'Fran! What is it?'

She sat down on Billy's toy box, pulled some wet wipes from the box and blew her nose.

'Sorry, sorry . . .'

I was trying to feed Billy and liked to be calm when I did this but Fran needed my sympathy.

'Go into the kitchen, sweetheart, and put the kettle on. I'll get Billy down and then we can talk.'

Fran got up and I transferred Billy to my left breast and he sucked contentedly, his teething pain forgotten. I looked at my watch and saw it was after eight already and Markus was due back around eight-thirty. No food cooked and I wanted to go through my presentation again. But needs must – clearly Fran was going through some kind of crisis. Fran was good with Billy and I relied on her; I needed her to be OK. Billy, now replete with breast milk, had fallen asleep in my arms so I laid him down gently in his cot. His little cheeks were still flushed and his hair a bit damp around the temples, otherwise he seemed fine.

I went into the kitchen. Fran had stopped crying and had made a pot of tea and I poured us both a cup.

'Now, tell me what's wrong, sweetheart.'

She gave a shuddering sigh. 'Andros dumped me last night!'

'Andros . . .?'

And it all came out: how she had been dating this Andros for nine months; how she'd helped him by paying the fees for his motor maintenance course and how last night, out of the blue, he had dumped her. She'd had her suspicions for a while, that he was after this Greek Cypriot girl who lived on his estate. He had taken her money and used her and then dumped her, and she was clearly wretched.

I tried to console her as much as I could. I said she was a lovely young woman with so much to offer. It was far better to know now that he was a rat than to waste years on him. There was someone much better out there for her. I don't think it helped much though she had calmed down.

'I'd say have tomorrow off, Fran, it's just I've got this big presentation I have to do.'

'No, no, I'll be here. I'm better being at work.'

Just then we heard Markus letting himself in and Fran stood up.

'I'll be off.'

She was a bit in awe of Markus, I think. I got up and gave her a hug. 'It will be all right.'

After she'd gone I told Markus what had been going on. It was now after nine and I felt drained and a bit headachy. We ate a late supper and I decided I was too tired to go through my presentation again. I'd set the alarm for an early start.

The alarm went off at six-forty and I unglued my eyes. I was so tired and longed to sleep more but knew I would feel better if I'd prepared properly for the board meeting. I made myself get up, showered and dressed in my smart black and orange dress and proper grown-up shoes. I had learned that you needed to look the part of editor when meeting board members. I brushed my hair vigorously and put on mascara and expensive earrings.

Markus was stirring as I went into the kitchen to get my folder of notes. There were some expense claims on the top of the pile, which was odd as I was sure I'd put my presentation notes on top. I flicked through these. Below were Aisha's hand-over notes and then some invoices and that was it. My presentation notes weren't there. Puzzled, I went through the papers in the folder again – they were not there. I wondered if I had taken them out last night. I got my handbag and searched through it. No. I looked at the various piles of magazines and flyers on the kitchen table and started to riffle through them with an increasing feeling of anxiety. Then I went into my study to look for the notes. My dress was close fitting and I was starting to sweat. Markus was now in the kitchen, making coffee.

'Do you want coffee?' he called out.

'I can't find my notes!'

He walked out into the hall and watched me checking through the papers on my desk with increasing desperation.

'When did you last see them?'

I thought back. 'I looked at them in the office. Then I took a taxi home. Oh, shit! Could they have fallen out in the taxi?'

'They'll be on your system at work. Go in now. You've got time.'

'They're not on my system. They're on Aisha's!'

I grabbed my mobile phone and rang Aisha's number. I was pacing up and down the hall now as it rang and rang, and remembered that she was taking an early flight to Crete. It went straight to her recorded message. Then I heard Billy making his waking-up noises.

'No answer from Aisha! She's probably on a plane by now. Markus, I need you to change and feed Billy. I have to go into the office at once. Sorry, I have to go. Fran will be here soon.'

I grabbed my bag and the folder and left the flat. I didn't wait for the lift. I hurried down the stairs in my high-heeled shoes.

It was already nearly eight and the board meeting started at nine-thirty. I hailed a cab on Baker Street. We got caught up in the usual rush-hour congestion and by now I was feeling quite panicky and light-headed. I knew I had to calm myself down somehow. I remembered that I had an earlier draft of my notes on my computer. It lacked the polish I had given it and the analysis of our readers, which was the key part of my presentation. Finally we reached the office. I unlocked my room and switched on my computer. I printed off the earlier version and for the next forty minutes I tried to remember the detail that Aisha had gathered for me so painstakingly. I remembered some of it. It was not the comprehensive survey I had been planning to present.

Philip, clad in a smart suit, put his head round my door at twenty past nine.

'You ready? Some of the board members have arrived. Come and join us for coffee.'

I stood up. Should I tell him? No, he would think I was

flaky. I followed him out of my room, clutching my draft notes and feeling as if I was being led to my execution. Just before I went into the boardroom I saw Heja and Stephanie at their desks. Heja was looking coolly immaculate, as ever, and was turning on her terminal. Stephanie mouthed, 'Good luck,' in my direction. Philip closed the door behind us.

It was dreadful. I tried to excite the board members about the wonderful sites we would be covering in the guide, some of the most famous buildings in Europe. I hadn't managed to shake off the panicky feeling and I spoke too fast and breathlessly. I know I was not convincing. I must have given the impression that I was unsure about the project. One kind board member, a woman in her sixties, nodded encouragingly at me as I struggled through my notes.

The worst bit was the question-and-answer part after my presentation had ended. I was less than assured in my answers on the figures, and it is the figures that board members always want to talk about. I told them I would send them all a detailed analysis of the demographics of our readers, their travel patterns and which companies were likely to advertise in the guide. That was what they wanted to be convinced about, that the advertising would pay for the guide. Finally Philip moved the meeting on to the next item and I was allowed to leave the room.

I came out of the boardroom and headed for my office. Most of the desks were empty, thankfully, though Heja was sitting there and she glanced over at me with her usual inscrutable expression. I nodded at her and could say nothing. I walked back to my room feeling very low and full of self-doubt. The temp from the agency was sitting at Aisha's desk. I asked her if she would mind getting me a coffee and a croissant. I remembered I hadn't eaten anything all morning and my head was starting to pound. I gave her some cash and then sat at my desk, took off my high-heeled shoes and pulled Aisha's folder over to me.

I wanted to go home very much and lick my wounds. I knew that Philip would come and find me as soon as the board meeting was over. I opened the folder and found Aisha's handover notes under the expense claims. And there, at the very top of her notes, she had written her username and the password to her computer. If only I had kept my head I could have got into her system and printed out the presentation we had worked on so carefully, the version that had all the figures I needed.

At lunchtime, after the board members had left the building, Philip came to my office. I had been expecting him with a feeling of rising apprehension. He came in and shut the door behind him and I stood up. There was no preamble. He launched straight in.

'That was not up to your usual high standard.'

'I know. I'm sorry, Philip.'

'I mean it's all very well offering to send an analysis of our readers, today was your opportunity to *give* them that analysis. That's what I was expecting and I thought I'd made that clear to you.'

'You had. I'm sorry.'

'Is everything all right with you?'

He gave me one of his penetrating looks. He was doubting me; doubting my ability to be a top editor with a baby at home. Should I explain about the lost notes?

'I'm still adjusting and still a bit tired.'

'I'm a bit concerned about your performance, Kathy,' he said. I felt sick. I had always excelled at my work.

'You're still on probation, you know,' he said. 'This role comes with a six-month probation period.'

I lifted my head and made myself look straight into his eyes.

'I understand. I'll prepare a really detailed analysis for the board. You'll have it by the end of the day.'

'OK.'

He walked out.

His criticisms were fair, although they made me feel wretched. I have lost some of my clarity since Billy was born and the old Kathy would never have lost her notes or fluffed her presentation. I went to the Ladies, locked myself in a cubicle and allowed myself to cry for five minutes. Then I spent the next three hours trying to put things right. I used Aisha's password and got into her system. I wrote a concise and persuasive explanation to accompany the table of figures we had produced. I printed it out and handed it to Philip just as he was leaving the building at six.

HEJA

JUNE

Kathy is unsure about her role as editor. And it does not take much to destabilize her. I saw her as she came out from the board meeting. She did not say a word and she looked devastated. She can never hide her emotions. Her face is an open book. It was wonderful to see her looking so brought down.

It had been so easy to go into her office while she was in the Ladies and take her notes. Aisha had left for the night. The folder was lying there on her desk. It was a matter of moments to flick the folder open and grab the notes. I put them in my desk drawer. Then I tapped on Philip's door and said could I have a quick word. He invited me in with alacrity and offered me a drink, which I accepted. He keeps a bottle of whisky in his office. I dislike whisky and toyed with the glass. He didn't notice because he was sitting back and talking about the magazine. I knew it would unnerve her seeing me sitting in there with him. She would wonder what we were talking about.

She does not know how to manage Philip yet he is easy to manage. If I gave him the slightest encouragement he would ask me out. Stephanie told me he has had affairs with colleagues before. There was a woman on their team, Andrea, who became his lover. She was riding high for a while, Stephanie said, and started to throw her weight around and cause resentment.

Finally another member of the team alerted his wife. The very next week Andrea was gone. I asked Stephanie who had told Philip's wife about the affair. She said she did not know. Whoever it was had done them all a favour, she said. I am sure she does know but she was not going to tell me. Perhaps it was her. I established that it had happened two years before and that Kathy was working on the magazine.

I have been watching her flat for the last few days and something has happened to change the nanny's routine. She still takes Billy out for his walk. She goes in the opposite direction now. Today I saw her leave the building. I took the lift to the third floor and let myself into the flat. I went straight into Markus's workroom. I like being around his things, his books and his plans. It makes me feel close to him. I was looking at his books when I saw the old album that had belonged to his grandfather Billy Hartman, the news photographer and communist. I pulled it out and sat on the floor and looked again at the best of his grandfather's work.

Billy Hartman worked all his life as a photographer on the *Helsingin Sanomat*. He was proud of his work and over the years he had pasted his best pictures into this album. Markus loved his grandfather dearly. I remembered his fury when his parents put his grandfather into a nursing home when he got ill with Alzheimer's. Markus fell out very badly with his parents over that. He thought they should have kept him at home with his familiar things around him.

The nursing home was miles away from his grandfather's usual haunts. Markus was still at university, in Helsinki, and it was a long way to go. In spite of this he would visit him regularly. Sometimes I went with him. I remember one of my first visits there. Markus was carrying this photo album. We were sitting in the station, waiting for the train to come.

'What's that?'

'Can you believe my parents? They exile him to this place and they don't even pack his album!' he said.

'What's in it?'

'Only his whole life . . .'

He said when he was a kid he used to ask his grandfather to go through the album and tell the stories behind each picture. Billy Hartman's work had taken him to every kind of news event: shipping accidents; political rallies; and strikes. There was one picture that made a deep impression on Markus. I looked at it now. A young man is lying stretched out on the ground. There is blood coming from the side of his head and it makes a sticky shadow on the ground. His eyes are open and his look is one of surprised pain. There is the trace of a moustache on his upper lip. One arm is trapped under his body in an awkward way. The other arm is flung out with his fingers curled as if in a gesture of calling to someone. He is wearing jeans and one of those rough blue work jackets. Close to his body a crate lies smashed open, spilling the metal parts it contained.

'It's a very powerful picture,' I said.

'My grandfather was at the dockyard when the accident happened. He'd been sent to photograph some visiting trade delegation. He got there early and was walking around the yard to see where he could take his pictures. He always said to me: "Time spent in reconnaissance is never wasted." That was one of his favourite sayings. So he saw the crate fall and hit the young man on the side of his head and saw him crumple and die in front of his eyes. He decided he would record it.'

'What a terrible accident,' I said.

'It was an outrage. That dockyard had a bad safety record.

He'd heard that from some of the dockers who were in the Communist Party with him.'

As it turned out, his grandfather's shocking photograph kick-started a campaign to improve safety at the dockyards in Finland. His work had made a difference.

When we reached the nursing home Markus walked in front of me and found his grandfather sitting on a bench under the trees. It was one of Billy Hartman's more lucid afternoons and he was very happy to see Markus and to get his album back. He was a committed communist. On other occasions when we went to see him he would say to us over and over again: 'From each according to their means, to each according to their needs, it's the only thing that will work. You'll see.'

I am sure she knows none of this. She has no idea what a special man Markus is or what matters to him. I remembered that man at the window, the man holding Billy while Markus was away. I put the album back exactly where I had taken it out and went into her study. I went through the drawers in her desk. She had stuffed all kinds of things in there. Old floppy disks, some used-up cheque books and in the bottom drawer I found a pile of loose photographs. I scanned through them. I found what I was looking for. There were quite a few photos of him. In one he was stripped to the waist, his torso tanned, standing in a garden. Her lover . . . I took this photograph and placed it right in the centre of Markus's drawing table. His table was clear and he could not miss it.

KATHY

JUNE

I was in the kitchen, trying to decide what to make for supper. I felt the need for comfort food. Billy was playing at my feet and I was so despondent. Philip had given me no feedback on the paper I'd done for him and the board members. I knew he had sent it out because I'd asked his PA. He hadn't mentioned it to me once. Philip is very unforgiving. It takes a long time to gain his respect and then you can lose it very quickly. I heard Markus unlocking the front door and he came into the kitchen and kissed me and Billy.

'I feel like a night off,' he said. 'Let's take Billy for a walk.'

It was rare for Markus to suggest such a thing and I agreed at once.

I was glad to get out of the flat. It was a mild and luminous evening and we headed for Regent's Park. There were quite a few couples strolling along the paths of the park, arm in arm, enjoying that peaceful after-work time, and I wished that I felt more peaceful. As we walked around the boating lake, pushing Billy, I confided my fears to Markus.

'I'm having a bad time at work and I'm not sure I can hack it as the editor.'

It was hard to voice my feelings of inadequacy to him but I needed to talk about it.

'It's still early days,' he said in a kind voice.

I could feel my eyes filling with tears.

'I seem to be messing up, losing things, forgetting things. And the more I doubt myself the more mistakes I make.'

'You lost your notes and that was a pity. You came up with a good idea for the guide,' he said. 'And it's still going ahead, isn't it?'

'Yes, it is. Philip reminded me that I'm on a six-month probation. I think he's lost faith in me.'

'I doubt that. Perhaps you try to do too much. Let your team do more. Let them do the writing and you sit back and be the calm and benevolent boss.'

'I like doing the writing.'

'Do some, then, but be generous with them. Let them have the pick of the sites. You'll get them onside and with a loyal team behind you Philip can't touch you.'

It was good advice and his support made me feel better. I decided I would do as he suggested: yes, I would hold individual meetings with each member of my team and ask them which sites they wanted to cover. It would make them feel valued and it would help me get back my good feelings about the project. I squeezed his hand.

'Thank you.'

We walked some more and admired the light shining on the lake. As we were both enjoying being out we decided to make an evening of it. We found a café with tables on the pavement that was serving tapas. We sat down, parked the buggy next to us and ordered two beers.

'You're bound to be a tapas expert,' Markus said, 'so I'll let you do the ordering.'

'It's true, lots of tapas during my childhood, though Dad always remained a meat and two veg man.'

'Well, mine was a pickled herring, potatoes and rye bread childhood,' he said with a rueful smile.

I looked at the menu. 'We have to have garlic shrimp, patatas bravas, marinated anchovies, tortilla and some chorizo, I think. I'm torn between fried squid rings and stuffed mussels. Do you have a preference?'

'I've never had stuffed mussels.'

'Well, they're stuffed, breaded and fried, and very tasty.'

'Do we need another dish?' he said.

'Maybe not, maybe I'm just being greedy. It's a bit of a treat, though.'

Our plate of tortilla arrived first and I cut off a small piece for Billy to chew on. He wasn't very interested. His eyelids were getting heavy and I tipped his buggy seat back and Markus rolled him back and forth till he was asleep.

We had a second beer and the rest of our tapas arrived. I told Markus to close his eyes and I would feed him random forkfuls and he had to tell me which dish he liked best. I fed him garlic shrimp and then patatas bravas and then the other dishes, and we were both giggling and being a bit silly. He said he liked the bite from the Tabasco in the potatoes' sauce. His overall favourite had to be the marinated anchovies.

'That's your pickled fish heritage coming through,' I said.

'And I'm guessing your favourite is garlic shrimp.'

'Spot on.'

When we had finished the food and wiped our bread around the plates to catch the last bit of sauce, we both looked at our sleeping son next to us.

'Nothing prepared me for the feelings I have for him,' Markus said. 'It's really quite primitive, isn't it, how you feel?'

I put my hand over his. 'It really is.'

We walked back to the flat and there was a lovely united feeling between us. It was quite late and I carried Billy into his room and was putting him to bed.

'Did you put this on my table?' Markus said, coming in.

He held out a photo to me and it gave me a jolt because it was my favourite photo of Eddie. In it he is standing in a garden, one of the places where he often worked. He is stripped to the waist, his chest and arms are tanned, his face is freckled and he is grinning broadly into the camera. He looks the picture of healthy male sexiness.

'That's Eddie, my ex. I told you about him. Where did you find it?'

'On my work table just now . . .'

I immediately felt a bit defensive.

'That's strange. I didn't put it there. I haven't seen this in ages.'

'Maybe Fran, then?' he said.

'Where would she have found it?'

I was sure that I'd tucked all my photos of Eddie away in my bottom desk drawer. I remembered doing it just before Markus moved into the flat with me as I thought it was the tactful thing to do in the circumstances. Markus just shrugged and left Billy's room. He didn't seem to be irritated about it, just puzzled. It had made me feel uncomfortable and guilty as I hadn't told him about Eddie's arrival at the flat. It was possible he might have been annoyed about that late-night visit. I'm no good at keeping secrets and I don't like to do it. Now this photo was a potent reminder of my not telling Markus and I'm sure my face had given me away.

I covered Billy with a light blanket. Then I looked at the photo again; Eddie on a good day. I went into my study and opened the bottom desk drawer and there were all my photos of my life with Eddie, just as I'd thought. I added this photo to the pile. It was a shame because it had created a slightly jarring note to the end of what had been a loving evening together.

HEJA

JUNE

This afternoon I had my meeting with her. She called me into her office and we sat at her meeting table. She is always very scrupulous to sit at this table. She would never conduct a meeting with her sitting behind her desk. She had a sleeveless red linen dress on. I noticed dark crescent-shaped marks of sweat on the dress under her arms.

'It's very hot, isn't it?' she said as I sat down. 'I can't open the window any further and anyway there's no breeze today. Would you like a glass of water, Heja?'

'Yes, please, if it is still water.'

'Sure.'

She walked over to her bookshelves and produced a large bottle of Evian and two ugly plastic tumblers, which she placed on the table in front of us. I waited while she poured me some water.

'Thank you.'

'So, the heritage series is going to keep us busy well into next year and I'm very keen to know which sites you'd particularly like to cover,' she said.

'Do you have any ideas?' I asked her.

I did not see why I should go through the motions of appearing excited about her project. Tim and Stephanie had already had their meetings with her and they were full

91

of it. Tim had bagged Italy and Stephanie was going to do the sites in Greece.

'I was hoping you might have a preference, Heja.'

I shook my head.

'Well, I guess you could do the Finnish sites. Would that appeal to you?'

She moved a list in front of me.

'There are seven sites and you probably know them all. We wouldn't include the burial site or the landscape sites. We'd like to cover the other four.'

I looked at the list – the Fortress of Suomenlinna, Old Rauma, the Petajavesi Old Church built of logs and the Verla Groundwood and Board Mill.

'I visited them all as a schoolgirl. I did not find them very inspiring then. I do not think I could find anything interesting to say about them now.'

'Oh, OK. I was just thinking that having the language you might get more out of any interviews . . .'

'The curators of these sites will all speak excellent English.'

'Of course, of course . . .'

She twiddled the ring on her right finger. It is a thick gold Wright and Teague ring with words etched on its circumference. I have noticed that she always plays with that ring when she is thinking. She looks down at it and turns the ring so that one particular word is uppermost. She rarely looks at the rather modest wedding ring on her left hand. She pushed the list of all the sites in front of me.

'You're sure there's nothing here you'd really like to do?'

I scanned the list. There are many famous sites throughout Europe. I do not want to travel anywhere. When I reached the United Kingdom I saw that Durham Castle and Cathedral were on the list, and the island of St Kilda and Hadrian's Wall.

'I would like to do the British sites, especially those in the north of England and Scotland,' I said.

'Are you sure?' There was sweat on her face, I noticed.

'Quite sure.'

'Well, OK, thank you, Heja, that would be great. I'm sure you'll bring a fresh perspective to them.'

She stood up. I remained seated.

'Will you give me more details of the format you want us to follow?'

'Oh, yes. I've created a template on Siena – let me make a copy for you now.'

She grabbed a board from the side of her desk and hurried out of the office. I looked over at her desk. There was a new photo frame by the phone and I could not see the picture from where I was sitting. I got up and walked over to her desk and turned the frame round. It was a medium close-up shot of Markus seated in a chair by a window with Billy on his lap. Markus has his large hands round the baby's body. Billy is leaning his head back against his father's chest. Both are looking straight into camera. The baby's face is serious. Markus has a quizzical, almost embarrassed smile on his face. A shaft of sunlight illuminates the right side of his face and his hair is almost white in its light. I did not recognize the room. I do not think the photo was taken at her flat. I turned the frame back and continued to look out of the window as she walked back into the room.

'You have a good view from here,' I said.

'I love it. That maple tree is a joy, especially in the autumn. Here's a copy of the sample board. I'd like us to give some historical background and key details on each building. Not too much text, though, you can use this as a guide.'

I glanced at the A3 sheet. 'I see. I'll get started on it, then.'

'Thank you, Heja.'

Sometimes I talk to Tim when the others are not there. He has been at the magazine a long time and I find him the least irritating of the team members. I was asking him about the Andrea business. He told me it had caused major trouble when Philip started his affair with her. He said Andrea had been one of the gang before that, she was a lot of fun and then she changed. He thought she was very ambitious.

'She started to call herself Arndrea,' he said.

'Did Kathy get on with her?' I asked.

'Sort of, I think, until Andrea became the bloody queen bee!'

Tim looked over towards Philip's office. The door was closed.

'Bit of a taboo subject, Heja, around the boss.'

This evening it was still warm and I put down the roof on my car and drove to Richmond to sit in the Great Park. I often come here. How quiet it is. The tall and ancient trees are still. There is no breeze to stir even the topmost leaf. The children have all gone home. There are three silver birch trees that stand apart in a triangular formation. Their barks are ivory white and etched with grey horseshoe markings and they gleam in the evening light. I like these trees even better in the winter when the leaves have gone and their delicate branches are silhouetted against a leaden sky.

There is something resilient about Kathy. She was cast down by her failure at the board meeting. Now she has bounced back. I noticed at our meeting that she seems to have recovered her zest. I think she must have parents who made her feel secure and loved as a child. That is why she does not see the threats around her. She and Philip are going through a bad patch, though. She may have got the team on side. I can make Philip my ally.

A large crow flaps by the white trees and makes a clumsy landing. He squats on the grass and examines his oily wings, digging with his beak between the black feathers with energy, almost with aggression. Then he lifts up his head and lurches back into the sky. I sit until the light fades.

I will not go back to Finland this summer. My mother is a carrion crow. She would peck at my body in its weakened state. I miss my father. I miss Arvo Talvela. I miss Markus most of all.

KATHY

JUNE

When I was born my dad said with fond amusement, 'Why, she looks like a little wrinkled olive.'

'No, no,' my mum protested, mistaking my father's humour for criticism. 'She's our little dove.'

This became the great family joke, told again and again, and explains my ridiculous name, which is Katherine Paloma Olive. My mum, Luisa, is Portuguese. She came to work in London in the late sixties and when she met my dad she introduced him to olives. Dad was Norfolk born and bred and at that time Norfolk had barely seen an olive! You could get carrots, onions, turnips and swedes in winter and lettuce, tomatoes and cucumber in summer. So he thought that olives were the height of exoticism, a bit like my mum really.

She is flamboyant, warm and expressive and my dad was crazy about her; he still is. They've had their difficulties. A year after I was born my mum was diagnosed with cervical cancer. She had to have a hysterectomy. My father was terrified that she would die and he'd be left with a one-year-old baby girl to look after. The gods smiled on them, she made a good recovery and the cancer has never come back, thankfully.

My mum was stricken that they couldn't have more children, though; she had planned to have a big family, so I became the beloved one and only child. My dad told me that Mum's cancer changed his view of life. He became less ambitious, he said, and found more pleasure in simple things – cooking, walking, spending time with us. During my childhood we spent every summer and many Christmases in Portugal and those are the times that I remember my mum at her happiest. Now that Dad has retired they have settled there permanently. He did that for Mum.

I stepped off the plane with Billy at Aeroporto Da Portela. It was the last week of June, a lovely time to be in Lisbon. I've noticed that when you step off a plane there is always a different smell to the air and I'm convinced that every country has its own unique smell. I love the smell of Portugal, which is slightly sweet with a peppery edge to it. My parents were waiting for us at the airport and after exuberant hugs all round my dad drove us to their apartment. Lisbon is an easy city to live in because it has kept its human scale and charm. As we were driving to their flat I pointed out the yellow trams to Billy.

'When he's a bit older I'll take him on the trams,' I said.

My mum and my grandmother used to take me on the yellow tram to the parades on saints' feast days and I remember many such days during my childhood. When I was little I was frightened of the giant wooden figures that would be paraded through the streets, especially the effigy of the Devil. I could exactly recall his painted bright red angry face with black horns on his forehead and his grotesque smile; a fearsome grimace. My grandmother had a strong sense of sin and she would talk about the Devil as if he was a real person; a person you might encounter at any time. You had to be prepared and your rosary and your prayers were your best defence.

Sometimes my dad came with us too, although he is not

big on religion. He is an easygoing man who does not like extreme views of any kind. When he came along he would lift me onto his shoulders so that I could see the parade better. Men would carry the giant wooden effigies through the streets and I did like the figure of the beautiful lady who wore a white lace mantilla. The procession of figures was always led by a band of drummers who beat out an ecstatic rhythm and we would follow them into the main square. In the winter months there would be a bonfire as well as the parade. The band of drummers would beat to a crescendo and then the bonfire would be lit to cheers from the crowd.

Afterwards Dad would take me to the street stall selling candied nuts. There would be the most delicious smell of melting sugar as the vendor swirled the nuts in his large metal bowl and coated them with hot caramel. Dad would buy me a bag and I would crack the sweet crunchy nuts between my teeth.

My grandmother was a formidable woman and I think my mum loved and feared her in equal measure. I wondered sometimes if Mum had come to England to get away from her mother's loving but oppressive care. Certainly there was conflict between them. I know they sometimes argued about how I should be brought up; and of course my mum had married an English Protestant. As Mum grew older, though, the pull of Lisbon and of her Catholicism seemed to strengthen its hold on her and she was certainly happy to be living there again now.

My parents have an apartment with a view of the river Tagus from their large balcony. This is their favourite space in the flat and they eat most of their meals out there. There's a canvas canopy over the balcony that used to be dark blue. The sun has bleached it to paleness, like a weathered sail,

and the raffia chairs round the table have a comforting sag
to them. We sat around that first afternoon and had a long
rich lunch of pork with clams – *carne de porco à Alentejana*,
one of my mum's best dishes. Then Mum said, 'Now you
must sleep,' so I went to bed for two hours, pulling the blind
down against the brilliant sun, while they took Billy for a
walk up the cobbled streets.

In the evening I helped with the dinner. Mum was pulling
out all the stops for us. She had soaked a large piece of salt
cod in the pan and she asked me to peel and slice some garlic.
She poured us each a glass of white wine and sat at the table
with me.

'Dad looks well, don't you think?'

'He looks great. Retirement suits him.'

'What about you, sweetheart . . .?'

'I'm not as tired as I was. For months I was in a kind of
daze. Mum, did you and Dad have any difficulties when you
first got married – I mean, coming from different countries?'

'Oh, yes, many times. We had lots of rows. Dad thought
I was far too emotional. Sometimes he couldn't put up with
it, especially if I cried, and he would just walk out of the
house and not come back for hours!'

'Men hate tears! What happened?'

'Most often we just hugged and made up. We couldn't
bear to be cross with each other for long. And then we got
used to each other's ways.'

'Did he tell you much about his life, before he met you?'

'Not so much. There was another woman before me, an
English woman. He didn't say much about her, and I didn't
want to know about her. I was usually the one telling him
my stories.'

'Me, too. I did all the talking when we first met. Maybe

99

it *is* a male–female thing. You know with Markus I think it goes deeper than that. He is *so* reserved.'

'Yes, he is. I saw that at the wedding. That's his way, darling. It's not a bad thing.'

My mother had been delighted and relieved when I got married and I had expected her to stick up for Markus.

'Now, have you two talked about the christening?'

'Not yet . . . One thing I do know about Markus is that he's very anti-religion.'

'Your dad wasn't a believer either but he let me christen you. He knew it was important to me.'

'We're still reeling from being new parents.'

'Talk to him about it when you can. It's important, sweetheart.'

The next morning I set off early for the Torre de Belem, leaving Billy with my parents. I had arranged for a local photographer, Hector Agapito, to meet me there. I'd seen examples of his work and thought it was first class. We had never met. I was standing on the pavement, looking at the tower, and the sun was so dazzling that it hurt to look at the brilliant white façade. I was getting my sunglasses out of my bag when this man with a camera case in one hand and a tripod in the other called my name out loudly.

'Kathy?'

He was dressed in black jeans and a grey T-shirt. I studied him as he walked over, noticing his long black hair curling around his neck.

'Hello, I'm Hector.'

He put down the tripod and we shook hands. He looked at me in a way I can only describe as thorough, as if he was assessing the contours of my face.

'How did you know it was me?' I asked.

'I thought you looked like someone from London.'

'Really?'

'Maybe it's your clothes that look London,' he said.

I looked down at my black Capri trousers, my sleeveless red tunic top and my black sandals and couldn't quite see it, yet his remark made me feel cheerful.

The tower is located at the entrance to Lisbon's harbour, on the right bank of the Tagus, and we both stood and looked at it. It had been built as a defensive fortress to the entrance of the river estuary and was completed in 1520. Now, after centuries of silting, the shore has grown to meet the tower so that it stands as if moored to the riverbank.

Hector said, 'We'd be much better off doing the establishing shots from the river if we get on one of the ferry boats later.'

'That's a good idea. We've got permission so let's start at the top. Can you get shots of the vaulting on the fourth floor? That's the only original vaulting left.'

'Yes . . . and you'll want the rhinoceros?'

'Yes, please.'

On the sentinel box there's a carved rhinoceros and it was the first depiction of the animal in Europe.

It was cool inside the tower and I breathed in that distinctive smell of stone and plaster that you find in old buildings and which I sometimes think I'm a bit addicted to. I offered to carry his tripod. Hector said he could manage, thanks, and he sprinted up the stairs in front of me as if he couldn't wait to get started. From the window I could see the wide estuary and the western side of Lisbon stretching out before me. I took out my pad and started to make notes.

'See those three-centred arches, they have an interesting perspective,' he said.

He walked round the space for several minutes, stopping in front of the triple arches, then set up his tripod and took a long time photographing them. Then we went out on to the jetty and the view opened out onto the Tagus and the sky and I could smell a whiff of drains from the river.

'Nearly finished here. Come on, I want you in this shot.'

'I don't think my boss would appreciate this narcissism! OK, just one with me.'

Hector positioned me against the wall. Then he moved in closer and took half a dozen close-ups of me. He had warm brown eyes that met mine over the eyepiece. Yet his look did not connect with mine. Again I felt that he was examining me as a series of shapes, of planes of light and shade.

We bought our ferry tickets and as we moved out onto the Tagus I watched him shooting the tower. It does look its best from the river and you can see the Moorish influence very clearly. I sat on the bench at the front of the ferry, which was half empty, and watched how he worked. His body conveyed the same level of intensity that Markus has when he's bent over his drawing table.

Finally he turned to me and said, 'Now I'm happy! Shall we get some lunch? I know a good place to eat on the other side.'

'I want moules with lots and lots of garlic,' I said.

'That won't be a problem.'

Just at that moment an old man, who had been sitting on a bench near me, staggered to his feet and tried to grab the ship's rail. His arms went all stiff, his body rigid and he started to have a fit. His eyes were open and staring but they did not seem to register anything and his jaw hung open as he gasped for breath. I saw that he was going to fall. Then Hector was there. He had leapt forward and had caught the full weight of the old man's body, which was now shaking violently.

'Kathy, here, now!' he shouted, in Portuguese.

I ran to his side and we held the old man's body under his back. It was a dead weight and I was afraid I wouldn't be able to hold on to him. Somehow we both managed to kneel down very slowly and lower the old man to the deck. I saw the stubble on the grey skin of his face and a trickle of blood from the right side of his mouth where he had bitten his tongue in the fury of his fit. His body was still shaking although the tremors were subsiding. Hector rested the old man's head on his knees, holding his face in his hands, stroking his cheeks and speaking gentle words to him. By this time one of the ship's crew had come up.

Hector said, 'We need medical aid at once. Can anyone help?'

He was still speaking reassuring words to the old man. The steward arrived and knelt down by us. The old man's body had stopped shaking. His eyes were open and unseeing. Hector laid his head down very gently on the deck. The steward bent over his body and checked the pulse in his neck. I knew he was dead and I started to shake. I sat down with my back against the bench and closed my eyes.

Some minutes later I felt Hector's hand on my bare arm. I shuddered.

'I've never seen a dead body before,' I said shakily.

He put his arm around me then. 'He was an old man and he died quickly,' he said. 'I don't think he knew much about it. And now I'm going to buy you a drink.'

I opened my eyes and saw them lifting the old man's body on to a stretcher. His grey flannel trousers were wet around the crotch and I noticed his nicotine-stained fingers protruding from his brown cardigan. I had witnessed how tender Hector had been with the old man in his last moments and realized again that kindness was such an important quality in a person, the most important quality really.

Hector came back with two brandies in plastic tumblers and we sat on the deck with our backs against the bench. I felt the breeze on my neck, the sun on my face and the vibrations of the ship beneath my thighs. I heard the slap of the waves against the boat and the shriek of a bird overhead. I felt the brandy burn its track down my throat and into my stomach and I was very aware of Hector sitting next to me. My body was prickling with life. The old man was dead and I was alive.

The next day I met Hector at the Mosteiro dos Jeronimos. It was early and there weren't many people about. He looked at me and asked quietly, 'OK?'

I nodded and spoke quickly to cover a feeling of sudden breathlessness. 'I think this is one of the most perfectly beautiful buildings on earth.'

We walked around the cloister, examining the detail of the carvings. On every span of every arch and on every slender column we saw the stonemasons' unique designs – faces tormented and divine, garlands of flowers and fruits, animals mythical and real. The sun cast fantastic shadows on the stone walls and floors. We spent five hours at the Mosteiro as Hector kept finding more details he wanted to shoot. While he was working I walked around, taking notes. There's a formal garden in the centre of the cloister and it's a perfect Mediterranean garden, with small paths crisscrossing an arrangement of low shrubs with triangles of gravel in between. I sat on a bench and closed my eyes and let myself be still and I felt happy. Then I heard Hector's footsteps on the gravel.

'I owe you a bowl of moules,' he said.

It was a small place and you wouldn't have known it was a restaurant from the outside. Hector ordered moules for both of us and a bottle of white wine. They brought us bread and green olives and a saucer of olive oil.

'I can do Porto now,' he said, breaking off a piece of bread, dipping it in the oil and chewing it with strong white teeth that were slightly crossed at the front.

'Great. Your agent wasn't sure if you'd be free.'

'She's rearranged things. This is a big project, isn't it?'

'It is. A year-long survey of World Heritage Sites, just the ones in Europe.'

'That should keep you busy . . .'

The waiter brought us a casserole of steaming moules and two wide bowls. Hector ladled a pile of black shells into my bowl then poured the milky white liquor over them.

'Fantastic amount of garlic, just how I like it,' he said.

'Me too, though I have this odd English anxiety about smelling of garlic.'

'It's good for you.'

'I know. If you eat a lot it comes out through your skin and your sweat, and that seems a bit too physical for us uptight English.'

'You're Portuguese too, though?'

'Yes, my mum . . . and I do take after her when it comes to food!'

We both ate with great contentment as the pile of empty shells grew between us.

'Do you ever work outside Portugal?' I asked.

'Yes, quite often in Spain and sometimes in Brazil . . .'

'And you like working abroad?'

'I do, but I loved doing the Mosteiro today even though I know it's been photographed a thousand times. I like to think of those stonemasons, each man creating his own unique piece of work. It must have felt good knowing his carving would be there long after his death.'

'Yes, his very own personal monument . . . Seeing the old man on the boat made me think about my grandmother. I often think about her when I'm here. She was a bit of a fearsome granny actually.'

'Oh, I had one of those too.'

'Did you? Mine loved the saints, especially Anthony of Lisbon. She'd tell me bedtime stories. Her heroes were never princes disguised as frogs; no, her stories were always about the saints and the battles they fought with the Devil and the temptations of the flesh!'

Hector laughed.

'And she would use such funny phrases. She would say solemnly that Anthony of Lisbon was the Hammer of Heretics. I didn't know what she meant except that it sounded very alarming.'

'That's enough to mark you for life! Now, my granny, who I'm sure would have got on famously with your granny, had a thing about the popes. She would do these jigsaws of paintings of the popes and they were really difficult because of all that white clothing!'

We were both laughing now. It was so easy being with him. He had a lovely mouth and somehow his slightly crossed teeth made it even more attractive.

I waved to him as he drove off on his scooter. Then I walked back to my parents' apartment. It was very hot and still and most people would be sleeping off their lunches. I took a turning up a road that ran parallel to theirs and saw a small chapel, which the afternoon light was gilding, turning the stone into the loveliest shade of pale gold. I decided to take a quick look inside and crossed the road towards it. I had the wrought-iron ring in my hand and was pushing the heavy door open when I found I could not bring myself to walk over the threshold. My heart jolted as my head filled with a vivid image of the Devil sitting cross-legged and malevolent on the pulpit. He had a blackened body and scaly legs that ended in hooves. It was the expression on his face that paralysed me at the chapel door. He was grinning with a look of utter malice in his smoky black eyes.

When I arrived at the train station the next morning for our trip to Porto, Hector was sitting in the coffee bar, as we had arranged. He was reading a newspaper and drinking an espresso. His head was bent over the paper and his dark hair curled around the nape of his neck. He saw me walk in and stood up as I came towards him, and what started as a hug of greeting became a passionate embrace and I tasted the coffee in his mouth as we kissed.

HEJA

JUNE

She is away in Portugal, recording her precious sites. She is not back until next week. Ever since I looked at his drawings and his books again a longing has been growing in me to see Markus. I feel that anything is possible. Markus is not like other men. He can never abandon a deeply held commitment and he told me I was the love of his life.

I called him at his office. He works at an architectural practice in Clerkenwell. The receptionist asked who was calling and I said, 'Tell him it is Heja.' He came to the phone straight away. His voice was tense and he spoke to me in Finnish.

'I was wondering if you would ever call.'

'I think we should see each other.'

There was a long pause. Then he said, 'I'm not sure that's a good idea, Heja.'

'Markus, it *is* a good idea. I want to know how you are. Are you happy and well? How is your work going? Come and have dinner at my new home. It is right on the river and I want to show it to you, to see if you approve.'

Another long pause and I knew I had chosen my moment well. He agreed to come to my flat for dinner the next evening.

*

I took the afternoon off work and took my time getting ready. I wore a black satin sheath dress and kept my hair down. Markus always liked me to wear my hair down. When we were students he would tease me about how I always wore my hair in a plait. Tonight it felt good to wear it down.

I live in a loft apartment that overlooks the Thames, near Blackfriars Bridge. My main living area is one huge high-ceilinged room. When the buzzer sounded I trembled, with fear as much as desire. He had not seen me for seven years. How much had I changed?

I opened the door to him and was able to say, 'Welcome, dearest Markus.'

He did not kiss me as he stepped over the threshold. He just looked at me and said, 'So many years, Heja . . .'

He has matured. There are some lines around his eyes and mouth that I have never seen before. Then he walked into the room and looked around slowly. The floor in the living area is pale limestone. The walls are parchment white, except for the back one, which is dull silver. The wall that fronts the river is all glass and on fine days it becomes a screen of light. I have kept the room uncluttered, almost empty except for two pale grey sofas. On the back wall there is a mosaic, which I made myself. It is in the shape of a giant conch shell and the tesserae are fragments of glass and shells – green, turquoise and mother of pearl. Against the left-hand wall is the kitchen area with a long bar that fronts pale wood cupboards.

He walked over and examined my mosaic. Then he crossed the room and looked at the kitchen fittings with an expert eye. Finally he walked over to look at the riverfront from my giant window. Turning round, he looked over at me, his eyes bright with appreciation.

'It's so good, Heja, and the colours are really subtle.'

'I learnt so much from you. It's not too rich for you?'

'It's all money you've earned, by your own labours.'

'That's true.'

We have always loved the same things. It is one of the deep things that connected us, but he does not allow himself to have them. Seeing him standing in my flat, which I created always with him in mind, I felt I could get him back. I walked over to the bar and offered him a glass of white wine. I asked him to pour the wine as my hands shake when I am deeply moved. He poured the wine. Then he sat down on the bar stool opposite me. He looked at me very intently and asked me the question I knew he would.

'You *must* tell me the truth, Heja. Why are you working at Kathy's magazine?'

'I love writing about buildings. You taught me to look at them properly.'

'But *Kathy*'s magazine?'

'It's the best one there is. I came to London to change careers, Markus, and I was stunned when I discovered the connection.'

'So was I when I heard you were working there. I couldn't understand it. Magazine writer? You were a household name . . .'

'The whole thing got so it sickened me. I'd had enough. I had to get out. You can imagine how furious my mother was when I walked away from all that.'

'They can't like you being here, so far from home.'

'She always preferred her dogs to me. Dad misses me and I miss him. How is your family?' I said, remembering his great rift with them.

'I hardly see them any more, not since Granddad died. They still regard me as the black sheep!'

'You haven't told Kathy about us, have you?'

'No.'

His 'no' hung in the air. I had prepared a simple dinner of smoked salmon and pickled herring, knowing it was a favourite with him, and tomato and cucumber salad. He sliced some rye bread for the two of us and poured more wine.

'It's a very large secret to keep,' I said gently.

He didn't reply. I leaned forward and put my hand over his.

'Markus, we should never have parted. We shared too much too early. It isn't possible to start again with someone else after all that.'

His skin was warm. He put his other hand on top of mine and said, 'Always such cold hands . . . I've thought and thought about it over the years. We were so young, Heja, we met too soon.'

'It's not like catching a train; I'll wait for the next one!'

'And everything was going so well for you . . .'

'Is that why you left – because I was doing well?'

He was quiet for a moment. Then he said, 'I suppose it did come between us a bit, the way you embraced the media world.'

'It was my job!'

'How could you stand some of those people?'

I could feel myself flushing.

'You thought I was turning into one of them, didn't you?'

'No, no, I didn't. Sooner or later the press would have got hold of it. There would have been stories about Heja Vanheinen and the student revolutionary! You might have resented me then.'

He took his hand off mine and looked out of the window

and his face had the anguished look I remembered from years before.

'Is your work going well?' I asked, wanting to pull him back.

He looked rueful. 'Sometimes.'

'Tell me what you're working on.'

And later I was brave, very brave, because I asked him about being a father. He went into raptures about Billy and showed me his photograph with such loving pride. I said all the right things, about what a fine boy he was and how much he looked like Markus. It hurt to see how much he adored his son by her; how Billy had become the centre of his life. He gave a great deal away, though, without meaning to. He told me how it had all happened so quickly. He'd only been seeing her for a few months; the pregnancy was unplanned but he was so glad it had happened. I knew then what I had suspected all along. He does not love her. Markus is only with her because of Billy.

He stayed late with me. We sat on my sofa and listened to some of our favourite pieces of music. He had walked over to my CD collection and studied the ranks of CDs.

'Still into the Russians, I see.'

Then he looked more closely and laughed.

'Only you would organize them alphabetically and then chronologically within the alphabet!'

'Look who's talking. I remember your books! Can I look at your plans for Durham?'

He agreed. We are meeting again in two days' time, while she is still away. As he was standing in the hall about to leave, he briefly touched my hair and the nape of my neck.

'I wanted to say all evening that I'm sorry I left you so abruptly,' he said. Then he was gone.

I stood at my large window and watched the river. I know I am what he needs. She would get the smells and the flavours and the colours all wrong for him. She does not know his history. She does not understand his anger. Soon her mess will start to corrupt him. He will lose that incredible clarity he has always had.

KATHY

JUNE/JULY

On the train to Porto we sat across from each other and played with each other's hands and tried to rationalize the kiss as an emotional reaction to the old man's death.

And I did not kiss Hector again. We worked hard and in harmony all day, ate together with pleasure in the evening and then we parted in the hotel corridor with glances at each other as we opened the doors to our separate rooms.

Markus has been different since I got back from Lisbon; he's being kinder and gentler with me. He's still working every waking hour on the Durham project. He's making an effort too and he came to meet us at the airport. When I walked through the gate with Billy asleep in his buggy I saw him standing at the barrier, waiting for us, and he looked care-worn. I felt a pang then that I had left him alone when he had so much work to do. We hugged for a long moment.

I said, 'Have you been looking after yourself?'

'I got a huge amount of work done. Can we get something to eat here now? There's not much in the flat.'

'And you forgot to eat all day?'

'Something like that . . .' he said, smiling ruefully.

We sat in the airport restaurant and Billy slept on while Markus ate his way through soup, steak and chips, and apple pie. He kept looking at Billy, wanting him to wake up.

'Your parents are well?'

'They're both really well and so in love with Billy. They took him out every day while I got on with it. Dad said he got fit climbing up the hills pushing the buggy!'

'Did the photographer work out?'

'He was excellent and he worked very hard. His shots will be a bit special, I think.'

I didn't want to talk to Markus about Hector. I knew I would falter under his gaze if I said anything more, so I didn't tell him about the old man dying on the ferry. It was one of those experiences that breaks through the mundane, that I would always remember, and it was something I shared with Hector alone. Afterwards it felt as if we had known each other for years and it had led to that amazing transgressive kiss.

I did nonetheless regret the secrets and the silences that were building up between Markus and me, like a drystone wall, each secret another stone to hide us from each other.

Billy finally woke up and as I lifted him up Markus said, 'Let me have him.'

He hugged him close then kissed his cheeks and said: 'My best boy; how I missed you.'

When we got home and were sitting in the kitchen I saw that Markus had mended my little apple green jug that I liked so much. It was standing in the middle of the table. I picked it up.

'Oh, thanks so much for doing that, Markus. It looks beautiful, as good as new.'

'Almost . . .' he said.

I searched in my bag and found the package, which I handed to him. 'And this is for you. I saw it in this shop near my parents' place.'

He opened the paper bag and pulled out the crystalline

rock I had bought for him. The outside of the rock was rough and dull grey-brown. Its interior was a mass of brilliant sparkling crystals. I had seen it on my last day and thought that he would like the contrast between the rough exterior and the brilliant interior. He held the rock in both hands and moved it back and forth so that the kitchen lights hit the crystals and bounced rays of light around the room.

'I like it very much. Thank you.'

'You can put it on your desk at work, as a paperweight or something.'

Hector's photographs are remarkable. They arrived at the office this morning. Some of them are really beautiful and some of them are high contrast and striking. They are all the product of his intense way of looking at the world. The art director, who is designing the guide, wants to put one of these shots on the front cover of the first issue. I haven't shown anyone the photos that Hector took of me.

On my last day in Lisbon we had met at the ferry and had taken the boat to the other side of the river. It was his idea to go on the boat again.

'To exorcise memories of a sad event,' he said.

We sat on the bench on the deck and looked at Lisbon from the river. I was leaving the next morning and the city looked so seductive to my eyes. I could understand why my mother had wanted to live here so much.

'I love that church,' he said, pointing to a rose-washed façade. 'Sadly, when you get close up you see that the stone is decaying and the frescoes inside are just crumbling away.'

Hector handed me two large envelopes. In the first were contact sheets of all his shots of the Torre de Belem, the Mosteiro and the Porto and Sintra sites. In the second envelope were six shots of me standing on the jetty by the Torre de Belem. He had printed them all up and had mounted one of them on to card.

'That's my favourite one,' he said.

I put his photos of me away in my desk drawer and started working on some early proofs of the copy. The guide was starting to come together and thankfully Aisha was back from her holiday. My team was excited about the guide and I felt more in control of things although Philip was still being distant towards me.

At about six, as I was packing up to leave, Aisha put her head round my door and said, 'Kathy, Eddie's downstairs, asking for you.'

I looked at her. 'Is he OK?'

She knew about him and pulled an anxious face. 'I think he's been drinking.'

'Shit!'

I locked the office quickly and hurried downstairs. The last thing I wanted was for Philip or any of my team to see Eddie if he'd been drinking.

When I got down to the reception area he flung his arms wide with a silly grin on his face and tried to embrace me.

'My darling K . . .'

I had to let him hug me and I could smell the drink on his breath. At that very moment Heja came walking down the stairs into the reception area and she saw Eddie embracing me. I pulled myself away from his hold.

He grabbed me again and said with a slight slur, 'Don't go . . .'

It must have been obvious to her that he was drunk. She looked over at him for a moment, then nodded to me and walked out of the office doors without saying a word. I watched her cross the car park towards her car. I felt embarrassed and ashamed. I hated anyone seeing Eddie when he was like this, but Heja of all people, the ice queen . . .

'You *can't* turn up at my work like this,' I hissed at him.

'I've got some great news I had to tell you.'

I watched Heja drive out of the car park.

'Not here,' I said through clenched teeth.

I steered him out of the building and into Regent's Park. We sat down on one of the benches.

'I just got the most fantastic job. I'm going to redesign this huge garden in Kent. Rich people and weeks of work. I'm going to get lots of money to do it.'

He spoke in that careful way people sometimes do when they've been drinking and they want to sound sober.

'That is good news. Congratulations.'

And then I looked at him without my usual indulgence and found that I was really angry that he had turned up at my place of work, really angry that he was drunk and that yet again he was blowing his chances.

'You won't ever get it done if you keep drinking. You're drunk now. I can smell it.'

'You always were a spoilsport. Can't you be pleased for me?'

'No, I can't be pleased when I see you sabotaging your life like this. Grow up. Stop drinking. Start working properly and leave me alone!'

I walked away from him quickly up the path through the park, fighting back tears of anger and pity and thinking how familiar that feeling was. In the six years of our relationship I had often felt ashamed of him. I used to worry about what other people might think of him and I would have to make excuses for him so many times.

One night my aunt Jennie had invited us both to dinner at her flat, which is now mine. She was planning her retirement and her move to Cornwall and she wanted to broach the subject of us taking on the lease of the flat. At that time Eddie and I were living in Paddington, renting an overpriced mews flat. She had made us a good dinner and the evening started well, with us looking around the flat and Eddie being charming. We'd brought two bottles of wine with us. He made quick work of them and then Jennie had opened a third. I watched with increasing concern as he drank his way through that. He was being expansive about his gardening design plans and as it was getting so late Jennie suggested we stay over. I agreed and we busied ourselves with towels and the like as Eddie stayed drinking at the kitchen table.

'Sorry,' I whispered to her in the bathroom. 'He's just getting a bit carried away tonight.'

She told me not to worry and she took herself off to bed. I got him into bed eventually and he fell into a deep sleep while I lay there worrying about him, as I so often did. Finally I fell asleep.

There was a crash that woke me up in the middle of the night. I was alone in the room. He must have got out of bed and not knowing where he was he would be staggering around the flat, banging into furniture. I leapt up and hurried into the hall just as I saw him blundering into Jennie's bedroom, stark naked and confused.

Jennie had woken in alarm and was sitting up. I grabbed Eddie and dragged him out of her room.

'Where's the toilet?' he said.

I steered him to the bathroom and then pushed him back to our room and into bed. I hardly slept the rest of the night.

I just lay there keeping watch over him and feeling waves of shame wash over me. Now my aunt would know just how bad things sometimes got with him. She would see that he was far more than a social drinker; she would realize he was a problem drinker.

He woke early, at around six, and as had happened many times before he had absolutely no recollection of what had happened in the night. I told him and he was mortified and said he'd go at once and please to say sorry to my aunt for behaving like such an idiot.

I wanted to go too. I felt awful and my heart was so heavy because yet again a happy evening had ended badly. It hurt to love him, but love him I did. I made myself wait there until Jennie was up and we sat in her kitchen and had tea and toast together. She stopped me as I started to apologize. She could see that I was wretched and she just said that if I needed a place of my own then her flat was mine for the asking. That offer of hers spoke volumes – a place of my own.

HEJA

JULY

I recognized him at once. That was the man I saw in Billy's room, the man in the photograph. He had visited her late that night while Markus was away. Now he was hugging her and she was hugging him back. Then she saw me and pulled away from him and she looked guilty as hell. I could not say a word. I was so angry. She has Markus and yet she does that.

I got into my car and drove to my appointment with Bernadita. She is a specialist in deep tissue massage. Usually I look forward to my massages with her. This time as I was driving to her place every instinct made me want to turn the car around and drive to Markus's office. I wanted to tell him what a traitor Kathy is. To do so I would have had to reveal that I was watching her flat, because that was when I saw that man holding Billy.

I parked my car on a meter and walked to Bernadita's garden flat. She always offers me green tea before we start the massage and today we sat in her garden and drank the tea. I gradually calmed myself as I sipped. I admired her lavender bush. It can wait; it will wait. I will choose the moment to tell Markus.

Massage can help with depression and weakness and I became interested in aspects of alternative medicine like aromatherapy two years ago, after Arvo Talvela died. How he would have disapproved of it all. He considered alternative medicine to be quackery. Arvo was an intellectually rigorous man and he had become the most important person in my life. I saw him twice a week. He could see the good in me and he loved me for who I was. And then he died. He died one morning in May from a massive brain haemorrhage. He was fifty-six years old. He died suddenly on a Tuesday, at half past eight in the morning. Tuesday was one of our days. We would always meet at noon.

I do not remember the days and weeks that followed Arvo's death. I was in deep shock. I handed in my notice. I told the TV station I had to take a sabbatical of three months. I knew they would have resisted if I had said I was going for good. They agreed reluctantly enough to the three month break. I knew I would never work there again.

I felt so alone. I would find myself standing on the street outside Arvo's consulting rooms at twelve noon on a Tuesday. The fact that he was gone for ever was too much for me to accept. He was the only person in the world who understood my troubles and he had been my compass and my anchor. Now he was gone. I would never hear his voice again, the inescapable finality of it. Grief is like fear, you are diminished by it. You are a shameful thing. You skulk around the streets and avoid the gaze of people.

I do remember what pulled me out of that blank horror. At the end of that summer I met Ilkka in the street. He told me he had heard that Markus was working for an architectural practice in London. He gave me the name of the company. For the first time in months I felt some stirrings of interest. Of course, I had to find Markus again. I had to tell him everything even though it had been years.

I started to feel a sense of purpose. I travelled to London

and after a few months of renting I bought my beautiful flat on the river. Having a lot of money has its compensations. Then I found out that he was with someone. I tracked down her address and the magazine where she was working. An architectural magazine; it made sense. She must have met Markus through the magazine.

I remember the first time I saw her. It was late one evening and I had been sitting outside her flat in my car. Suddenly she and Markus came out of the main door together. It was a shock to see him with her. I felt electrified by it. Should I drive away? He might see me and recognize me. I could not drag my eyes away from them and anyway they were oblivious to the cars in the dark street. They stood there talking together and then she turned to go in and I saw that she was pregnant – four or five months pregnant! The fabric of her top was stretched over her distended stomach. He pulled her round to him and kissed her. It was such a public place to do that, out there on the street. How smug she looked as she turned to go into her building. She thought she had everything: the good job, the baby growing inside her, and him.

If only I had found him a few months earlier. When I worked in television I was told that my sense of timing was impeccable. I was able to time my links into the news headlines on the hour perfectly. This time my timing was out. I was a few months too late. She was already carrying his child.

KATHY

JULY

Tonight, after Billy was tucked up asleep, I told Markus that I was keen to do the Alhambra and Segovia heritage sites in Spain if he would come with me. I said it wouldn't be till September so maybe we could work it? I felt sure he'd be bowled over by the sites and it could be part of our summer holiday. Markus didn't say no. He was cautious in his response.

'Maybe, they would be great places to visit. If I get the Durham project then probably not . . .'

'Surely we can fit in a short summer break?'

'You wouldn't be on holiday, would you? You'd be working. What about sorting something with Fran? Maybe get away for a few days to Spain?'

'I suppose I could leave Billy for a day or two. I'm not sure, I might feel anxious.'

We were in his room and Markus was sharpening his pencils. He turned the pencils in the sharpener until he had achieved a perfect point on each one and lined them up in front of him in a straight line.

'Who is doing Finland?' he asked.

'Laura, she's doing all the Scandinavian sites. I asked Heja first. She was dismissive of the idea. In fact, she gave the impression that she thought the whole project was a bit of a bore.'

And then it suddenly struck me.

'Markus – do you want to go to Finland? Here I am going on about Spain. I could organize that so easily. We could take Billy to see your family.'

Markus stood up. 'Really, I don't. I've no wish to go back there at all. You're keen to do the Spanish sites so stick to that. Do you want some coffee? I think I'll make another pot.'

'I'll do it. You get on with that drawing.'

I got down his coffeepot and the jar of coffee out of the fridge. Markus ground coffee beans every morning and he insisted that I keep the ground coffee in the fridge, he was such a perfectionist about these things. So there was another clear rejection from him of any idea that we should go to Finland and meet his family. I unscrewed the coffeepot and filled the bottom half with water, just under the valve.

I thought about my own trip to Lisbon. Why didn't I want to show Markus the photos of me? I spooned the ground coffee into the funnel and pressed it down with the spoon. The shots were rather good, though not how I saw myself at all. I looked Portuguese in them. Maybe it was the light or maybe it was the way that Hector had shot them, but I exuded a kind of Mediterranean sultriness in the pictures. I screwed the top on the pot and lit a low flame under it. Although Hector had said he thought I looked like someone from London; he'd said that on our first day, at the Torre de Belem. The pot started to burble and I waited until it got to an insistent hiss, then turned off the flame and poured the rich dark coffee into a bone china mug. I took the mug through to Markus.

'That smells great, thanks. Aren't you having any?'

'No, way too late for coffee for me. Are you planning to work long?'

'Probably a couple more hours . . .'

'I think I'll turn in.'

I kissed the top of his head and touched the hair on his forehead. I could see him struggling not to show impatience with my gesture. When he's working he's untouchable. He bent over his drawing. Then he looked up and said, 'Kathy, I'm so glad the project's going well for you.'

I checked Billy, who was lying on his back in his cot, deeply asleep. He's going through a good sleep phase at the moment. I stroked his white-blond baby hair, his downy face and chubby arms. He's the image of Markus when he was a baby. I have this one photograph of Markus, which he gave me when Billy was born. Markus was about one year old and he's sitting up on a blanket, his wide face smiling into the camera, and it could be Billy sitting there.

I went into our bedroom and undressed and stood naked in front of the long mirror on our wardrobe. I've always been insecure about my looks. People say I have a striking face, an attractive face, which means they don't think I'm pretty. My eyebrows are so thick and dark. When I was a teenager I wanted to reinvent myself and started to pluck my eyebrows into thin high arches that gave me a permanently startled look. It was painful and my mum tried to talk me out of it. She said I was embarking on a lifelong struggle against a very tenacious part of myself and that I should accept my eyebrows as they were.

I ignored her advice, as you do when you're a teenager. For weeks I sat in my bedroom in front of one of those magnifying mirrors, tweezers in hand, my eyes streaming with the pain as I pulled out the thick dark hairs. In the end I gave up and my eyebrows grew back thick and dark. My hair is thick too and I usually keep it chin length as when it gets any longer it just becomes too much of a good thing.

I looked at myself for a few minutes. My breasts were still larger than usual because of the breastfeeding. I put my hands under each breast and felt the weight of them. Then I turned sideways and saw how my stomach protruded a bit. My clothes were a bit tight on me at the moment, after the pregnancy, and I needed to lose a few pounds. Maybe that was why I looked sultry in those photos: my clothes were clinging to me! I stroked my stomach and held it in and pulled my hands down over my hips and thighs. My skin felt dry so I rubbed some body lotion in, enjoying the feel of the cream on my thighs.

Lying in bed, I thought about the heritage project and what lay ahead. Philip wants us to have some kind of launch in the autumn to coincide with the first issue; a high-profile launch, he said. He has warmed to the idea and now seemed willing to spend money on it. I felt vaguely guilty about wanting to do the Spanish sites, which I hadn't yet allocated to anyone in the team. Why wasn't I being honest with myself? I had been strongly attracted to Hector. I rolled over and checked the clock; I didn't want to go to sleep; I wanted to have sex with Markus.

This weekend Markus and I tried to buy a sofa. We had long agreed that the sofa Jennie had left behind had served its time. It was a perfectly reputable sofa, a Wesley-Barrell, in fact. It had an old-fashioned look to it and a gold and orange geometric pattern that we often joked about. I suggested we go down to this furniture showroom I knew in Highbury that had lots of sofas on display. We could take Billy with us and walk around the showroom and try out a few sofas to see if there was anything we both liked.

When we got there I made a beeline for a lovely squashy

yellow fabric sofa that was bright, cheerful, and was called the Cuddler. Markus picked out a tubular grey leather and chrome sofa, which was sleek and Scandinavian in look. I tried sitting on the Markus sofa and it wasn't just firm, it was actually hard.

'It's no sofa, it's a bed of nails,' I said, laughing. 'We couldn't cuddle up on this!'

He looked at my Cuddler sofa then and thought it was just as unsuitable.

'It's got no structure' he said. 'It's far too soft and it wouldn't last.'

We stood in the showroom smiling sheepishly at each other and scanning the many sofas on display. Was there anything we could compromise on? We both quite liked a cream fabric sofa. Neither of us loved it. We eventually decided it was a hopeless quest and left to have lunch at a nearby restaurant that was advertising Thai street food. It was a funny and fruitless afternoon and Aunt Jennie's old sofa was spared.

HEJA

JULY

Today I had my regular appointment with Mr Banerjee, my Ayurvedic physician. We meet every two weeks. How Arvo would have disapproved of Mr Banerjee's methods. Arvo had a strong puritanical streak. He believed that suffering honed one's character; that the ephemera fell away and the essential person was left. I felt that Mr Banerjee was helping me even though today he made me drink a disgusting herbal infusion. He said he was pleased with my progress.

I parked my car and was walking towards the entrance to my block when I saw Markus standing in the hall. I stood quite still in the car park. He had not called me. Why had he just turned up like this? Two residents walked past me and swiped open the apartment block door. Then he turned and saw me and waved at me, his face happy and excited. I hurried over to him, swiping the door with my card and pushing open the heavy glass door.

'We've won the contract! I just heard. I had to tell you at once.'

I hugged him.

'That's wonderful . . . just wonderful . . .'

'I really wanted this job.'

'You're a great architect.'

'I feel so good, Heja.'

'Come upstairs. We'll have a drink to celebrate.'

We went up in the lift together. There were three other residents in the lift with us and we just stood there smiling joyfully at each other. Once out of the lift I took his hand and pulled him towards me. We hugged each other tightly and then we kissed; standing in the corridor outside my flat we kissed each other again, the first time in over seven years. Then he pulled away, looking confused, and followed me into my flat. I went through to my dressing room where I keep a few bottles of very good wine. I brought one out with me. Markus was looking out of my riverfront window.

'I've always wanted to build a cinema,' he said.

'Just make sure it's more comfortable than the Biology Theatre!'

He laughed in delight. I held the bottle out to him.

'Please, open this.'

He looked at the label. 'I don't know much about wine. This looks expensive. Are you sure?'

'We're celebrating.'

I got down the glasses while he opened the bottle. He poured us each half a glass of the wine. We held our glasses up to each other.

'To great buildings . . .' I said.

'That we try to make better than ourselves,' he said.

'And that live on long after us,' I said as we clinked our glasses.

'So you will have to spend a lot of time in Durham now.'

'A lot, I like it there. I'm enjoying getting to know that whole area. You did help me; your comments made a real difference. Can I take you out to dinner to thank you?'

If only I could have gone. It hurt me to turn him down.

'I can't. I would have loved to, more than anything, someone is coming round soon.'

'Someone . . .?'

'Robert Mirzoeff. I mentioned him to you.'

'The analyst . . .'

'Yes. He got us tickets for a concert at an art gallery near here. He knows the musicians.'

'That sounds a bit challenging, a bit highbrow . . .'

I nudged him playfully. 'Probably will be; I wish I'd said no. Have some more wine.'

He poured wine into our glasses.

'Markus, you never know what's going to happen so savour this moment now. I am *so* happy for you and proud of you too. You will build an outstanding building and it will stand in Durham for many years. That is enough.'

'When did you get to be so wise? Come and sit here next to me.' His voice was very affectionate.

I walked round to his side of the bar and sat on the stool next to him.

'You're wearing shoes exactly like the ones I bought you,' I said, touching his brown brogues with my toe.

'What do you mean, "like"? These *are* those shoes . . .'

'They've never lasted all this time?'

'Shoes like these are made to last a lifetime. I did have them resoled.'

'I'm so glad you're still wearing them.'

'They're my lucky shoes.'

We laughed and clinked our glasses again.

The doorbell buzzed and I jumped. I did not want Markus and Robert to meet and for a brief moment I wondered if perhaps I could pretend not to be in.

'That's Robert. He *would* be early!'

I sighed, got up and pressed the buzzer to let Robert in, and waited at the door. He came down the corridor dressed in his usual sober grey suit and white shirt.

'Come in and meet a very old friend of mine,' I said.

Robert kissed me on the cheek and walked into the flat in front of me.

'Markus and I were at university together,' I said, getting a glass for Robert, which I handed to Markus to pour some wine into.

They shook hands a bit formally.

'Thanks,' Robert said, taking the glass from Markus. 'Are you visiting London?'

'No, I live here. I've been here some years now . . .'

'This wine is fantastic, Heja.' Robert looked at me. 'Where did you get it?'

'Some years ago I made a documentary and it won an award for our station. And my boss, who was a devotee of wine, gave me a case of it. He told me to keep it for ten years and it would get better and better. I have a few bottles left.'

'It's quite something. Are you keeping it in the right conditions?'

'Probably not; I keep the bottles horizontal and in a cool dark place. Will that do?'

'Sounds fine. What's your field, Markus?'

'I'm an architect.'

'What buildings do you do?'

'Public buildings usually, libraries, health centres, that sort of thing . . .'

'Office buildings?' asked Robert.

'I've never done one. They don't interest me,' Markus replied flatly, without any further explanation.

I broke into the frisson that was building up between them. 'Markus has just won a commission to build a major arts centre with a gallery and a cinema,' I said.

Robert raised his glass to Markus. 'Congratulations.'

'Thank you. Heja told me you're training to be an analyst?'

'I completed my training this spring.' Robert gave an ironic smile. 'Now I'm let loose on real people.'

'Heja, I must be off. Thank you for the drink. It was good to meet you, Robert.'

Markus got up and I walked with him to the door.

'Thank you for coming to tell me your wonderful news. I just wish we could have celebrated it over dinner.'

'So do I . . .'

I walked out into the corridor with him, pulling the door to behind me.

'Markus, let's have that dinner, let's have it in Durham. I have to go there to do some research. We could meet up when you're next up there. You could show me the site. It would mean so much to me to see it.'

He agreed to us meeting in Durham. He walked down the corridor away from me. I was happy he had wanted to tell me his news.

I closed the door and walked back towards Robert, who was looking at me with a slightly aggrieved expression on his face.

'You are a mystery! I didn't know you worked in television.'

'That was years ago, in Helsinki.'

KATHY

JULY

Markus won the project and I am so happy for him! This means he won't be able to come to Spain with me in September, he said. It doesn't matter. What matters is that he won a major commission, the most important project he has ever secured. What really excites him is that they've supported his innovative designs. It's going to be a landmark building in Durham. I've decided to cook a special Portuguese dinner tonight, for my friends Fiona and Douglas, who are down from Glasgow, and to celebrate Markus winning the project. I'm going to make my mum's signature cod dish, *bacalhau com natas*.

When I was eleven years old my parents sent me to a Catholic secondary school while my all friends went to the local high school. I was unhappy about this and determined to hate the new school. On my first day there they sat me next to a Scottish girl called Fiona. She had light red hair, the colour of barley sugar, which she wore in bunches on either side of her face. We took an instant dislike to each other and she became the focus of my rejection of the school and all it stood for. She hated the school too because she was new to London and missed her friends in Glasgow. She thought I was 'loud and Londony' and our mutual antagonism enlivened us both.

When I returned from the Christmas holiday I met her in the corridor. She had had her hair cut into a bob and we stopped in the corridor and started laughing at each other. I found myself delighted to see her again. I realized I'd missed her and from that time on we became the best of friends, did everything together, talked every day and shared every secret. Then, when school was through, Fiona decided to go back to her beloved Glasgow. She took her degree there and lives there now, with Douglas. They're coming to London for the weekend and tonight they'll meet Markus for the first time as they couldn't get to our wedding.

I took Markus's car for the day because I had to do meetings all over town and also had to buy the ingredients for the meal. It was hot, even at nine in the morning, as I drove to our printers in Mile End to discuss the printing of the heritage guides. Later I drove from Mile End to a lunch near Islington to talk up the guides to one of Victoria's advertising clients. The traffic from Mile End was terrible, and the sun was beating down through a pollution-heavy haze.

Victoria had booked us into a fashionable Lebanese restaurant in Exmouth Market and thankfully it was cool in there. The waitress was a tall, striking Arab woman dressed in a billowing white blouse tucked into black satin trousers. She wore a gold chain-link belt low over her hips. The advertising client was a real creep, who leered at the waitress as he ordered arak for the three of us. Victoria suggested we get the meze and she chose nine small dishes, falafel, and kibeh, bright green tabouleh, baked aubergine and Lebanese salad, which had this crunchy bread in it. The food was delicious and decorative. The waitress kept whipping the plates away as soon as we had eaten the offerings, as if she wanted us out of there. The creep had clearly annoyed her.

I did as Victoria had asked me to do and described the guide in glowing terms. I mentioned the most glamorous sites that we would be covering and emphasized the quality of the photographs and the production values we would achieve. There would be a dedicated website too where he could advertise. Then I left Victoria and him before the coffee as I still had to buy the ingredients for the celebration dinner. I didn't envy Victoria her job that afternoon; she had to be nice to guys like that.

I reached the car just as the meter had run out and a traffic warden was lurking. He looked hot and uncomfortable in his uniform and I wondered if he was going to book me. He let me get into the car without writing a ticket and I thanked him through my open window. I drove to Highbury where there's a really good fishmonger and a delicatessen that sells Portuguese cheeses. I needed cod for the main dish and then bought some Azeitão, Serra and Castelo Branco for the cheese board. I put the ingredients in the boot and drove back to Primrose Hill. The sun was still blazing and the tarmac of the car park felt slightly soft and sticky under my feet. I imagined the cheeses sweating and the fish going off in the furnace of the boot, so I carried all the ingredients into the office and asked the receptionist if we could store them in her drinks fridge.

For the next two hours I rushed through my tasks because I wanted to get home early, if possible, to start cooking the meal. Just as I was clearing my desk Philip called me and said please would I join him in his office as he wanted to know where we were on the heritage guides schedule. He kept me in there for over forty minutes, cross-examining me on which writer was doing which site, and how much was this going to cost the magazine? That is his way, to summon you out of the blue. If he'd given me any notice I could have prepared a spreadsheet for him. I left his office feeling flustered and cross.

When I got to the car park I saw Heja in front of me, getting into her car. She has this beautiful dark green convertible and she had put the roof down. Now I understand how she affords such an amazing car. It must be from the days of her TV work. You could never buy such a car on our salaries. She looked as cool as ever, her blouse uncreased and her hair neat in its French plait. I waved to her and followed her out of the car park. She turned right towards Belsize Park and I headed left to Camden Town. I still needed to get some parsley and there's a stall I go to in Inverness Street market.

The market was closing down and there was more than the usual pile of rotting fruit and vegetables in cartons at the side of the road. I saw a man in oil-stained trousers, rummaging through the discarded fruit, looking for something to eat. Then he turned his attention to the waste bins. He plunged his hand into one of the bins and pulled out a half-eaten baguette. Without a moment's hesitation he put it in his mouth and started to chew.

Finally, I was on my way home. I was driving down Park Street towards Baker Street when I noticed that the right-hand lane was closed for roadworks and there was a worse than usual bottleneck going into Baker Street. I stayed in my lane, cursing the delay.

A small red car drew up on my left and started to try to move in front of me. I glanced at the driver. He gestured rudely at me to pull back and let him in. I was hemmed in by the car behind so I just shrugged at him and stayed in line, looking ahead at the lights. My windows were open to try and let in some air and the man in the red car started to shout at me. I turned to look at him. He had a shaved head and a thin, pointed face that was tracked with lines of resentment. A woman was sitting next to him and a teenage girl was seated in the back. Both women had their hair scraped back in high ponytails and they were staring at me in a vaguely hostile way.

I shrugged my shoulders again as if to say I couldn't let them in, and this seemed to infuriate him further. As the lights turned green and we all inched forward he moved even closer to me so that our wing mirrors collided with a small crunch and his smaller mirror was bent back by the sturdy one on Markus's Saab.

He screamed at me, 'Look what you've done. You've broken my mirror, you cunt!'

I quickly closed the windows and pressed the car locks down. The lights were turning amber and I was indicating to turn right. I stopped now to let him get in front of me. He revved in front of me then braked hard and leapt out of the car to look at his mirror. He was a short, wiry man, dressed in pressed jeans and a sweatshirt. It didn't look to me as if the mirror was broken as it snapped back into place, but he made a great show of examining it. The lights turned red and I was trapped behind him now. He spoke to the woman in the passenger seat and she shook her head at him. Then he looked back at me and I avoided his gaze and thought, Please, let this be an end to it. It was so hot in the car and I could feel my face and hands sweating.

The lights were changing. He got back into his car and turned right too and parked his car on the corner. I drove past him and was heading up the road, then had to stop at the lights again. I saw that my hands were gripping the steering wheel so tightly that I'd left sweat tracks on the wheel. I tried to loosen them and took a deep breath. I was about to open the window for some air when he was suddenly there, right at my window, his face close to the glass as he screamed at me.

'Open the window. Open the fucking window. You broke my mirror.'

I would not acknowledge him. I knew if I looked at him it would only make things worse. Then he started to thump his fists on the roof of the car. He hit the roof with such force that I could feel the vibrations shiver right through the bodywork.

'Stop the car. Stop the fucking car,' he shouted.

The lights turned green. I put my foot on the accelerator and roared ahead into Dorset Square. He leapt back on to the pavement. In my rear-view mirror I saw him run back to his car. I realized he was going to chase me! I sped down Dorset Square and jumped the lights into Rossmore Street. This is not the way to my flat, but the road was empty ahead and I wanted to put as much distance between him and myself as I could. I kept checking the rear-view mirror, expecting to see the bonnet of his red car behind me. I was breathing short, shallow breaths and felt dizzy. I turned left then left again. Finally I parked and waited, my heart hammering. I had shaken him off.

'People are so damned angry these days. They don't know why they're full of murderous rage,' Douglas said.

We were sitting in the kitchen over dinner with Fiona and Douglas. 'Things are tough out there now, for many people, and, yes, people are turning against each other,' Markus said.

'You know I'd had a bad day,' I said. 'These things seem to happen when you're already wound up. I guess I could have let him overtake me . . .'

'Oh, the smallest thing can trigger it,' said Fiona. 'I mean, what was at stake? Being one car further up the line.'

We had just eaten my *bacalhau com natas*, layers of cod

and onion and fried potatoes in cream. Usually cooking calms me down. Tonight it hadn't worked and I was still hot and headachey. I got up to clear the plates away. Fiona helped me, and then I heard Billy grizzling in his room.

'I think I'll get Billy up,' I said to Markus. 'His cheeks were really red this evening and I'm sure he's teething again.'

I brought Billy into the kitchen and he stretched out his arms towards his dad and Markus took him on to his lap.

'He didn't want to miss the party,' Fiona said.

I brought the salad and the cheese board to the table.

'Three favourite Portuguese cheeses,' I said.

'Wonderful,' said Fiona. 'Where do you find all this stuff?'

'There's a great place in Highbury, and they do the best olive oil too.'

Markus passed Fiona the salad bowl. He had made the dressing for it and it was very garlicky and almost startling to eat.

'This is so good,' she said, piling radicchio, cress and rocket, viscous with his dressing, on to her plate.

Douglas spread thick butter on his water biscuit and then piled a wedge of Serra on top.

'Douglas, you don't need butter as well as the cheese!' Fiona wailed.

'I like it like this. I like the taste of butter under the cheese.'

'Think of the cholesterol!'

I gave Billy a piece of bread to chew on.

'I was in Finland a few years ago, on a research project,' Douglas said. 'We were trying to gauge attitudes to change; mainly in Helsinki, which I really liked. I also spent some time in the villages along the coast. I think small communities can be pretty angry places too.'

Markus nodded his agreement.

'Oh, yes, angry and narrow and mean-spirited,' he said.

'When were you there?' I asked Douglas.

'About four years ago.'

'Well, one of my team used to be a well-known TV presenter in Helsinki – Heja Vanheinen.'

Markus stood up and said to Fiona, 'Will you have Billy? I need to get more wine . . .'

'I thought you'd never ask,' she said, taking Billy on to her lap and bouncing him up and down gently.

Markus picked up the empty wine bottle and took it to the recycling box.

'What does she look like?' Douglas asked.

'Very blonde, high cheekbones . . .'

Markus got down another bottle and started to tear off the foil.

'There's one cooling in the fridge,' I said.

He nodded and turned towards the fridge and I wondered why he was looking a bit grim.

After Fiona and Douglas had gone I scraped the plates on to a spread newspaper before putting the leftovers into the bin. My head was pounding from the heat and stress of the day. I watched the oil from the cream sliding into the newsprint and felt a wave of disgust and weariness.

Fiona rang the next morning.

'Thanks for last night. That was a fantastic meal.'

'It was great to see you, and Markus really liked you both. Sorry I was a bit on edge.'

'You were fine. I see why you fell for Markus. He's gorgeous!'

'He is easy on the eye, isn't he?'

'Why didn't you tell me he was famous?'

'Famous? What do you mean?'

'Douglas said it was niggling him all night because Markus looked familiar. Then this morning he remembered. Apparently Markus was a well-known radical in Finland.'

'No!'

'Yes! There was some big student protest and Markus led a mass demonstration in Helsinki. It got nasty and he was arrested. Hundreds of students marched to the police station and demanded his release.'

'I can't believe it.'

'It's true, you know Douglas and politics. Your Markus was a pin-up for thousands of university students!'

'Incredible. I knew none of this. Nothing . . . it would explain a lot.'

So ask him about it.'

'I'm not sure. He's touchy about talking about his past. I'm almost scared to raise the subject.'

'You should be able to talk to him about it.'

'I should but . . . well . . . things aren't perfect, Fiona. Markus can be so reserved and some days I find his coldness really gets to me.'

'I'm sorry to hear that.'

'I keep thinking give it time. It's been a major adjustment for us both. I just wish he'd be more open with me.'

'You should have called me.'

'And Eddie pitched up here the other night.'

'Oh, Kathy you're not . . .'

'No, no, of course not; he just turned up out of the blue.'

'His drinking made you very unhappy.'

After our call was over I did something that it hadn't occurred to me to do before. I looked up Markus on the internet. I typed in 'Markus Hartman Finland' with a feeling of guilty apprehension, as if I was doing something mildly stalkerish. What would I discover? Five photographs of a much younger Markus came onto my screen. Three of the pictures looked like a student demonstration as there were banners and a crowd and Markus was at the front of the crowd. The text was all in Finnish, from various newspaper reports, so I couldn't get a lot of information from it, only the dates and that these demonstrations had happened years ago. There were also two solo shots of Markus, a head-and-shoulders shot and one of him standing in front of a building. Again there was no English text so I couldn't establish where these had been taken.

It seemed that what Douglas had said was true – Markus had been involved in student politics and had been a kind of leader. Could this be what he was keeping quiet about? It was nothing to be ashamed of. Or had something else happened to him that made him reluctant to talk about his life in Helsinki? I stared at the photos and he looked so young and fired up and handsome and I knew I wouldn't ask him about them.

While I was at it I decided to look up Heja too. I typed in her name and lots of pictures came up this time. There were a series of glamorous shots of her seated behind a news desk, and what looked like several PR shots of her that had a glossy edge to them. There was a picture of her interviewing a man who looked like a politician. There was some accompanying text in English that described her role at the TV station and some information about programme ratings. It seemed that she had indeed been one of the top news presenters in Finland. It was all information about her work, who she had interviewed and the events she had covered.

There was nothing personal. I could find no links to Facebook or LinkedIn or Twitter. Well, that figured. Heja would be the last person to share information about herself on any social media sites. Why, she shared little enough with her colleagues who she saw every day. I still could not understand why she had left such a high-profile television job. She was in her mid-thirties and would have had more TV years ahead of her surely; and all to make the jump to writing about architecture for a magazine? It was odd.

HEJA

JULY

Early in July I received a letter from my mother, Solange.

My dear Heja

    You are proving so elusive this year that your father and I have decided that if Mohammed won't come to the mountain we will come to you.

    Your father has not been himself and I am concerned about his health. He will keep working and pushing himself quite unnecessarily. However, I have persuaded him to take a four-week holiday. We will be taking a ten-day cruise in August. We start in London, then on to Paris for two nights before taking a train to Marseille to board the ship. We then visit Genoa, the Amalfi coast, Sicily, Carthage and Barcelona. The cruise returns us to Marseille. We then plan to spend two weeks in Provence. It will all be very comfortable and Father is keen for you to join us on the cruise. I too think it will do you good to have a break from your work. Father is happy to pay for everything.

    If, however, and as I expect, you say that you can't get away for so long we plan to fly to London early so that we can spend some time with you. We have been recommended a good hotel right in the centre, the Brownsage Hotel in Charlotte Street. I would be grateful if you would check it out for us before I confirm the booking.

Let me know as soon as possible if you wish to join us, as Father will need to reserve your cabin on the ship.

With love, as ever,
Solange

I can think of few fates worse than spending ten days on a ship with my mother, vying with her for my father's attention. She is the most jealous woman in the world. Why, if Dad fills my glass before hers there is a scene. And it is quite clear that she does not want me to join them.

I remember when I told her I was leaving my job in television. She was furious with me. She may not have loved me but she had enjoyed having a famous daughter. I couldn't tell her the real reason I was giving it up. I hoped she might see the suffering daughter beneath the façade I presented to her. She saw nothing. She could not have been more icy or critical. I gave up on her then. I do not even call her mother any more. She is Solange to the world and Solange to me.

When my parents arrived in London a couple of weeks later I took Robert along to act as a buffer and to stop the usual questioning I always got from her. She was standing in the foyer of the Brownsage Hotel, elegant in a dark green shirt-dress and jacket. Robert kissed her on the cheek and she gave him a little smile. It had been obvious she liked him the night before when we had joined them for dinner at their hotel. She turned to me.

'Pieter won't be coming with us this morning. He had a bad night and needs to rest. He'll meet us for lunch.'

'He didn't look well last night,' I said uneasily.

'I made that clear in my letter, Heja. He's not been well.'

'What is it?'

A spasm of irritation moved over her mouth and cheeks, a passing tremor.

'He's got a heart problem,' she said, lowering her voice.

'How serious is it?'

'He needs to be careful.'

'Can't they do anything?'

'They are doing all sorts of things and it's under control. He just has to take it easy sometimes.'

Robert could feel the tension between us. He pulled his mouth down in the way he does when he is holding back words. He stroked my arm and said to Solange, 'Do you still want to go to Tate Modern? We could call it off.'

'No, no, I very much want to go and Pieter wants me to buy him a catalogue.'

I was looking at the geometric pattern on the floor of the hotel's foyer. There were grey and white blocks of marble cut and laid with precision. Robert pressed my arm again.

'Shall we go now?'

'I'd like to stay and keep Dad company here. Would you mind terribly?'

I looked up at him and then over at her.

'Your father needs to sleep,' she said crisply.

'I wouldn't wake him. Give me the keys to the room. I'll sit in there and when he wakes up I'll make him some tea.'

'You were going to show us around.'

How I hated her. I had not seen my father for months and months and yet she resented us having any time on our own.

'I'd be delighted to show you around,' Robert said.

'Thank you, Robert.'

She turned to me. 'We'll see you both at the restaurant, then.'

'The table is booked for one-fifteen,' Robert said, giving me a conspiratorial look as if to say, yes, he could see she was a difficult woman.

Dad was not asleep. He was sitting in his dressing gown in an armchair by the window.

'Darling, where are the others?'

'They've gone to the Tate. I wanted to keep you company.'

He stood up and we hugged tightly.

'I'm so pleased,' he said.

I sat next to him and looked at his face lit by the light from the window. His colour was not good.

'Did you have a bad night, Dad?'

'I didn't sleep very well, just wanted to take it a bit easy this morning, nothing to worry about.'

I stroked his hand. 'It is exhausting going around the Tate. It's huge,' I said.

'Yes, I read all about it.'

'You can't do it all in one go, although I bet Robert will try!'

My father smiled. 'I liked him. He's a clever man.'

'Yes, he is, very clever and civilized . . .'

'Now, those are not very warm words to use about him.'

'Robert is excellent company. I'm not in love with him.'

'Oh, dear, I think he's mad about you.'

I shrugged. My father knew how much I had loved Markus and how much it had hurt me when he left.

'How are you, Dad, really?'

'I'm OK. I have to take a few pills and not overdo it. That's all.'

I was still stroking his hand. His skin was thin and dry.

'Let me rub some cream into your hands. It will feel nice.'

I went into their bathroom and found a small bottle of complimentary body lotion. It was Persian Lilac.

'You'll make me smell like a Turkish harem,' he said, grinning at me.

I poured a generous amount of lotion onto the top of his left hand and gently worked it into the skin, then massaged each finger, his knucklebones and his wrist.

'It does feel rather nice,' he said.

I started to work on his right hand. Every time I see him now I think it might be the last time. And there is still so much unsaid between us.

'I sometimes think our family is cursed,' I said, as I worked the lotion round each knuckle of his right hand.

'Why do you say that, darling?'

'Tomas and Aunt Tanya . . . Maybe our genes are cursed.'

'Tomas died of an infection.'

'And Tanya?'

'Tanya's early death was tragic, such a terrible waste, but every family has its share of tragedy. Have you been worrying about this?'

I could tell him now, at this very moment. It would be such a release for me to confide my troubles to my father. I looked at his dear, kind face, his poor colour. He had already buried one of his children. He needed to believe that everything was going well with me.

'It had an effect on me, of course.'

'Is it stopping you having children?' he asked gently.

I shook my head.

'You told me Solange was never the same after Tomas died.'

'No, she wasn't. You see, we just thought he had a cold and that's why he had the temperature. The doctor said keep him cool and your mother sat up through the night, bathing his limbs to get his temperature down. She fell asleep on the floor of the nursery for maybe an hour and a half. When she woke up Tomas was much worse. He was very pale and did not respond to her at all. She was frantic. We drove him to hospital straight away. He died the next evening. Meningitis comes on so suddenly, so devastatingly.'

'I'm sorry to have brought it up, Dad. I didn't want to upset you.'

'You haven't upset me. You could never upset me. I know it cast a long shadow over your childhood. Losing Tomas was almost unbearable for your mother. She adored him, you see. I was almost jealous of her feelings for him. I felt profound guilt after he died. I hadn't helped her enough that night.'

'You couldn't have been a better husband to her, Dad. You do so much for her.'

He smiled sadly at me then as if he still felt he had fallen short.

'She was ill for a couple of years. There was a time when she didn't want to get out of bed or do anything at all. I bought her a puppy then and she made herself get up to take him out. Slowly she got better. It made me realize how fragile she was, still is in a way.'

'She never seems fragile to me! She wanted sons and finds it difficult to like me, a mere woman.'

Now he put both his hands under my chin so that my face was cupped in them.

'She may not show it very often but we are both so proud of our beautiful, talented daughter. Don't be afraid of having children, darling. They bring such joy.'

I buried my head in his chest then. Of course he wanted me to have children. They were waiting for it. I could hear the faint *lub-dup* of his poor diseased heart.

We met them at the Connaught at one-fifteen precisely as instructed. Solange was in a good mood. Robert had invited my parents as his guests this time and it was just the sort of place he relished. Over the aperitifs, he told us how General De Gaulle had used the Connaught as his London residence during the war, and that General Eisenhower had been a regular at the restaurant. Robert always chooses these opulent places with their rich food and hushed tones. He recommended the chicken pie, which he said was a speciality of the house. Dad chose it; I think to thank Robert for looking after Solange that morning. They brought him a whole chicken pie in a ceramic pie dish. He cut into the crust of the pie and found a perfect soft boiled quail's egg nestling under the dome of the crust.

'Now, that's a brilliant touch,' Dad said, slicing delicately into the egg. The rich yolk ran out and mingled with the chicken gravy. He ate a mouthful of the pie.

'Fantastic. You know that saying, "Little things please little minds"? I've often thought it was wrong. Little things can give great pleasure. Take this egg sitting on top of these chicken pieces. That's a little thing but it raises this chicken pie from the merely good to the great.'

We all laughed.

Robert nodded. 'Never underestimate the importance of small details. In analysis we think that small things can carry great meanings.'

'You look better, Pieter,' Solange said. 'The rest did you good.'

'Being with Heja did me good,' he said, smiling over at me.

I glanced across at her. She let it pass. She was full of Tate Modern and the art and the views and her new-found alliance with Robert.

'The views of St Paul's are quite stunning. I think I prefer the views through those magnificent windows to the actual art in the rooms,' she said.

Now, if I had ever chosen to invite Robert to dinner at our family home in Helsinki she would most certainly have brought out the porcelain and the silver for him!

Wednesday morning and she called a team meeting at short notice and told us that she is going to be away next week: in Cornwall; St Ives; a family holiday. She said if we had any problems we were to let Aisha know. Aisha would contact her if necessary. She was sure, she said, putting on her friendly face and smiling at each of us in turn, that there would be no need to contact her; we were a great team and she appreciated our efforts.

I sat there feeling icy cold. I could just imagine it: the pretty little family staying in the hotel; the days on the beach; Billy with a sun hat on; them both playing with him on the sand. She would wear a bikini, her large breasts on show. She is proud of them. He would rub sun-cream into her back and over her shoulders. He would have his camera with him. She would go for a swim and as she came out of the sea her breasts would almost be slipping from her bikini top. He would take photos of her then as she picked her way up the beach. He always likes to take unposed shots. He would wait until she was drying herself with a rough beach towel, rubbing herself awkwardly behind a rock, laughing and wriggling underneath the towel. And with every shared experience, with every photograph he took of her and Billy, they would be building their life together, giving it stronger foundations.

I had to see him again before he left for this week away with her. I wanted us to have our dinner in Durham. He said he would show me the site where he is going to build the arts centre. I left the office as soon as the team meeting had ended. I called his work number. The receptionist told me he was away in Durham for three days and would not be back until Friday. I felt myself filling up with silent fury. They were going away on Saturday so there was no way I could see him now until his return from Cornwall. Why hadn't he suggested we meet in Durham this week? It would have been the perfect time to do it.

I walked back to the office slowly. She was walking down the stairs with Philip Parr. He nodded in my direction and I made a point of stopping in the foyer as they crossed the floor towards me.

I smiled at them both and then turned towards her and said, with a concerned look on my face, 'So we are to contact Aisha if there's a problem?'

She flushed slightly. 'Yes, please, though I'm sure you'll all cope brilliantly. It's only a week.'

Philip said. 'Or speak to me, Heja, if something crops up.'

I thanked him with a smile and she did not like that. I could tell by the way she pushed her lips together in an effort not to grimace. They walked out of the building together.

That night I sat outside her flat in my car. At first I thought I would not go in again. I was just sitting there, watching the building. The last time Markus was away that man had showed up. I wanted to see if he would show up again. As the lights in her flat were gradually turned off until the only light remaining was the orange light from Billy's bedroom, I found myself standing at the entrance to the block. I let myself in. And then I was walking up the three flights of stairs to her flat. And then I was standing outside her front door. I knew I was taking a big risk. I'd done it before and she had not woken up. She might wake up this time. That thought made me feel very alive as I turned the key in her front door.

Perhaps I was less careful than before. Perhaps I had made some slight noise as I walked down the corridor, but once I was standing in her bedroom, watching the mound of her body under the cover, she stirred and made a little moan. I glided out of the room and into Markus's room. I heard her come out of her bedroom and walk down the corridor to the bathroom. She put the light on and then I heard her flush the toilet. Then she walked back along the corridor right past Markus's room, where I was standing in the shadows. She went into Billy's room. After a few moments, she walked back into her bedroom, carrying Billy. She must have taken him into the bed with her. He was making funny little noises and she was making soothing sounds back.

I stood and I waited, my hand resting on Markus's drawing table. Gradually my breathing settled. My eyes got accustomed to the dark and to the outline of his things. How I loathed her. This room is the only room that is truly Markus. Everything else is hers – her furniture, her mess, her sticky cooking things, her baby. She has spread her mess everywhere and she is gradually sucking him into her orbit.

I would not leave the flat until I had seen her again. I waited for a long time, sitting on the floor in Markus's work room with my head resting on his chair. The flat was silent and eventually I got to my knees and then stood up. I walked to the threshold of her bedroom and looked in. She was lying asleep, with Billy in the crook of her arm. I stood and watched them, the rhythmic rise and fall of her chest, the smaller movements in the baby's body, mother and son sleeping peacefully.

KATHY

AUGUST

'Wake up, Kathy, it's time to get up.'

I pulled my eyelids open. Markus put a mug of coffee down next to the clock, which showed 05.27.

'Five more minutes,' I murmured.

'You need to get up. I want to leave by six to avoid the traffic. You and Billy can sleep in the car.'

Markus had finally agreed to a one-week holiday, at short notice, so I had rung around and booked us into a family hotel in St Ives that my aunt Jennie recommended. I struggled into a sitting position and sipped the very strong coffee he had made me.

'If we get there by lunchtime I might be able to get a dive in,' he said. He was moving around our bedroom full of energy, willing me to get up.

I let Billy sleep on while I had a quick wash and got dressed. Markus had arrived back late from Durham the night before so I had packed all the bags, including his clothes.

'You'd best check I put in everything you need,' I said, going into the kitchen to get some baby jars for Billy.

Billy and I slept until Exeter. Markus pulled over at a motorway service station and as he switched off the engine we both woke up. We had a quick coffee and a Danish pastry and then we were back on the motorway and speeding towards Plymouth.

'That coffee was undrinkable,' he said.

'I don't think you'll get much better in St Ives.'

'I should have brought my own supply *and* my coffeepot.'

I laughed and he grinned over at me:

'Am I getting obsessive compulsive about my coffee?'

'You are a bit . . .'

We crossed the Tamar Bridge and we were in Cornwall. As we drove over the bridge I looked down and saw a small fleet of sailing boats tacking across the sunlit water. My spirits started to lift. It was great to be having a week without feeling pulled in two directions all the time; a week to recharge and to spend time with Markus and Billy. Markus looked buoyed up too. He was explaining which dives he would do while we were in Cornwall. He belongs to a diving club and they often dive off the Manacles on the Lizard. He told me it's one of the best places in the country as there are ship-wrecks along the seabed there.

And then he suddenly said, 'I'd like us to live in Cornwall.'

'It's beautiful, isn't it?'

'It would be good to get Billy out of London and living by the sea while he's little. Maybe we could look at some properties while we're down here? At least see what the prices are like.'

'Whoa, that's way too fast for me.' I looked at him and was puzzled at what he'd just said. Look at properties in Cornwall?

'This hasn't got anything to do with that road-rage incident, has it?' I asked him.

'I hated that that happened to you. No, it's more about the life we want Billy to have. I know you grew up in London, but I don't think it's a good place for a child.'

'It can be.'

I thought about this for a while. I had this vision of us living in Cornwall in a cottage near the sea. It would have a garden for Billy, and Markus and I would both work from home. There would be no more Philip Parr and the pressure he put on me. I'd be working for myself as a freelance writer and have peace and calm and . . . isolation! No, I knew I was a city person through and through. I liked living in the centre of town and I loved our Baker Street flat.

'I'm not ready to leave London yet,' I said.

'You can write articles from anywhere.'

'Yes, but I couldn't edit the magazine from Cornwall. How long have you been thinking this?'

'A while . . .'

This surprised me again because I'd assumed he was committed to his architectural practice in Clerkenwell, especially since he'd won the big commission. Perhaps that was the point; perhaps he felt more secure about his work now.

'You'll be tied up with the Durham project for ages.'

'Yes, I will. I still think we should think about it. Children need fresh air and wide open spaces,' he said. 'And I sometimes feel trapped in London.'

And then we got trapped behind a tractor for the next few miles of the single-lane Cornish road. Markus is not brilliant in these situations and I could feel his impatience building as he wanted to get to the coast. My mobile phone rang.

'Oh, no! I bet that's work.'

'Ignore it,' he said. 'You're on holiday.'

I pulled my phone out of my bag and saw that Eddie was ringing me. I let it go to voice-mail. I wasn't going to talk to him with Markus sitting next to me.

'They can leave a message,' I said.

*

We finally arrived at the hotel and were shown up to our family room. It was a large double-aspect room with slightly shabby furniture. It had a great view of the sea and we both thought it would do fine. I unpacked our stuff quickly and then went into the bathroom to listen to the voice-mail Eddie had left me. It was a long message. He said that he was off to Kent to work on the major garden redesign; that he was sorry about turning up at my work like that; I had been right to be angry. He just hoped we could stay in touch. I stood in the bathroom and thought about whether I should try to find a time to call him back later and wish him luck. Then I decided, no, enough of this. I was building a new life with Markus and we were going to have a good holiday together. I turned my mobile phone off.

It was too late for Markus to get in a dive as he still needed to fill his air bottles. We did get down to the beach before dinner and we both held Billy's hands as we watched him have his first ever excited paddle in the sea. It was a lovely moment.

We had been in St Ives for three days and I'd asked my aunt Jennie over to our hotel for dinner.

'Markus, if you like diving you must go to Botallack. There's the most stunning natural swimming pool there, made from a ring of granite rocks. At high tide it fills with seawater. It's a place only the locals know about.'

'How do you get there?'

'It's a bit of a walk, about an hour from the village of Botallack, which is west of here. A pretty walk, though. And you'll see the old mine head.'

'If it's an hour's walk I can't go diving. That's too far to carry my gear. We could go snorkelling there.'

'Let's go tomorrow,' I said enthusiastically.

'I don't think you'd want to take Billy. The climb down to the pool is very steep and slippery. I can't look after him tomorrow. If you can wait till Thursday, I'd be happy to have him.'

'I'd like to go tomorrow if we can,' Markus said. 'The forecast for Thursday isn't great.'

'Let's go, then,' I said. 'You can swim in the pool and I'll stay above with Billy. We can have a picnic.'

We were having a good time and had both started to relax. The weather had been good, Billy was sleeping well, Markus had got in two dives already and I had been enjoying lying on the beach, reading purely for pleasure. Markus and I had made love the second night and it all felt a long way from the office and the tensions I'd been feeling there. I was so glad we'd found the time to come away and were beginning to pull down the wall that had built up between us.

HEJA

AUGUST

Tonight I slept in Markus's bed. I lay on his side and could smell the faintest trace of his body.

I had not intended to sleep in her flat. I got there at nine o'clock and planned to work for a few hours. I put the hall light on and went into Billy's bedroom. There is a small white chest of drawers by the wall and I got down on my knees and went through the clothes in the drawers. He is not yet one year old yet a lot of the clothes had labels for twelve to eighteen months old. He must be big for his age. His clothes were neatly folded, with jumpers and cardigans in the bottom drawer, T-shirts and dungarees in the next one up and vests, Babygros and socks in the top drawer. There is a row of little hooks on the back of his bedroom door and a padded jacket was hanging there. The seagull mobile had gone from above his cot. Perhaps they had taken it with them to Cornwall? Perhaps Billy can only sleep with the seagulls stirring above him.

Under the window there was a padded fabric toy box with a Noah's Ark design. I lifted the lid. It was full of toys – a squeezy rubber giraffe that squeaked when you pressed it, a painted wooden clown with jointed arms and legs, lots of coloured wooden bricks and a red plastic tipper truck with large wheels. The rubber giraffe was rather horrible. It had hooded eyes and long black rubber eyelashes.

I walked into their bedroom next. I saw that she had left

161

their bed made up. I would have thought she would have stripped the sheets before she went away. I wanted to lie down where he lies every night. I took off all my clothes, pulled back the dark quilt and climbed into his side of the bed. I slept well in that large strange bed. And I had the most vivid dream. I was standing in my kitchen. Markus was sitting at the breakfast bar. I took a knife and made a deep incision in the flesh above my right ovary. Markus was watching me intently. I pressed the sides of the wound carefully until a raw egg emerged through the slit. I caught the egg in a white china bowl. I was glad that the yolk had not broken. I heated butter in a frying pan and fried the egg for Markus.

When I woke up next morning it was nearly eight so I dressed quickly and got to work. Her study is small; there is hardly room to move. There were some new photographs of Billy on the back of the door. I sat on her chair and looked at the shelves in front of me. What a mess they were. I pulled the first batch of papers from the shelf and looked through them. They were a mixture of paid bills, postcards from friends and a few charity Christmas cards. Then there were some reference books and a second batch of papers in one of those plastic wallets. I skimmed through these. They were mainly letters from her parents in Portugal. I had not known that her parents lived abroad. She must have some place where she kept important documents.

I stood up and looked at the shelves. There was a purple box file wedged into the space above the books on the top shelf. I stood on her chair carefully and took the box file down. This was it. On the spine of the file she had written: *Birth Certificates, Pension, Will.* It was one of those box files with a spring that holds the documents down. I pulled the spring up and took the papers out. Her birth certificate was on the top. She is two years younger than me. Her father is English and her mother Portuguese. She was born in London. Billy's birth certificate was under hers. He was born on 3 October at University College Hospital. He has no middle name. He is just plain Billy Hartman. I find it moving that Markus has named his son after his grandfather, the news photographer and communist. He was the member of his family that Markus loved most and the one who had the greatest influence on him.

He told me that when he was eleven years old his granddad took him to the fishing village where he had grown up. His granddad had not been back there in forty years. His wife had died in the spring and that had prompted the journey. This visit meant a great deal to Markus and he often talked about it. His older brothers had sneered at the idea of going away with their grandfather, so it was just the two of them. Markus told me his grandfather always had time for him, always listened to him. And he had his own special name for him too, which was Poppa.

On their first morning in the village they walked to the site of his grandfather's house. It was on the outskirts of the village and the house had been pulled down and a new single-storey building stood in its place. His poppa was troubled by the disappearance of his old home. Then he noticed that the trees from his childhood were still there. He told Markus that the trees had been his world when he was growing up; that sometimes they became a pirate ship, sometimes a chariot. So Markus climbed his favourite tree for him.

Then they walked back into the village and stopped in front of an old-fashioned store that sold clothes. It was in the best position in the village, Markus said, and Poppa told him that when he was a boy the family that owned this store were very big fish. He knew the son of the family, Jari Varpe; they had been schoolmates. They went into the shop and his grandfather noticed a man standing behind the counter. He had grey hair and a lined and disappointed face.

He had looked startled and said, 'Is that you Billy Hartman?'

'It is, Jari. It is indeed. And this is my grandson, Markus.'

The two men shook hands, looking into each other's faces with amazement, and established that they hadn't seen each other for forty years. And afterwards – and this was the bit that Markus often talked about – his grandfather walked with him down to the harbour and said, 'Just imagine Jari's life here all these years. Imagine him getting up every morning to unlock his shop and to stand behind that counter and see the same old faces coming in. When I was your age we all thought Jari Varpe had the world at his feet. The family business trapped him here.'

He told Markus that he must live his life to the full, fight for his beliefs and not be afraid of taking on new challenges.

Years later Markus often visited his grandfather in that miserable nursing home in the middle of nowhere and I told him once that I loved the way he always wanted to take responsibility for the weak and the vulnerable. He got quite cross with me then and said he did not see his grandfather as weak or vulnerable. He was still a big man to him. He ended his relationship with me the year his grandfather died. I have often wondered if the two events were connected.

I will take the birth certificate and get a copy made. Her will and testament made interesting reading. She had left everything to Billy. She did not have that much. She does not own the flat. She rents it and it has a long lease, which she has assigned to Billy in the event of her death. What about Markus? She had also made provision for Billy to see a named child psychotherapist . . . *should I die suddenly*. What had driven her to put that in her will? She was not ill. She had a number of pension plans with smallish sums of money in them.

Just then I heard a key in the front door and the handle being turned. I leapt up and stood behind the study door. It was a bad moment. Could they have come back? I did not have time to move the documents or close the box. I heard footsteps coming down the hall and someone saying to herself, 'She left the hall light on.'

It was a woman's voice, not Kathy's. I heard her go into the kitchen. Then there was the noise of someone rummaging in a cupboard and of water being run into a bowl. It must be the cleaner come to do the flat. She would have her own set of keys. After a few minutes I heard the radio come on and then she was fiddling with the tuning switch to change stations. The kitchen filled with a country and western song. Kathy's study was right next door to the kitchen and I would have to walk past the open kitchen door to get to the front door. So I had to stay in the study until the cleaner moved into another room. Would she come into the study? It did not look as if it was ever cleaned. She had probably been told to leave it alone. One option would be to stay in the study until she had finished her work. That could be two or three hours. I did not have the strength to stand behind the door for that length of time.

I would have a better chance of getting down the corridor unnoticed when she was in the bathroom or one of the bedrooms. Of course, she would strip the sheets from their bed. That might be my chance. She worked in the kitchen for about twenty minutes. I heard her sweeping the floor and putting china away. I was getting very bad pins and needles in my legs. Then she put the kettle on and made herself a drink.

She came out of the kitchen and went into the bathroom.

I could hear her put on the bath taps as she scoured the bath. This was my best chance. I picked up Billy's birth certificate and walked noiselessly down the corridor, opened the front door and pulled it to. I did not actually close it as it might have made a click. She would think she had left it open when she came in. I will have to go back later this week to replace the documents and put the purple box file back in its place. I walked down the three flights of stairs with shaking legs, crossed the entrance hall and escaped into the street.

I was walking up the stairs to the office when Philip Parr came up behind me, taking the stairs two at a time, and said, 'Heja, how are you? Have you got a minute?'

I followed him into his office. He motioned me to take a seat. 'It's been a while since we talked.'

I do not like his face. There is something angry and compressed about it. It is as if all the features are pushed into the centre. He thinks he is attractive because of his power. He is not attractive. He moves with quick, jerky movements. He is not at peace with himself or with his body.

'How's the heritage sites project going?'

'OK, I think.'

'Which sites are you doing?'

'Scotland and the north of England – Durham Cathedral, Hadrian's Wall . . .'

'Was that your choice?'

'Yes, it was.'

'I expected you to choose somewhere more exotic . . .'

'Maybe I find them exotic.' I smiled at him. 'I've never been to the north of England or to Scotland.'

'And you think the project's going well?'

I hesitated, so that he noticed my hesitation.

'I think so.'

'You don't sound very convinced.'

'I just wonder if our readers will want to stay with the topic for a whole year, that's all. Perhaps interest will wane after a while.'

'That would be unfortunate.'

'There are some wonderful places on the list. Some of the more obscure sites are perhaps less interesting. The Verla Groundwood Mill did not interest me when I was twelve, and it still does not. Perhaps it would be better to select the sites of greatest interest and focus on them.'

'Then it wouldn't be a comprehensive survey. Have you talked to Kathy about this?'

'No.'

'Perhaps you should discuss your doubts with her.'

I made a point of looking at him doubtfully.

'I don't like to seem negative,' I said.

He sprang up from behind his desk then and I had this image of him as a type of manic marionette.

'I'm meeting a big advertiser tomorrow. With Kathy away I was going to ask you to come along and enthuse about the series. Would you be able to do that?'

'Oh, yes, I would be happy to enthuse . . .' I said archly.

'Good. I look forward to it, then.'

He opened the door for me and I went over to my desk. I saw that Aisha was watching me, storing this information to share with Kathy. Watch away.

KATHY

AUGUST

We walked for about an hour. Markus was carrying his diving bag with his mask and fins and our picnic and I had Billy in a baby carrier on my back. Shortly after we set off we saw the ruined engine house from the old mine that Jennie had mentioned. She said it was once a major tin mine and when its waste poured out into the ocean it would turn the sea red. It's built of pale gold bricks in contrast to the squat houses of the village, which are uniformly grey and hunched and look as if they're bracing themselves against what the weather might throw at them.

We'd chosen a perfect day for our picnic as the sun was high and brilliant overhead and gilded the landscape before us. We walked over a wide heath without a single tree in sight. There were sturdy bushes at the perimeter. These had been bent out of shape by the pressure of the wind that swept over them. The path was shaley and here and there outcrops of granite reared up from the earth. The grass was yellowy-green and tussocky and scattered with purple wild flowers. The sea was to our right and foamed against the granite cliffs. Most of the walk was level until we reached a steep hill that led down to the cliff-top we were looking for. Here the loose shale made it precarious with Billy strapped to my back, so Markus went in front of me and helped us down. At the bottom of the hill the cliff-top opened into a plateau with an expanse of heather in full bloom stretching all round us.

Where the land ended there was a steep granite cliff leading down to a jagged rock formation, which indeed formed the outer perimeter of a natural pool. The sea surged in through the gaps in the rock circle to fill a central crevasse and the water was so clear in the centre and you couldn't tell its depth.

'This is fantastic!' Markus said.

We unpacked the blanket and our stuff a good distance from the cliff's edge.

'I think I'll go straight in,' he said eagerly.

'Don't you want something to eat?'

'No, I'll wait. That water looks so inviting.'

He pulled his wetsuit out of the diving bag. I set Billy down on the blanket and helped zip Markus into the tight-fitting suit that stretched over his firm shoulders. I kissed him on the back of his neck and he turned round and kissed me back.

'Is it safe to go in on your own?'

'Quite safe. Don't worry, I'm only snorkelling.'

He put his mask, snorkel and fins into a string bag over his shoulder and climbed nimbly down the rock face. I could never have made it down there with Billy on my back. I saw him reach the plateau and sit down to put his fins on. He looked up, grinning with anticipation, waved at me and jumped into the pool. I walked back to the blanket and rocked Billy in my arms until he fell asleep. I laid him down on the blanket in the shade thrown by the diving bag and walked back to watch Markus in the water. He was swimming round and round and then diving down, his fins poking up in the air. He was a strong and graceful swimmer and looked completely in his element.

I stretched out next to Billy and watched the seagulls wheeling overhead. It was so peaceful. There was the faintest breeze rustling the heather and the air smelled good. Someone once told me that heather only smells when the sun shines on it and today I could smell its subtle scent. I decided to unpack the picnic and turned onto my stomach. I saw the name label on Markus's diving bag written in his strong handwriting. He had written his name and there was an address below it. I sat up to examine the label more closely; yes, it was definitely an address in Helsinki. The name label was coming out of its leather case so I pulled it out fully so I could put it in again more securely.

Behind the name label I found a section of a photograph, cut to fit behind it. I pulled the photograph out. I saw a young Markus in a white T-shirt and khaki shorts sitting on a harbour wall. He had his arm around a woman's slender shoulders. She was tanned and dressed in a turquoise halterneck sundress and her blonde hair was hanging free around her face. Her body was turned towards Markus, nestling into his, her face in half-profile. He looked so happy and she was beautiful; radiant. And the woman was Heja. I turned the photograph over and read the words written there.

You will find this one day and remember how happy we were.

I shuddered deeply and felt I might retch. It was as if the sky was full of seagulls screeching her words again and again.

How happy we were.

How happy we were.

I knelt on the blanket with my arms over my head and rocked back and forth in shock and pain. It was a physical pain, like a prickling all over my body. And not just physical pain, also a feeling of intense humiliation that I had been lied to for months. My harsh, truthful, puritanical Markus was a liar. He had lied to me all along and shut me out and made me feel shallow because I wanted to know more about him and his past. And what made it even more painful was that she knew all the time. She knew that he was lying to me. I saw her face then, as she sometimes looked at me across the office, curious and supercilious at the same time.

I could not stay there a moment longer. I could not bear the thought of seeing Markus and his lying face. I picked Billy up, waking him to put him in the baby-carrier, and he cried at being woken like this. I had to shut my ears to his cries. I took the photograph and a bottle of water and left everything else lying there.

I walked to the hill and tried to scramble up it. It was difficult to get up with Billy on my back and I slipped on the shaley path, scratched my ankles and slid to the bottom. I abandoned the water bottle then and tried to get up the hill again, using both hands to scrabble to the top. Sweat was pouring between my breasts, my hands were grazed and the strap of the baby-carrier was rubbing against my shoulders. These physical discomforts were as nothing compared to the rage and misery I felt.

Somehow I reached the village with its ugly crouched houses and only then did I get my mobile out and phone for a taxi to take me to the hotel twelve miles away. There was no taxi company in that small village and the car took a long time coming. I paced up and down the main street of the village, with Billy bobbing up and down on my back, terrified that Markus would catch up with us. Finally the taxi driver arrived. He was intrigued at me calling him out to Botallack.

'Bit of a distance to St Ives, with the baby and all. Did you walk here?'

'No, I didn't,' I said weakly.

'The buses here are few and far between.'

'I made a mistake,' I said, wishing he would leave me alone.

When we reached the hotel I nearly ran up to our room and packed my things and Billy's as fast as I could while my jealousy and my rage pounded in my temples. Then I sat at the table and wrote him a message.

I found this photograph in your bag. You and Heja were lovers and perhaps you are still lovers. You lied to me. I asked you about her and you lied to me. It's all been a great big lie. You made me feel stupid but I knew something was wrong. The great big rotten lie of you makes me sick to the stomach.

HEJA

AUGUST

'I like that dress,' Tim said from behind a pile of his corrected proofs. 'It's very Jackie Kennedy.'

I was wearing a duck-egg-blue linen dress for the lunch with Philip and the advertiser.

'Thank you,' I said.

'It's more Audrey Hepburn,' said Stephanie.

'No, she always wore black,' Tim retorted.

They pulled silly faces at each other, as they so often did.

Philip gave me a quick briefing on the Mr Chudleigh we were going to meet as we walked down the stairs. He ran the marketing for a large and successful travel company, he said, and had spent money in the magazine before. Victoria looked put out when she saw us leaving the office together. Philip's PA had booked us a table at Odette's, which was a ten-minute walk from the office. On our way there I mentioned to Philip that I had once compèred an award ceremony for the advertising industry in Finland. This seemed to impress him, as I thought it might.

Mr Chudleigh was late joining us and Philip had already started on the good red wine he had ordered. Then he walked into the restaurant and I saw him squeezing his way between the tables. This was a man who went to a lot of business lunches. He was wearing a pinstriped suit that seemed inappropriate for an August day. He and Philip knew each other quite well and a lot of easy banter went back and forth between them. They ate rich food: rabbit stew and roasted wood pigeon. I chose pea and mint risotto.

We did not talk much about the heritage guides, in fact. As I had suspected, I was there to add glamour to the lunch. At one point, fairly late on, Philip made a reference to the award ceremony I had compèred, so I had to explain that I had once been an anchor for Finnish TV news. Mr Chudleigh expressed surprise that I had left that world. Did I miss television? I was more forthcoming than I usually am as I need to keep Philip on my side. After Mr Chudleigh left us we sat on and Philip ordered a calvados.

'That went well. I could tell he was impressed by you. I'll have to take you along another time.'

'I'd be delighted.'

'So you're enjoying your new career?'

'I'm happy to be working on the best architecture magazine there is,' I said.

'No downsides? It must be less lucrative?'

'I put money away during the TV years. I guess the only downside for me is that I am not good at the whole team thing. I find the joshing and the gossip tiresome and, occasionally, unpleasant.'

'And are they a gossipy lot?'

He appeared blasé but I knew he was keenly interested.

'Of course they are. It was the same at the TV station.'

'And what do they gossip about?'

'They gossip about you, Philip.' I smiled at him playfully. 'Teams always gossip about the boss.'

'That's gratitude for you! It's my efforts that keep the magazine going and pays their wages.'

I had taken a risk. Had I hit a raw nerve? That was enough for that day. It would be too much to plant the idea now that it was Kathy who had told his wife about his affair with Andrea. That would be the next conversation; that would be the unexploded mine that would get her into serious trouble.

Philip paid the bill and we left the restaurant. I decided to play it contrite.

'I'm sorry if I offended you just now. I didn't mean to. I really enjoyed our lunch.'

He stopped in his tracks and looked at me as if I had excited him. 'So did I. You didn't offend me at all.'

Then he said he was going away for his summer break next week. He was spending three weeks in Tuscany. He would very much like to take me to dinner on his return. And I agreed, of course.

KATHY

AUGUST

I took another taxi to Jennie's. As the taxi was drawing up outside her cottage in Newlyn I remembered she'd said she would be out most of the day. I paid the driver – thank goodness I had the holiday money on me – and then tried her front door, just in case she'd left it open. It was locked. I wheeled Billy round to the back garden and the back door was locked too. I lugged my suitcase round and left it on the path at the back. Odds were it would be safe here, this was Newlyn, not London. It was just after three and Jennie would probably not be back till six so I had to get through the next three hours somehow.

I took Billy for a walk and was remembering every exchange Markus and I had ever had about Heja. I remembered his 'She was much admired in Finland.'

I pushed his buggy fast along the seafront past the large car park. There was a seagull on top of the pay-and-display machine and two gulls were examining the grit at its base. Billy pointed at the gulls so I let him get out. He's not quite walking yet. He can do a few steps if I hold both his hands and help him. As we walked nearer the gulls launched themselves into the air and flew off towards the sea. Billy stood there, a bit unsteadily, looking after them. The feeling in my chest was now like very painful heartburn as I remembered his cold, dismissive 'Why should you care?'

I picked Billy up and hugged him tight and then I pushed him in the buggy up to the centre of town. Newlyn is not as prosperous or as touristy a place as St Ives and it feels more like a working town. I passed one of those cheap bakeries with yellow glazed sausage rolls in the window and the smell of hydrogenated fat wafting out of its open door. Next door was a charity shop and then a surfers' shop. I kept seeing that photograph of her nestling into his body; it was as if her body fitted his and they looked so in love.

After an age of tormented walking up one street and down the next, Billy started to grizzle and I realized that he must be hungry. We hadn't eaten for hours and I remembered our abandoned picnic on the cliff-top. I spotted a small café in a side street called Sea Breezes, which had a blackboard outside with the day's specials written up in coloured chalk. I couldn't see through the windows as they were steamed up so I pushed the door open and saw that most of the tables were taken. There was one table with three chairs by the window that was occupied by a young girl with a baby in a buggy next to her. There was a seat free so I asked if we could sit opposite and she nodded.

She was reading a book and rocking her baby to get him to sleep. She was a thin little thing with a pointed, wistful face and shadows under her eyes and she looked about eighteen or nineteen. Her sharp shoulders protruded from a purple strappy top. She was engrossed in her book, which I saw was *The Beach*. It had a plastic wrapper on it, as if borrowed from a library. Her fingernails were bitten and every now and then she chewed on the corner of her thumbnail.

I ordered a pot of tea and treacle tart with custard and took out a jar of parsnip and carrot for Billy. I spooned it into his mouth. He was hungry and ate it all so I gave him a second one of puréed apple. The young mum closed her book with a sigh and drank from her can of Diet Coke. Her baby was very bonny with a mass of dark curls and was nicely dressed in a red T-shirt and striped dungarees. His eyes were getting heavy as she rocked his buggy gently from side to side. My treacle tart arrived and I ate it hungrily, letting the warm sweetness melt in my mouth. It was comforting and I wanted to cry. I gave Billy a rusk to suck on. Her baby had gone to sleep and our eyes met.

'How old is he?' she asked, nodding at Billy.

'Ten months. And yours?'

'He's just had his first birthday.'

'He's gorgeous.'

'Best thing that ever happened to me.'

'What's his name?'

'Rory – Rory, Peter, Patrick. The Peter and Patrick are from his granddads and I chose Rory. What's yours called?'

'Billy.'

'He's very blond.'

'Yes, and I think he'll stay blond.'

'And you're so dark.'

'I know. His dad is very blond. He doesn't take after me at all.'

'Rory's the image of his dad too.'

We both gazed at her baby. Rory had plump rosy cheeks and thick dark lashes.

'You visiting . . .?'

'Yes, my aunt lives here. What's it like living here with a small baby?'

'It's OK really. There's a drop-in place for mums and kids. They look after the babies so we can have a coffee and a break.'

'Sounds good . . .'

'It's all right. I go there most mornings. They have DVDs and books you can borrow.'

She put her novel in her bag and stood up to go. 'Been nice meeting you . . .'

'And you. I'm Kathy.'

'Tina,' she said.

Later I walked back slowly to Jennie's house. Talking to Tina had helped me forget my misery for a while. Now it had come back full force. Markus and Heja had been lovers. Then I saw that Jennie's car was parked in the road in front of her house and I nearly cried with relief. I could tell her everything. I needed her support and her special brand of warm good sense so much.

HEJA

AUGUST

My body always lets me down. I had been feeling fine for several weeks and then on Wednesday I started to feel sick and shaky. I went into work but left early. It was evening and I was lying on the sofa wrapped in the kimono Robert had given me. I was about to go to bed when the phone rang. It was Markus. He said he would be over in fifteen minutes. He sounded tense. I did not understand it. He was supposed to be in Cornwall with her all week. What had happened? I opened the door to him in my kimono.

'Come in. I've made you some coffee how you like it,' I said.

'You look very white. Are you OK?'

'I think I may have flu. I'm a bit shaky.'

I poured coffee into a large cup and pushed it across the bar towards him.

'Aren't you having any?' he asked.

'I don't drink it any more. Markus, you look really tired. What's wrong?'

'I just drove back from Cornwall.'

'Why?'

He took a photograph out of his pocket and slid it over the bar towards me. I looked down at it. I could feel my face get hot. I picked it up and gazed at it for a long time. Then I turned it over and read my words. *You will find this one day and remember how happy we were.*

'I haven't seen this in ten years. It was that summer at Aland.'

'I know. Kathy found it in my diving bag. Where did you put it?'

'It was under your name label. You were supposed to find it after that row. It must have been there all this time. You look so young.'

'So do you.'

I turned away from him with the cafetière and took my time rinsing it under the tap. My hands were shaking. I knew that I looked ill and old and that he was contrasting me with the young Heja in the photograph.

'Heja, I *can't* go on seeing you.'

'Why not . . .? Because of a photograph?'

'I'm so sorry. I have Billy now.'

'I would *never* come between you and Billy.'

'This has to end now, tonight,' he said.

I waited for a moment and then I said it. 'Kathy still sees her ex.'

He sat up and pulled his shoulders back as though he was about to face an enemy.

'What are you saying?'

'Just that: she still sees her ex. I saw them hugging in Reception at work a few weeks ago. Why shouldn't we still see each other?'

He looked so lost, so unhappy but he did not respond to what I had just told him. And what I couldn't tell him was that I had also seen her ex in their flat, holding Billy. If I had said that he would have known I was watching the flat. He stood up now.

'I've made my choice, Heja. It was wrong. I'm so sorry; I've made my choice.'

'You chose me too, Markus.'

I longed to press my body against his so that we could comfort each other. He turned and walked out of my flat without another word and the door clicked shut behind him. And I know Markus. When he has made a decision he sticks to it.

I was so shaky I had to lie down again. That photograph, I had forgotten all about it. And now she had found it and she finally knew about us. He had left me again; a second rejection; another unbearable blow.

I remembered how Markus had left me before. We had had one of our rows, a bad one this time about a woman in his office. We made up eventually, as we always did, and we went to bed and made love. I assumed things were all right between us again. Markus thought otherwise. He left me. He left Helsinki. He wrote me a letter, which I got three days later. He had written that he loved me still, he would always love me but he could not go on with the endless cycle of jealous rows followed by reconciliations. We seemed incapable of having a calm, happy life together, he said. The relationship was hurting both of us. He had to end it. He was leaving Finland. He could not tell me where he was going.

It was a brutal rejection. I was at the height of my fame. I had money and a beautiful apartment and I was completely bereft. I made frantic enquiries about him, using my many contacts in the media. I could find no trace of where he had gone; just that he had definitely left Finland. He could have gone anywhere.

Then about three weeks into this torment I noticed that my period had not come. I put it down to the agonizing stress I was going through over Markus. I woke a few mornings later feeling queasy. I bought a pregnancy test and I tested my urine and it confirmed that I was pregnant. As I looked at the positive test I felt the most profound joy of my life. I was carrying our child. Everything would be all right now. Markus would hear of my pregnancy somehow. It would become news in a few months anyway when I started to show my bump. There would be coverage on TV and in the papers. Somehow he would hear about it and he would come back to me and we would have a new beginning. What a precious moment to get pregnant.

For the next two months I hugged my secret to myself. The world looked a different and kinder and more hopeful place. Everything in my life shifted in focus. I had a strong sense of purpose that made me feel fulfilled. Now I was glad of all the money I had earned and the position I had reached in my career. Markus and I and our child would have a good life. I started to think about where we should live. I knew Markus would want us to live by the sea. I registered with some property companies. I longed to find him and tell him the news. I wanted him to be the first person to know about the pregnancy but could not see how I could make that happen.

And then, when I was nearly three and a half months pregnant, I started to feel really ill. I was getting bad dizzy spells and days of feeling very sick. I started to feel afraid about the welfare of my baby. My doctor was worried and he kept taking blood tests. He was our family doctor and I had known him for years. Then that day came when he called me and said I needed to come to the surgery as soon as I could and perhaps I should come with a friend. The moment he said that I knew the news was bad. And when I saw his face all my fears were confirmed.

'Sit down, Heja,' he said quietly.

'Is my baby OK?'

'We've had the results back and it's not good.'

'Tell me! Is my baby OK?'

'Heja, I'm so sorry to tell you that you have a genetic disease.'

'I don't understand . . .'

'The illness that's in your family . . .'

I couldn't take it in.

'Your great-aunt Tanya . . .'

'You're saying I've got what Tanya had?'

'I'm afraid so.'

I started to tremble violently. My mind was racing. I remembered that day in the garden: the brilliant sunshine; the feathery grasses; hearing her cry; and her funeral.

'They couldn't save her . . .'

He looked rather white. 'We can do much to help you, Heja.'

'I'm twenty-eight and you're telling me I have a terminal disease?'

'You have the same disease.'

'She was dead at forty-seven,' I shrieked at him.

'This must be the most terrible shock. Can I call your parents?'

'No! Don't you dare!'

I was still trembling violently. 'But my baby's OK?'

He didn't want to tell me but he had to. My baby was not viable. Those were the words he used, 'not viable'. I would have to terminate my pregnancy as soon as possible as I was already four months pregnant.

And I remembered what Tanya had said to me that day in the garden: 'Don't be afraid, Heja. Sometimes tears are good. They make new life grow.'

Make new life grow? I had thought I was carrying new

life in my body but I was carrying her death gene. It had been there inside me from the beginning: from the day I was born; from that day in the garden; from the day I met Markus; and today. It meant our baby had to be aborted. I had to agree to the termination that afternoon in the doctor's surgery. No one to help me; no one I could tell. He pleaded with me to call my parents so that I would have someone with me when I woke up from the general anaesthetic. He said it was a very difficult moment. I refused. He gave me strong tranquillizers to deaden the horror of that day and the days that followed.

Why didn't I tell Markus this evening, when he was standing in my flat, saying he would not see me again? He needed to know that Billy was not the first baby he had made. He needed to know about our poor little aborted baby.

People thought I had everything – the looks, the fame, the money, the handsome boyfriend. I had nothing. All I had was the death gene working in me, waiting to claim me.

KATHY

AUGUST

'I've been a complete and utter fool,' I said.

Jennie was walking round the kitchen with Billy propped against her shoulder. She was rubbing his back with gentle circular movements and she stopped by me now and gave me a sympathetic pat.

'Stop beating yourself up . . .'

'There I was thinking Markus's great secret was his politics and all the time his great secret was Heja!'

'He's asleep. I'm going to put him down, and then I'll make us some tea.'

I'd spent a bad night in Jennie's back bedroom and I wondered if she'd heard me pacing up and down. The floorboards were bare, except for a rug, and they creaked when you walked on them. If she had heard me she didn't say anything about it. I had finally made myself lie down and got to sleep as the light was turning the curtains pale. Jennie had taken Billy when he'd woken up and she'd let me sleep on. Things felt a bit more bearable when I finally got up. There was no word from Markus.

Jennie came back into the kitchen, filled the kettle and sat down at the table.

'I was going over it all last night,' she said. 'It's no coincidence, her turning up at your magazine. When did she first show up?'

'I was pregnant, maybe five or six months pregnant. I remember because when we interviewed her she kept looking at my bump.'

'Oh, dear . . .'

'And I gave her the job! In fact, there was another candidate I liked better, a man who had all the right experience. She was my second choice. Philip Parr wanted to appoint her. I remember we had a bit of a tussle about it and I gave in.'

Jennie filled the teapot and brought it to the table.

'Can you remember the first time you told Markus about her?'

'I've been trying to remember that. He wasn't living with me then; it was just before he moved in. He'd come over for supper and I told him we'd employed a Finnish journalist that day, and I told him her name, Heja Vanheinen.'

'How did he react?'

'I don't remember him saying much at all. He certainly didn't mention that he knew her! We were absorbed with my pregnancy, and getting on so well. Ages later I asked him if he knew she'd been a TV presenter in Helsinki, and he said, yes, she was much admired, and that was it. He shut the conversation right down. And I put that down to his not wanting to talk about his life in Finland, not that he'd been involved with her!'

'I don't think Markus had anything to do with this, I mean with her coming to your magazine. It was probably a huge shock to him.'

'Then why didn't he tell me about her the moment I mentioned her name? Can't he see what a huge betrayal it was not to tell me?'

Jennie poured us each a mug of tea and put some lemon biscuits on a plate in front of me. The tea was richly brown and strong, how she always made it.

'And he left Finland seven years ago. She hasn't been in London very long so it doesn't make sense. Why has she come now?'

We drank our tea.

'It's clear to me she wants to sabotage your relationship. She found out about you and that's why she got the job there,' Jennie said.

'You mean she's been stalking me?'

'Yes, that's exactly what I mean.'

'Bloody hell! I've felt uneasy about her for quite a while, especially about the way she is around Philip.'

'I think she's very jealous of you. Some women won't let go. It must have been horrible for Markus knowing she was working with you. Now at least it's out in the open and you can talk about it.'

The tea was strongly fragrant and the biscuits light and citrusy and they did make me feel a bit better.

'They looked so in love in that photo.'

'They were very young,' Jennie said.

'And I'll never have that with him.'

'You've got something else.'

'We've got a baby we both adore. I was crazy about him when I met him and really happy. It's changed since Billy was born. We're just not that comfortable with each other. They looked comfortable together in that picture, like they fitted each other.'

'It's very early days to be giving up on this relationship. Don't let her ruin your marriage. He's worth fighting for.'

Jennie looked at me with such affection and patted my hand encouragingly. She was remembering my troubles with Eddie, I'm sure. She wanted my marriage to work out.

'I don't want us to break up. I really don't. But he can't have these secrets from me. On our way down here he suddenly said he wanted us to leave London and come and live in Cornwall! Out of the blue it was. He said he felt trapped in London.'

'She's making him feel trapped,' Jennie said.

After lunch I took Billy to a playground Jennie had told me about. It was one of those days when it's sunny one moment and cloudy the next. The play park was full of young mums and their children. It was such a normal everyday scene yet I felt alienated from it. I was wondering how many years Heja had been with Markus. When had they split up? When he came to London? I parked the buggy by the sandpit and took Billy's shoes and socks off and sat him in the sand. He was happy enough wriggling his toes and grabbing handfuls of sand. I showed him how to fill a bucket. I turned it upside down and made a small castle and Billy squealed with delight and squashed the castle. A toddler sitting nearby picked up a handful of sand and threw it at Billy.

'No, Johnnie. That's naughty,' his mother said.

The toddler did it again. This time some of the sand landed in Billy's hair and I shook the sand out and checked his eyes.

'I said *no*, Johnnie.' His mother slapped his hands quite hard and the toddler started to cry. I didn't like her doing that.

'I don't think he meant any harm,' I said, trying to placate her.

She threw me a contemptuous look then picked him up roughly and marched him over to the swings. Just then I saw Tina from the café by the park gates. She was standing talking to a dark-haired young man who had to be Rory's dad. He had the same cherubic features and curly dark hair as his son. They were having an argument. He was trying to convince her of something and she kept shaking her head angrily. Rory was in his buggy, cramming some plastic toy in his mouth and watching his warring parents with huge round eyes. The young man turned and walked away fast. Her shoulders slumped, then she bent down and took the toy out of Rory's mouth and wiped his face gently. She saw me and I waved at her.

She walked over slowly with Rory.

'Hello again,' I said.

'Hi,' she said.

She took Rory out of the buggy and took his sandals off. I noticed that he was very smartly dressed again, this time in matching yellow shorts and T-shirt.

'He loves this sandpit,' she said dully.

She sat on the wall next to me. I made another sandcastle for the two of them to squash.

'Do you mind if I have a ciggie? I'll blow the smoke the other way. I don't usually smoke anywhere near him, it's just I do need a ciggie.'

'Not a problem,' I said. 'In fact, can I have one?'

'Course . . .'

She reached for the cigarettes, offered and lit mine and then lit her own and inhaled deeply.

'I gave up when I got pregnant. Then I started again. I don't smoke in the house with the baby,' she said.

I hadn't smoked since Eddie but I enjoyed that cigarette. It seemed to calm us both as we watched our babies.

'That was Sean, Rory's dad.'

'He looks so like him.'

'I know.'

She inhaled deeply on her cigarette again.

'He loves Rory. It's just he finds it too much, being a dad at his age.'

'Do you live together?'

'At the moment we do, at my mum's. He'll be off before the summer's out. He's got the travelling bug bad.'

'That's tough on you.'

'He says we should go with him, to Thailand. Find bar work out there. But he's not thinking straight. I know it's no good Rory being moved from pillar to post. He needs a routine.'

'That's true enough.'

'Part of me really wants to go.'

'I saw you were reading *The Beach*.'

'Yeah, we'd all like to escape. But life's not like that, is it?'

'Not for mothers,' I said.

When I left I gave Tina my email address and told her to keep in touch. Here was this nineteen-year-old girl about to be left on her own in Newlyn with a one-year-old baby and probably very little money. I could see that she was a very good mum to her little boy. She made me realize what a privileged life I had.

I walked back to Jennie's and saw Markus's Saab parked in Church Road and my heart lurched hard. The car was quite muddy and one of Billy's soft toys lay on the back seat. Where had he been? He was standing in Jennie's front room, looking out. As soon as he saw me he came out and knelt by Billy, unstrapped him and hugged him close.

'It's time to go home, Kathy,' he said in his stern voice. 'Pack your things and I'll drive us home.'

'Not so fast,' I said. 'We need to talk.'

'Not here. Not in front of your aunt. We can go back to the hotel.'

'No. I need answers, Markus, and I need them now.'

I took Billy from him, went into the house and asked Jennie if she would look after him. Markus was pacing up and down the front path.

'We can walk down to the seafront,' I said.

When we were some way from Jennie's house I burst out, 'How could you not tell me about Heja?'

'Hear me out,' he said. 'When I came out of the pool and you were gone I thought you and Billy had fallen over the cliff! That cliff has a sheer drop. I knew no one could get out alive if they fell there. I scrambled down and climbed over the rocks for ages. Then I climbed up again and walked and walked, looking for you both. Then I walked back to Botallack and thought you must be there, in the car with Billy. No sign of you. You had *no* right to take him away like that, without giving me any explanation. I was very frightened.'

'Don't you dare try to put me in the wrong! I had just found out that you and Heja were lovers.'

'Were lovers. Past tense.'

'You lied to me.'

'I didn't tell you about her.'

'Why the hell not?'

'It ended years ago. It was a bad ending. I was shocked when you told me she'd joined your magazine.'

'That's exactly when you should have told me.'

'I couldn't bring myself to talk about it.'

'Why not? I needed to know.'

'I couldn't understand why she was at your magazine. It was strange and worrying. Heja is very possessive. You were pregnant and needed calm. I decided it was best to say nothing.'

'Of course it wasn't! I've never understood why you won't talk about your past. How can we have anything real if there are all these secrets between us?'

My voice was rising, I knew. He, on the other hand, seemed to be getting calmer, colder and more rational.

'I don't agree. I'm sure you have secrets from me, Kathy.

Being married doesn't mean we have to share every thought, every impulse. That would be so oppressive.'

'Don't twist my words. Something as big as this, a major relationship in your life, and she turns up at *my* work! Can't you see that by saying nothing you were being disloyal to me?'

'It was over long ago, seven years ago. If I'd told you about it there would have been all kinds of trouble. I knew it would come out at some point.'

We had reached the seafront and I had to ask the question that was making me feel ill, that had kept me awake that long night in Jennie's back bedroom. I had to ask, yet I dreaded his answer.

'Have you seen her? Since she's been in London?'

Markus stood still and looked out at the sea. He would not look at me.

'Have you?'

'I've seen her three times. I drove to London yesterday and told her I won't see her again.'

'Three times since we've been together?'

'Yes.'

'You bastard!'

Tears came now, hot seething jealous tears that brought no relief. I forgot all my resolutions. I forgot my own behaviour with Hector. I wanted to wrench every last detail from him about his meetings with her.

'When did you see her?'

'She called me when you were in Lisbon.'

'Oh, yes, perfect timing. And you just fell in with her plans. Did you sleep with her?'

'Don't demean yourself, Kathy.'

'Why won't you answer me?'

'Because I won't let you, or anyone, tyrannize me. We're

not manacled together. I'm with you and you're with me out of choice. And we're only going to stay together as long as we both choose to.'

At that very moment Tina's image came into my mind. I saw her standing in the park, arguing with Sean with her thin little shoulders hunched and despairing. She knew the way it was. She had no illusions about what was owed to her. I am the naive one, expecting things to be better than they are.

I'm tired yet I cannot sleep. Markus must have got up even earlier as his side of the bed is cold. Last night, in our own bed, I lay facing his back and thought, How can a back express such hostility? It was as if there was this vast space between us and I couldn't move my hand to touch his back or stroke his neck. I lay there thinking, If I can only reach out and touch him tenderly on his neck it will be all right and he'll turn round and hug me and we'll make love. The sex will be angry at first and passionate and then healing. My arm would not move. I was frozen with my resentment against him. When you're lying next to someone and you are become like stone, the night is very long and dark and lonely.

I got up and dressed myself in jeans and a shirt. Markus was working in his room, apparently absorbed in his drawings. I dressed Billy and gave him breakfast and told Markus we were going for a walk in the park. He nodded but said nothing to me. Billy was cheerful, talking in his baby language to the little row of figures I've fixed across the front of his buggy and twisting them with his chubby little fingers. One block away from the flat I called her on my mobile. I found myself grimacing as I heard her cut-glass tones.

'Hello . . .'

'It's Kathy. I think we need to meet and talk, outside the office.'

'Why? Are you planning to dismiss me?'

'This is not about work.'

'Then I am not obliged to meet with you.'

'I didn't say you were obliged. I said I think we should meet, before I come back to work on Monday.'

There was quite a pause and then she said, 'Very well. I suggest we meet at the Royal Institute of British Architecture. There is a coffee shop there.'

'I know it. I'll see you there in one hour,' I said.

'Yes,' she said, clicking her phone off.

Then I called Fran and asked her if she would babysit Billy for the morning.

'I thought you were away till Sunday?'

'We had to come back early.'

'That's a shame. You needed that break.'

'Something cropped up. Could you look after Billy for a couple of hours?'

'I've got the plumber coming to do my overflow. I've got to stay in till he comes. Could you bring Billy here? I'd be happy to have him here, if that's all right with you?'

'Thanks a million, Fran. I'll bring him straight over.'

I used to enjoy going to the RIBA building in Portland Place, it was one of my places. Before I had Billy I would go to the exhibitions there, have a coffee, buy books and postcards. Today as I walked up Portland Place I passed an old man mopping the stone steps of the Institute of Physics. There was steam coming from his bucket and that pungent smell of bleach in soapy water. As I got to the building I saw a young Chinese woman sitting on her own on a mat she had spread on the pavement. She was wearing a yellow sweatshirt that said *Truthfulness, Compassion, Forbearance* in black letters on the back. She was a Falun Gong supporter and she held her palms open and concentrated her energy on the Chinese Embassy opposite. I looked at the Embassy, which seemed like all the others in this exclusive road, except that it had a huge communications aerial on its roof. The young woman gazed at the building with a determined expression on her face. Her placard told of the torture and death of Falun Gong members. She watched them and were they watching her?

The glass engraved doors were heavy against my hand and I walked across the marble floor to the stairs, saying, 'Truthfulness, Compassion, Forbearance' – I said it like a mantra as I mounted the stairs. Heja was already seated at a table at the far end of the coffee-shop, immaculate as ever and paler than usual. She hardly acknowledged me as I approached the table. I was looking at her differently, imposing the photograph of the radiant young woman on to this older, sophisticated woman. The radiance has gone. She made no greeting as I sat down and I made myself speak calmly to her. I was the editor and she was a member of my team.

'Hello, Heja, thank you for agreeing to meet. This is a difficult situation for us both.'

Heja looked over my shoulder at the waitress who was coming to our table. I ordered a cappuccino. She ordered lime flower tea.

'I do not see why what happened in my private life some years ago should impact on our professional relationship,' she said.

This was so cold. This was so Heja.

'You must see it's awkward,' I said. 'You were involved with Markus and I'm married to him now and we are colleagues.'

196

'Yes, I was with Markus for nine years.'

She looked at me with her usual inscrutable expression. The skin under her eyes was almost blue.

'This was in Helsinki?' I asked, trying to keep my voice level. Nine years was a long time. I had been with Markus just over two years. At this moment the waitress came up with our drinks and placed a little white teapot in front of Heja and a large cup of cappuccino in front of me. Heja was silent until the waitress was out of earshot. Then she spoke.

'I think "childhood sweethearts" is the phrase you English use. It was the first important relationship for us both. You could say we grew up together.'

She poured her pale tea into her cup. She was saying she had a prior claim on Markus. I knew that she had not ended the relationship. He had left her. What I really wanted to know was why she'd come to my magazine; why she had switched careers so dramatically. It had to be to get near him and me.

'Markus told me you used to present the news on Finnish TV. It's a big change isn't it – writing about buildings?'

Heja shrugged.

'I have a deep interest in architecture.'

I waited. She offered nothing further and it was a bullshit answer. I tried again.

'I suppose what I'm trying to say, Heja, is that I would like us to have a good working relationship, without any awkwardness about this.'

'If you recall,' she said, 'I offered to take on more of your workload back in April.'

'You did, and as it turns out that wasn't necessary,' I said crisply.

She looked quizzically at me then. I put sugar into my coffee and stirred it into the frothy milk. I wondered if she knew about the mess I'd made of the board meeting. Could Philip have said something to her?

'It's just rather a strange coincidence, isn't it; us both working on the magazine?'

'I don't understand what you are saying,' she replied.

'I'm keen that your former relationship with my husband should not unsettle our working relationship.'

'It makes no difference to me. It is irrelevant,' Heja said calmly. 'It was you who asked for this meeting.'

Yes, I had asked for the meeting but I felt she had all the power in this exchange and I didn't believe her, not for a single minute. How could it be irrelevant that she had ended up at my place of work?

'It's hardly irrelevant,' I said.

'It is not unreasonable that I wish to keep in touch with the man I was involved with for many years. You do the same.'

She looked at me directly as she said this and my stomach contracted. She was referring to Eddie, of course. She'd seen him that day when he came to my office and was drunk. She'd seen us hugging. Had she told Markus about Eddie coming to see me? Was that why Markus said I kept some secrets from him? I took a deep breath to steady myself and played my trump card.

'We have a young son now and Markus and I are trying to build a new life together.'

She smiled coldly and I regretted my use of the word 'trying'.

'Yes, Markus has a highly developed sense of responsibility.'

She looked at me now with undisguised contempt. She wanted to wound me with that remark and was saying that Markus was only with me because of Billy. She was so controlled and so full of malice. I wanted to throw the hot liquid in my cup at her contemptuous face. I wanted to see the coffee hit her face and stain her perfect powder-blue jumper.

'He's the most wonderful father,' I said.

'Yes, he would be. The pregnancy was unplanned, I believe?'

She looked at me directly again and I had to drop my eyes. I felt colour rising hotly into my cheeks. How could she have known that? Markus must have told her. Unplanned; she made it sound like something dirty and disreputable. She had told me nothing at all and had just made me feel even more insecure about my life with Markus.

'Sometimes unplanned things are the most wonderful,' I managed to say. I needed to get away from her fast as I was close to losing control.

'I'll see you on Monday.'

I stood up abruptly and as I did so I knocked our table. My cup of undrunk coffee splashed all over the table and she had to leap to her feet too. She gasped as some drops of coffee hit her.

'That was an accident,' I said angrily, as if she was accusing me of something. 'I'll pay for your clothes to be cleaned.'

I rushed out of the café, away from her.

I ran up the stairs to our flat, unlocked the door and hurled myself into his workroom. He was still sitting there so calmly in front of his drawing desk. His calmness made me even more furious:

'I've just met Heja and she implied you're only with me because of Billy. Is that what you said to her?'

He stood up. 'You went to see Heja?'

'Yes. Since you won't tell me anything . . .'

'Where's Billy?'

'Did you tell her my pregnancy was unplanned?'

199

'Where's Billy?' He reached for my wrist.

'Let go of me.'

'*Where's Billy?*'

I pulled my arm away from him.

'He's with Fran,' I screamed in torment.

'What did you say to her about us?'

'Look at you. You're like a madwoman. Control yourself.'

'I can't stand it! I can't stand your fucking coldness!'

I started to pull his books out of the shelves and fling them on the floor with all my strength.

'Leave my books alone!'

He grabbed me again and we struggled violently until he got me down on the floor, kneeling on me and pinning my arms down by my sides.

Then he said into my face with the greatest bitterness, 'Why did you have to go see her? It's because you want to bring everything to a crisis. You love drama, don't you? You want to make things even worse than they already are.'

He stood up.

'I'm going to get Billy. Get a grip on yourself.'

He walked out of the room and slammed the front door. I curled up into a ball and rocked back and forth on the floor, crying with rage and fear and frustration. I was out of my depth with these two.

HEJA

AUGUST

I was holding the photograph of Markus with Billy lying on his stomach. I lay in bed and looked at it. Markus had his hand resting protectively on Billy's bare back. His eyes were crinkled with laughter. Father and son; Markus with his beloved son . . . I have lost the will to get out of bed.

What a transparent and clumsy fool she was at our meeting. She tried to assert her authority. She thought she could defeat me by invoking Billy and by saying that Markus was her husband. I could defeat her but what is the point any more? Markus is like granite. He said he wouldn't see me any more. And he won't. I know he will not come near me again, because of Billy. He would leave her tomorrow. He will never leave Billy.

Our house was full of photographs of Tomas; photographs of Solange with Tomas on her lap, in her arms, on a sledge. He lived for twelve months – 378 days, to be precise. A life completed before it had really started. Yet Tomas was never forgotten. How strongly my mother held on to her grief. I was never good enough. I could never replace the son she adored. When I was a little girl I longed for my mother's touch. I longed to sit on her lap and have her arms around me. I think back and the only time I can remember her touching me was when she plaited my hair as a child.

There were two photographs of me in the house. One

was a school photograph taken when I was seven years old and had lost my two front teeth. Solange had wound my hair into tight plaits. She put this particular photograph in a cream and gold frame and gave it pride of place on the piano at home. I asked her why she put it there and kept it there all those years. She told me this was her favourite photograph of me 'because you look such a bright little schoolgirl with your plaits and your blue shirt and tie'. Perhaps she felt affection for me then, when I was seven.

The other photograph is a studio head and shoulders of me taken by the TV station. The photographer took ages lighting the shot and he made me look hard and glamorous – the enamelled face of Finnish news.

I have been quite ill for the last two days, drifting in and out of sleep. My dreams have been terrifying. I dreamt that the carrion crow was coming to get me. She was huge and blotted out the sun. Her wings were made of black rags, all shredded and tattered, and her face was a chalk-white mask. I was a little grey mouse hiding in the grass, rooted to the spot. She got me in her sights and swooped down with her talons bared, her mouth stretched back over her teeth. She pierced me with her claws and lifted me into the sky, broken-backed and bleeding.

From my large window I see that the sun is breaking through the clouds and I remember that Markus and I have a date in Durham. I cannot remember when we are meeting or where we are meeting. I will go there and I will walk through the cathedral looking for him. How difficult it is, it has been such a long, lonely struggle. But look, they are singing in the cathedral. They are singing Bach. Tanya is singing. The cathedral is full of people. Tanya is wearing a full-length velvet dress in the richest shade of royal blue. Her beautiful shoulders rise out of her dress. She opens her arms as she sings. Her voice fills the great barrel vaulted space of the cathedral. I am standing in a side chapel, watching her. She is singing Bach's *Mein Herze schwimmt im Blut*: My Heart swims in Blood.

She sings:

> *My heart is swimming in blood,*
> *For my teeming sins*
> *Make me a monster*
> *In God's holy eyes.*

The cathedral is full of women in coloured dresses and men in black. Their solid faces are turned towards Tanya and they are spellbound by her voice. As she sings the last words of the cantata there is a rapt silence. They long to clap but know they cannot clap in the cathedral. She bows her head once, then walks away from the musicians and sees me standing in the side chapel. She walks over to me with her arms open wide and her face full of love. I run to her and bury my face in her soft perfumed velvet breast.

KATHY

AUGUST

Heja has not been at work for the last three days and she's not phoned in sick either. It's been such a relief not to see her. I'm dreading seeing her again. Did I cross a line at our meeting on Saturday? Could she make a complaint about my behaviour? My team must not know what's been going on and somehow I have to appear normal towards her. It's going to be so difficult to work with her and I'd be happy if I never had to set eyes on her again. Her absence has meant I could get through all the routine questions about did I have a good holiday; yes, it was lovely, thanks, without seeing her hateful gaze contradicting me. And Philip is away for three weeks in Italy with his wife. That is also a relief.

The atmosphere at home is horrible and tense, and since our fight in his workroom Markus and I are barely speaking. He spends long days at his office. I wonder that I can get up every morning and come into work when I have this pain in my chest of undigested hatred; when my mind keeps rerunning that meeting with Heja, only this time I have the upper hand and I make the point that Markus chose to leave her and to marry me and nothing she says can change that. Then I feel tearful again when I remember how she implied that Markus is only with me because I got pregnant; because he is such a responsible man. Unplanned, she said. You trapped him, she implied. And I know that I will always doubt his feelings for me.

I realize now that she's obsessed with him and will not let him go. That's why she came to England, to London, to this magazine. That's why she is working a few hundred feet away from me. I've never felt hatred like this before, and the truth is that it's turning me into this ugly, jealous person I hardly recognize.

Yet the discipline of having to get up, get washed and dressed by a certain time is helpful. Here at the office I have a structure and a role that allows me to feel almost normal. Aisha greets me in the morning and we go through the diary. My team members come to me for advice, as they've always done. I work on the articles, trying to improve and polish them. You can go on working even when life at home is subject to intense pressures.

When I was living with Eddie I would sometimes return to find him drinking excessively and he'd be angry or maudlin. The flat would be in chaos and I couldn't get through to him at all. Yet most mornings I made myself go into work. Occasionally, when things got really bad at home, I would call in sick. My job was my salvation then. It enabled me to keep a grip on things and not sink into the mad spiral of Eddie's life at its worst. At the time I thought that must be an unusual state of affairs. Yet here I am again, wretched at home and keeping it together at work. I think now that there are many, many people getting up every day with hearts full of dread or sorrow, travelling to work, doing their tasks, holding it together.

Victoria has been working on the event for the world heritage guide and we're going to have a party in October to launch publication of the first issue. On my first day back she came to see me.

'I've confirmed the location for the party. Philip said it had to be an interesting building so I looked at lots of places. This one is perfect.'

'What is it?'

'It's the Locarno Suite at the Foreign and Commonwealth Office. It's a magnificent large room with a stunning decorated ceiling.'

'I've never heard of it.'

'It's not open to the public. They hire it out for events. It's expensive, but worth it.'

She laid out some photographs of the Grand Reception Room on my desk showing a long room with a high ceiling decorated with ornate stencils of classical figures picked out in red and gold on a background of brilliant turquoise.

'It looks amazing. Won't we need a lot of people to fill a room that size?'

'Leave that to me. It's great, isn't it?'

'Yes, it's quite something. Well done, you, for finding it.'

Thursday, and she finally showed up. She arrived at the office at about ten-thirty and asked Aisha if she could have an appointment to see me. I was sitting in my room and was on the phone when I saw her walk into view. She looked different. She has lost weight and was wearing her hair down, which I've never seen before. She was dressed in a tailored black suit with a pencil skirt. In fact, she looked rather incredible. I could see how men would find her sexy. That thought made my chest fill with acid again.

Aisha looked at me through the glass walls of my office. Heja had walked out of view. I was talking to a contributor and motioned to Aisha to come in. She came in and closed the door behind her and waited.

'It's Heja. She wants to talk to you. She was very formal about it. I think something's happened.'

I found that I was breathless.

'She looks different,' I said.

'Yes, she does. She didn't ring in sick, did she?'

'No. Not a word all week.'

Aisha made her eyes round and mischievous. 'Maybe she's getting married to that bloke I saw her with.'

'You think?'

If only, I thought; but I knew it was my husband she was after.

'I've got nothing on for a while, have I?'

'No. Shall I tell her to come now?'

I took a deep breath and nodded.

Heja stood at the threshold to my room. I did not move from behind my desk. I needed the distance the desk put between us. I asked her to sit on the chair in front of me and she did so with an expression of barely concealed contempt. I fought the urge to slap her face and scream abuse at her. I said nothing because she has a way of using my words against me. I would let her speak first.

'I have just heard that my mother is seriously ill and I am needed in Helsinki at once,' she said.

I couldn't pretend to be sorry and I didn't know what to say so I was silent.

'I plan to leave tomorrow,' she said with an insolent drawl to her voice. I sat up in my chair. I was finding it difficult to look at her face.

'I see. I take it you're asking for compassionate leave?'

'I am telling you that I need to leave the magazine straight away. I will not be able to work out my notice.'

Her weight loss had accentuated her cheekbones and her

hair lying loose around her face projected an image of fragile femininity. But I knew she was made of steel.

'Are you asking for compassionate leave or are you resigning?'

'I am resigning, with immediate effect. I am flying to Helsinki tomorrow.'

'Tomorrow,' I said. 'I accept your resignation but I'll need you to put in writing that there's a family emergency so that I can waive the notice period.'

She gave a small cold smile as if to say, *Make me*.

'You can send any papers to my London address.'

Then she stood up, smoothed her skirt over her thin hips and walked out of my office without another word.

Aisha came in two minutes later.

'Are you all right, Kathy?'

'I had a disturbed night last night. Heja just resigned.'

'Why?'

'Her mother's very ill and she's got to go home to Finland.'

'Good riddance,' said Aisha energetically. 'Sorry about her mum but, boy, is she difficult to like! I never trusted her, Kathy. And while you were in Cornwall she went out to lunch with Philip.'

I sighed and rested my head on my hand. 'I've got a bit of a headache.'

'Shall I get you a cappuccino? I'm getting myself one. And I've got paracetamol in my desk drawer. I'll get you two.'

'Thank you, Aish.'

I should feel relieved. She is my enemy and she is going away, but I don't feel free of her.

HEJA

SEPTEMBER

Robert has been away in America, visiting his mother and sister. He is back this week and he could prove difficult to shake off. He has tried to get closer over the last few months. He is sure things have advanced between us since I took him to meet my parents and he got on with Solange. I wrote him a short letter, which he will find on his return.

> *Dear Robert,*
> *I have just received bad health news from my parents and I have to leave for Helsinki in the next few hours. I am sorry we could not see each other before I left. It has all been so very rushed and concerning. I will be in touch as soon as there is some news to tell you. I hope your mother and sister are well.*
> *My love,*
> *Heja*

My answering machine is on, my lights are off. Robert will not come round to look for me here and he does not have my parents' address in Helsinki.

Kathy had to be told something specific, something serious that she would believe and could not question. I would never pretend that my father was very ill. I would never tempt fate like that even for a moment. But I didn't mind telling her

209

that Solange was ill, that a sudden and acute illness had struck her down.

Today I received a heavily embossed invitation to the launch of the World Heritage Sites guide. The launch is happening in three weeks' time at the Locarno Suite of the Foreign and Commonwealth Office. What a grand location and no doubt one that Philip has chosen. She will play a starring role at the event as the guides were her idea. Markus will go along to show his support, the husband supporting his wife the editor.

Last week I sold my convertible at a car dealership in South Kensington. Today I called the estate agent and put my beautiful flat on the market. I have hired a Volvo. I went down to the car park and started the engine. It is less easy to manoeuvre than my convertible but it is more practical for the journeys ahead. It is also less recognizable. It took me over two hours to reach Deal. Much of the drive was on motorways. How ugly parts of Britain have become: these hideous motorway service stations that loom up at you; these plain, utilitarian bridges spanning the roads. So much stained concrete, so many lost opportunities for built beauty.

I found the Crown and Castle Hotel in Deal without difficulty. It is right on the seafront. The woman at the reception desk looked very young. She was wearing an ugly navy and red patterned blouse, hotel issue. Her face was carefully made up to make her look older, with too much foundation and lipgloss.

'I have you down for two nights?' she said.

'Yes, that is correct.'

'Will you be requiring dinner in the restaurant this evening?'

'Yes, please, at eight o'clock.'

'And would you like some help with your suitcase?'

'Yes, there's a case in the boot, thank you.'

I gave her my car keys.

My room has horrible soft furnishings of a sickly peach colour. The curtains are made of that mock linen with a lace curtain in front. I pulled these back and opened the window. I do have a view of the sea. There was a tap on the door and a young man brought in my suitcase. I brought a large suitcase with me because I have a lot of things to buy while I am here. His hair stuck up at odd angles and his skin was poor. He looked about sixteen years old and he blushed when I tipped him. I lay on the bed and rested for an hour.

Deal is a slow-paced, old-fashioned town. I walked along the seafront on the path that runs along by the beach. I passed elderly couples and middle-aged women out with their dogs. There is a lifeboat station on the beach and this seemed to be the focus of the community. The high street has the usual collection of small shops and I counted four teashops. The place is perfect.

I found one estate agent that looked suitable. The man behind the desk had a name badge: Wayne Bevan. He was in his mid-twenties with a thick bull neck and a crew cut. His face had a hopeful look to it.

'I'd like to rent a small house for October and November,' I said.

'Yeah, there'll be quite a lot available then. How many bedrooms do you need?'

'Two will be fine.'

'Sea view, I suppose?'

'No, that is not essential. I want somewhere comfortable and quiet, a small detached house or cottage with a garden.'

He nodded and tapped keys on his computer.

'I've got some cottages, with gardens, a couple of places we could look at. I can put in the calls this afternoon and we can look at them tomorrow, if that's convenient.'

I chose grilled trout for dinner. It was watery with very little flavour. The vegetables were also watery. The hotel dining room had windows facing the sea. It would have been a good view except that there were three hideous bright orange glass vases on the windowsills with dried flowers in them and these obscured the view. I do not understand the point of dried flowers. Who wants to look at dead stalks and dusty flowerheads? The dining room was half full and the other guests were elderly and muted.

I saw one lone woman sitting at a table by the window in the corner. She looked a bit strange. She must have been in her late sixties. She had long grey hair that swarmed over her shoulders and down her back. She wore a low-necked purple top, which stretched over her large breasts. She was reading a book as she ate and her face was angry. Later I heard her speak sharply to the waitress because she had had to wait for her pudding. I wondered if she felt she had been slighted because she was a woman on her own.

Wayne picked me up at the hotel at ten o'clock the next morning. He drove me through the streets of Deal. The first cottage we looked at was not suitable at all. It had four steps up to the front door and was overlooked at the back by a large timber-framed house. I told Wayne it would not do.

'The next place costs more. It's a really nice little property, in a private road, on the way out of Deal.'

We drove out of Deal and turned into a road, Cremers Drift, that was not much more than a track. It was bordered on one side by a large field.

'That's part of a farm. You're allowed to walk along the path at the side and it's a nice walk to Kingsdown and to Deal.'

I nodded.

'The road is a bit rough,' I said.

'Yeah, there are a few potholes. It's a private road, you see, and the residents pay for its upkeep. It's nice and quiet here, though, and a good class of properties.'

Overstrand Cottage was at the end of the road. It was a small white-painted house with a neat garden and a trimmed hedge. It was spotless inside. There was one largish bedroom upstairs at the front and a smaller bedroom overlooking the back garden. The kitchen was well equipped and the bathroom was adequate. The cottage felt cared for. It did not have that depressing abandoned atmosphere you can find in rental properties.

'This is fine. I will take it.'

Wayne drove me back to the hotel.

'So, do you, ah, have family down here?'

'No, I don't.'

'I hope you'll enjoy it. The weather can get a bit changeable down here, though we do get some good days in the autumn.'

'When can I have the keys, Wayne?'

'You can pick them up from the office on your day of arrival.'

'Now, that will be a problem. I won't be arriving in Deal until very late that evening. Would it be possible to post them to me a couple of days before?'

'Don't normally do that, you see.'

'Could you make an exception for me? I will pay the two months' rent in full today and the deposit. I need to have the keys in advance. You could send them to me by registered mail.'

He drew up in front of the hotel. I held his eyes for a long moment.

'I'll see what I can do,' he said.

'Thank you, Wayne, I appreciate that.'

In the afternoon I walked along Deal seafront again. I saw the woman with the long grey hair walking in front of me. Her hair was flying free and she was dressed in a long black skirt that swept behind her. I saw her stop in front of a teashop. She was looking at the china plates loaded with cheesecake and meringues. I walked past her and we did not acknowledge each other. Further along the high street there was a Boots chemist. I went in and found the baby care section at the back of the shop. There was so much to choose from. I bought a set of baby bottles and milk powder. It was difficult to gauge what size nappies I should buy. In the end I bought a pack for babies of eighteen months. The woman in Boots told me where I could buy a buggy in Deal.

Eventually I had everything I needed. I packed the baby stuff in the suitcase and put the buggy in the boot. I wanted to get back to the calm and comfort of my flat so much but I knew the signs. I needed to rest again. My legs were feeling heavy. I dragged myself up to that ugly impersonal hotel room and lay on the bed until dinner.

When my doctor told me I had the disease he said I could take some steps to alleviate the symptoms. I could not be cured. I might have until my mid, even my late, forties. I lay there and thought about how Arvo Talvela had convinced me that I should try all the medical treatments that were available for my condition. Because of him I tolerated the painful examinations, the frequent blood tests and the drugs.

When he died everything changed. He had been my guiding

light. He had said he would be with me in this fight against the disease and that I would grow as a person even as I got weaker. He said I had no idea yet what the value of my life would be, even when I became paralysed. I told him how I had overheard Tanya's heartbroken tears in my grandfather's garden when I was just a little girl. He said Tanya had still been glad to be alive, that her comment to me had shown that. It was life itself that mattered. There would be something of worth in my last months, something I had no idea of now.

KATHY

SEPTEMBER

A strange and unsettling thing happened yesterday. I was sitting in my office, going through the proofs of the first issue of the guide, when Aisha tapped on the door. Standing behind her was a tall broad-shouldered man I hadn't seen before.

Aisha looked flustered as she put her head around the door. 'This is Robert Mirzoeff, a friend of Heja's. Is it OK if he has a quick word?'

My stomach did a double flip.

'Of course . . .'

I stood up behind my desk and he crossed the room quickly and we shook hands.

'Robert Mirzoeff. I'm sorry to barge in like this. I should have called beforehand.'

He had a low voice with an American accent and he fitted the description Aisha had given of Heja's boyfriend.

'It's fine, really.'

'I came on the spur of the moment because I was passing this way. I'm concerned about a dear friend of mine, Heja Vanheinen, your colleague.'

'Former colleague. Heja resigned a couple of weeks ago.'

'She resigned!'

'Yes. It was all very sudden. Her mother was seriously ill and—'

'Solange?' he said in a startled voice.

'I'm sorry?'

'Did you say her mother?'

'Yes. Heja was urgently needed in Helsinki to look after her mother.'

'This is so strange. I saw her mother last month. She was in perfect health. It was her father who was unwell.'

He had large serious brown eyes and he looked troubled. He said nothing for a minute and for some reason I found myself rushing on in a guilty way.

'It was all so sudden, you see. She said she had to go immediately. She'd booked a flight for the very next day and said she wanted to resign with immediate effect.'

'This is awful news. She said she'd be in touch as soon as there was more news. I've heard nothing. Obviously I'm worried.'

'Of course, you must be,' I said lamely. 'Please sit down.'

I indicated that he should sit at my meeting table. He sat down and he shook his head a couple of times.

'Could you give me her forwarding address in Finland? I know it's not the done thing but we are very close and . . .'

'I'm afraid I don't have a forwarding address, not in Helsinki. Heja asked me to send any stuff to her London address.'

'You don't have a number or anything?'

'Only for London . . .'

'I'm sorry to have disturbed you. I'm just so surprised to hear it's her mother who's ill. I assumed it was her father; he has a heart condition, you see.'

Now I was feeling sorry for him, left high and dry. He had come to the office because he was worried and had heard nothing from her. I felt an odd sense of kinship with him. We were both victims of her secrets and her icy coldness and I found myself wanting to help him.

'I'm just thinking, I do have Heja's application for the job here. There might be more details on that. It's worth a look.'

I got up and went over to my desk and pulled open the filing drawer.

'This is very kind of you,' he said.

I flicked through the files until I found her job application and scanned it quickly.

'No, I'm sorry. It's just the address in Blackfriars.' I looked at the second page.

'There's a number here for her reference; now, that might be a Helsinki number.'

'Can I see?'

'I probably shouldn't be doing this . . .'

I showed him that bit of the form.

'Ilkka Laine. Can I take the details down?'

I wrote down the name and number of Ilkka Laine on a Post-it note and gave it to him.

'Just between us,' I said.

'Of course. Thank you very much. I appreciate you doing that.'

And then I saw him look at my photograph of Billy and Markus, which I have on my desk. I'm sure I saw a flash of recognition in his eyes. He saw that I'd noticed him noticing the photograph and tried to cover that with a question.

'Is that your son?'

'Yes, Billy. It was taken a few months ago. He's nearly one now.'

'He looks very interested in the world.'

'He is!'

I walked him to the door. He gave me his card and I saw that he was a psychoanalyst. We stood there awkwardly as if there was much more we could both have said.

'I do hope you can find something out.'

'I hope so too. I would very much like to support Heja through this crisis if I can.'

We shook hands and he left.

I was shaken by this meeting with Robert. He had recognized Markus; I know he had. And he didn't want to acknowledge that to me. But how could he have recognized him? Does she have pictures of Markus in her flat? Could he have met him? And did he know that they were lovers for nine years? No, I didn't think so. She would have her secrets from him just as Markus had his secrets from me. He wanted to help her and she had just left him hanging. She and Markus were alike: they gave so little and they both held the most important bit back.

And I wondered why I hadn't asked him more about her. He has been her lover for months and he'll know stuff about her. I think what stopped me saying more was that it's obvious he's crazy about her and I could not have concealed my hatred of her.

Aisha had gone to lunch so I locked my office and went for a walk up to Hampstead to try to calm myself. What is it about her? When I think of Heja I feel my face go all hard and my lips tighten as if there is something very bitter in my mouth. I don't want to feel like this any more. I want to get back to how I felt on the walk to Botallack, with the sweet-smelling heather stretching out on either side of us, the sun high overhead, Markus at my side and Billy on my back. How I was before I saw that photograph of them. I was happy then and didn't know it.

Happy? I was living in a fool's paradise. There is this one lie, Markus not telling me about Heja when I first told him we'd hired her. At first it is only a single lie, but that one lie creates a chain reaction and it affects everything around it. That lie meant that Markus could never talk to me about his life in Finland. That lie meant that a distance gradually grew between us. It was the fault line running through our relationship, which I had begun to feel after Billy was born. But of course the trouble had already started when I was six months pregnant and we appointed Heja. That lie destroyed the intimacy and the pleasure we'd enjoyed in the early months of our relationship when we both felt we had been gifted a new beginning. That lie meant that every time I spoke to Heja, or passed her on the stairs, or gave her an article to write, she had this other knowledge, this other conversation running in her head. She knew what I did not know. She knew that Markus had lied to me. And Markus built another lie on the first one when I asked him about Heja and her job in television. Then one day the lies rise to the surface and bob in front of your eyes like pieces of excrement floating on greasy water. The lies spread and rot and destroy and it is immaterial that I found out that day in Botallack, or that Robert found out today about Markus and Heja. The lies could not have lived on much longer.

Today was truly horrible. Philip Parr got back from his holiday and was in early and Heja's poison is spreading.

His first meeting was with Victoria. While she was in with him I was going through my emails and saw that one had come in from Hector Agapito. We've invited all the contributors to the launch party, as well as the press and travel writers. I opened it at once and Hector had written that he was definitely coming to the launch, was looking forward to it. He was also going to be in London next week and wondered if we could meet for lunch. He hoped I was fine and that Billy was thriving and to let him know if we could meet. It was a really friendly email and his photos are going to be a big feature at the launch. We are planning to put a big screen up and we'll play a sequence of the best photographs blown up to magnificent size. Some of his shots have been chosen for this presentation.

My first instinct was to say no to the lunch with Hector. I'm a changed person since we met in Lisbon in June. My marriage is in difficulties and I'm filled with feelings of jealousy and inadequacy. Then I remembered our lunch of moules and how easy it had been to talk to him and how warm he was. And, oh, I needed some warmth at the moment. So I emailed him back that, yes, we should meet for lunch, that this time it would be my treat and I knew where we could get some great fish and chips. The phone buzzed on my desk and I jumped for some reason. It was Philip's PA, summoning me to his to office to report on what had been going on in his absence.

As soon as I walked into his room I could feel his aggression. He barely answered my polite enquiries about his holiday, grunting a response and waving it away then asking in a nasty tone of voice, 'What's this I hear about Heja leaving?'

'I was about to tell you. Heja came to see me a couple of weeks ago and had to leave at once to go to Helsinki. Her mother's very ill and—'

'Why didn't you clear this with me?' he barked.

'I beg your pardon?'

'Why didn't you consult me? I wasn't on the moon. I was at the end of a phone.'

'What was there to consult about? Heja virtually demanded that she leave at once. I offered her compassionate leave. She said no she wanted to resign with immediate effect; that she couldn't work out her notice. She'd booked a plane ticket for the very next day!'

'There's something not quite right here,' he said in an accusing tone of voice.

I could feel fear and anger building in me in equal measure. I felt simultaneously wronged and in the wrong.

'What do you mean?'

'Why would Heja give up her job just like that?' He snapped his fingers in an aggressive way near my face. 'She told me she liked working here. But she didn't like the team dynamics. Were you having a difficult relationship with her?'

'Philip, I object to the way you're talking to me. You seem to be accusing me of something.'

'While you were on holiday Heja made a few criticisms of the heritage guide, quite sensible criticisms, as it happens. She felt she couldn't talk to you about them.'

'This is the first I've heard of this.'

'Precisely,' he snapped at me.

'This is too much! Heja demanded to leave because her mother is very ill. If you want to accuse me of being a bad manager then go ahead and do it.'

Philip backed off at this point. 'I'm just saying it's very unfortunate to lose someone of Heja's abilities.'

'And good looks,' I hissed back.

I turned and walked out of his office. I was buoyed up by my rage.

Some time later Victoria came to see me. I had a great pile of papers on the floor and had been going through them, tearing up old articles and letters and stuffing them into my waste bin in fury. I was going to leave the magazine. I couldn't work with Philip Parr. I'd had enough. Before Botallack I would have called Markus and told him what had happened and asked his advice. Things had changed and I could not call him now – and certainly not to discuss Heja!

Victoria stood at the threshold of my office and raised one eyebrow as she said, 'I've been sent as the messenger of peace. He knows he went too far. He doesn't want you to resign too, just before our big launch.'

'He's outrageous. He accused me of driving Heja away.'

'Look, Heja was a difficult woman. No one liked her.'

'Except Philip . . .'

Victoria knelt down on the floor next to me with a sigh.

'He fancied her, for God's sake. You know Philip. And she made moves on him while you were in Cornwall. Went to lunch with him and he probably thought he was in with a chance.'

'It's so like her to go behind my back. How do you put up with him? He's vile and I would like to leave; just pack my stuff and go!'

'Don't, Kathy. You're a bloody good editor and we're about to launch your guide. It's your baby.'

'Bloody monster baby! And he said that Heja was critical of it.'

'She thought we shouldn't do all the sites. She was scathing about some of the minor sites.'

'So we should do a survey but leave things out!'

'Hey, I'm on your side! Come on, come out for a coffee with me.'

'Sorry, yes, let's get out of here.'

As Victoria and I walked through the office the place was charged with emotion. Word must have got round that Philip and I had had a big bust-up.

*

When Hector arrived at the office in the last week of September I hurried down to meet him in the foyer. I'd dressed with care that morning and had put on a summer print dress with sunflowers on it and a short yellow cardigan. Then I'd felt a bit awkward wearing the pretty dress all morning, even though the day was sunny. Was it too obvious that I wanted to look nice? At least there had been no Heja there to look at me with mocking eyes. Hector was in jeans and a white linen shirt and looked tanned and relaxed. He hugged me, kissed me on the cheek and complimented me on my dress.

We walked to a café I liked and found a table in the corner. Our tablecloth was red gingham and cheerful.

'They do good cod here but the haddock is great,' I said.

'I'm in your hands, Kathy.'

I ordered two haddock and chips with a side order of mushy peas and two giant gherkins.

'Mushy peas . . .? That will be a new experience. How are things?' he asked, giving me one of his direct and warm looks.

'OK; maybe a bit better than OK . . .'

'I sense a "but" there . . .'

I looked around the café and there was no one in there that I knew. To be on the safe side I slipped into Portuguese.

'My boss is a difficult man.'

'Bosses often are.'

'Yes. I haven't been editor long, only since April, and I'm still on probation. He makes me feel insecure. And when I'm insecure I make mistakes. *And* we had a bad bust-up last week.'

'What happened?'

'He took his temper out on me because a member of my team he fancied had resigned while he was on holiday.'

'He sounds a prick.'

'He really is. I'm still feeling sore about it.'

'But you're about to launch your guide.'

'Yes. I did honestly think about leaving the magazine. I've calmed down a bit now.'

'Do you like the rest of your team?'

'Yes, they're a great bunch. You know as editor you have to keep yourself a bit aloof.'

'I don't think I could ever work for a company,' he said. 'I've been freelancing all my life and it suits me fine.'

He smiled at me so warmly and it felt easy talking to him.

'And how is your Billy?'

'Just wonderful and on the point of walking. Then watch out, I won't have a minute to myself.'

'I kind of envy you that.'

'You don't have any children yet?'

'No, to the regret of my parents! They've made it clear they expect grandchildren some day soon.'

'Parents do that to men too, do they?'

'Oh yes!'

'I was in this relationship for about six years, before Markus. My mum in particular gave off this unspoken longing that I produce the next generation.'

'What happened?'

'We split up, eventually. Eddie drinks, you see. Not all the time, but he is a problem drinker. I adored him and wouldn't see it for what it was. I kept hoping he would sort himself out.'

Hector nodded, his brown eyes warm on me.

'That must have been painful.'

'It was.'

We ordered a second round of tea and coffee. I didn't want the lunch to end and Hector seemed keen to talk on.

'I made the final break and then I met Markus soon after and got pregnant really quickly. It's sort of left me reeling really, everything happening so fast.'

I sipped my tea, hoping I hadn't implied too much.

'I'm not surprised; and a prick of a boss too . . .!'

I giggled.

'That's enough about me. Are you with someone?'

'Not now. I was. I was with Lucia for about five years but it didn't work out.'

'I'm sorry. What went wrong?'

'She couldn't stand that I had to travel so much to do my work. We moved in together quite soon after we met. And she wanted me to be there all the time. Her neediness drove me crazy. It drove me away in the end. It was hard because I had really fallen for her.'

'Do you keep in touch?'

'No. She is married now and happy with a husband who does not go away. You don't realize when you're starting out and falling in love just how important it is to find someone who fits with you, who has similar expectations. I could never be happy long term with a needy woman. I tried so hard to make it work with Lucia though.'

We all have these failed relationships, I thought. Why is it so difficult to get it right?

'We're both battle-scarred,' I said.

'Yes, we are both veterans! Thanks for today, Kathy, it's been fun.'

'It's been great.'

I paid the bill, in spite of Hector's protests. We walked out onto Camden Parkway and I pointed him to the tube at the bottom of the road. I was going to get a taxi back to Primrose Hill. I'd been out of the office nearly three hours.

'See you at the launch,' he said, giving me a proper hug.

He turned to walk away and then turned back just as I was stepping into a taxi.

'Kathy . . .'

I looked up.

'You can always call me if you need to talk to a friendly, you know, veteran.'

'Thank you.'

In the taxi going back to work I felt better about things for the first time in weeks. Seeing Hector had made me feel more hopeful. And then I realized what it was. Hector made me feel like I was a good person after all.

HEJA

OCTOBER

The river is grey today. The sky is overcast and the wind is driving ripples across the surface of the water. The slope of the ripples has been growing steeper all day so the wind must be getting up. This is my last day in this, my beautiful room. The last time I will be able to stand at my large window and look at the river and the bridge. I have grown to love this view. Markus stood here when we saw each other again for the first time after our seven years apart. He always wanted to live by water. When he was a student he told me that one day he would have a place with an unbroken view of sea and sky. He told me that when we were first together and at that stage of telling each other everything we wanted from life. The psychic undressing you do when you start a love affair; the psychic undressing that is more important than the actual taking off of your clothes.

We were lying in bed in his bare student room. He lived in a commune and his room was at the top of the house. It was a noisy house. There were no carpets. You could hear his flatmates thundering up and down the stairs. His room was immaculate. He had painted the floorboards with white gloss paint. The bed linen was all white too. He had a table, a chair, a good radio and an old-fashioned built-in cupboard. That was it. He had stuck some of his architectural drawings on the walls. We talked about the house he would design and build for us one day by the edge of the sea.

Last week I received a handwritten letter from Philip Parr. He said that he hoped his letter would reach me as he knew I was in Finland. He was so sorry to hear of the trouble in my family. If he could do anything to help I was to contact him. He was also very sorry I had decided to leave the magazine. I had made a great contribution to it and if I changed my mind there would always be a role for me on his staff.

I am sure there would be. What would be the point of that? I have expended so much energy getting that job and working in her team. And what has it achieved? I may have caused her some uncomfortable moments. I may have dented her. All that effort has not brought her down. She has depths of resilience that she can draw on. And I no longer have the time.

I have kept the answering machine on for the last few weeks and this morning there was a message from Ilkka Laine. I have not spoken to Ilkka for many months. He said that a Robert Mirzoeff had been in touch, had asked him for my parents' address and should he give it to him? I called him back.

'Heja, it's wonderful to hear from you. I wasn't sure if you'd even get my message. I thought you might be here. How are things?'

'Very good, really very good . . . Now, what's this about Robert Mirzoeff?'

'He left a message, some days ago. I only just got it. We've been away. Said he was a close friend and wanted your parents' address. He'd heard Solange was very ill and that you were back here.'

'No, no, not at all; I am sorry, Ilkka. I don't know how he got your number. The thing is I want to end my relationship with Robert so I told him I had gone to Helsinki for the foreseeable future. I did not give him a forwarding address and I do not want him to have one!'

'He sounded very concerned. Said he wanted to help if he could . . .'

'He's a nice enough man, but it was never going to work out. He wanted to get serious and wouldn't take no for an answer.'

'Still the heartbreaker, I see. And your mother is OK?'

'She's fine. They are just back from a four-week holiday in France.'

'That's good, then. And when are you coming back to Helsinki?'

'I'm not sure. When I do, we must get together. Are you still enjoying work?'

'Not really. Not the fun it once was and not a job for mature people any more. The idiot children are in control these days. You were clever to get out when you did.'

'Thanks for the call, Ilkka. And please make some excuse to Robert.'

'Of course I will. Take care, Heja.'

Damn Robert. Damn him. How did he get Ilkka's number? And how could he know that I said Solange was ill? I did not say anything about Solange in my letter to him. There is only one possible explanation. He has been to see *her*. The only place I ever wrote Ilkka Laine's number was on my job application. She must have given it to him. I can just imagine the two of them meeting up in her office. She would be all fake reasonableness, ever the professional manager. He would probe gently until he got more information out of her than she meant to give, or should have given, him. He insinuates his way into people's confidence. He is someone who does not respect boundaries, whether it is my body or my plans. I have the same sensation of my inner self being probed as when he used to stick his fingers up me.

They will leave by six o'clock at the latest. The party starts at seven and goes on till nine-thirty. She will have to stay till the end and Markus will stay on to show his support. The childminder will be at their flat. She will watch television in their sitting room. Maybe smoke a cigarette with the window open. Or call that boyfriend of hers. It will just be a matter of choosing my moment. I will not go there till eight o'clock. Billy should be asleep by then.

I assembled all the paraphernalia for the journey in the middle of the room: my suitcase with my things and a holdall for Billy's things, including the pack of nappies. I had already stowed the buggy I bought on the floor of the car, covered with a blanket. Then I closed and taped down a cardboard box containing the bottles and baby foods. So much stuff! I do not want the caretaker to see what I am loading. He is an ex-cop. He takes a lively interest in our comings and goings. I have to get all this from my apartment into the boot of the Volvo. Then I will need to rest before the drive.

First I took everything out and put it by the lift. I locked my apartment and moved all the stuff into the lift. At the ground floor I moved everything out into the lobby.

The caretaker saw this and moved from behind his desk. He has a fat face and wears one of those absurd white shirts with navy epaulettes with brass buttons on them as if to convey authority. His shirt was tucked into navy trousers and his belly was hanging over the top of his black leather belt.

'Morning. Can I help you with that?'

'Thank you.'

He picked up my suitcase and the box. I followed him and he held the doors open for me. We crossed the forecourt. I knew he would ask where I was going.

'Going away for a bit, are you?'

'Yes, for a week or so.'

'This isn't your usual car, is it?'

'No. That is in for some work.'

'Got pranged, did it?'

'I am sorry?'

'Your car, it got damaged?'

I opened the boot. He lifted my suitcase in then placed the box and the holdall neatly by its side.

'No, it just needed a good service.'

'Right, right. Going anywhere nice?'

'The Lake District.'

'Ahh, lovely spot . . . May be a bit wet, though, this time of the year. Looks like there's a storm brewing today.'

I looked up. Great purple-grey clouds were forming over the river. I locked the boot and we walked back together.

'Thank you for your help.'

'I'll keep an eye on your flat while you're away.'

'I would appreciate that.'

I opened my bag and gave him a twenty-pound note. How I detest the English and their snooping ways.

I stood outside the front door of her flat and listened intently. No sound came through the door. I slid my key into the lock and turned the key and the handle softly. I pushed the door open one inch and listened again. I could hear the rise and fall of TV voices coming from their sitting room. I pushed the door open further and looked down the landing. The table light was on in the hall and light was coming from Billy's room. I stepped in, closing the door silently behind me, not letting the lock engage, then walked into Billy's room. He was lying on his back asleep in his cot.

I closed his door behind me and picked up the padded jacket hanging on the back of the door. The wind was getting up and he would need it. Then I leant over his cot and picked him up, bringing his blanket with him. He made a funny little noise as I lifted him. I wrapped the blanket securely around him and rocked him in my arms until he settled back to sleep. Then I walked back to the door and opened it carefully. Still the voices from the TV rose and fell. I walked down the hall through the door and pushed it to behind me, again not letting the lock engage. In three minutes I was out of the building. I lay Billy on the back seat wrapped in his blanket. It took me a few minutes to secure him there with the car seat belts. I had not bought a baby car seat. They are so visible and we would only be making the one long journey. I got into the front seat, started the engine and began the journey to Kent.

KATHY

OCTOBER

We arrived at the Foreign and Commonwealth Office at five-thirty p.m. A security guard lifted the outer gate for us and Philip drove in through the arch and stopped at the security window. A man checked the registration number against a clipboard, checked our names and then examined the underneath of our car with a torch and a metal detector. I wondered if all the guests would have to go through these security procedures. It was a government building, of course, and these days such checks were the norm. The security man handed Philip a square paper pass to put inside the windscreen. Philip drove slowly into the quadrangle and parked the car. Victoria and I got out and she pulled her skirt down as a strong wind whipped across the quadrangle, swirling grit into our faces.

'Hope this weather won't put people off,' Victoria muttered to me.

'What?' Philip asked. He had sprung out of the car, all fired up. He was wearing a brown linen suit that did not suit him and I wondered if he was nervous at all. I certainly was.

'I was just saying it's good we're so early – plenty of time to check the sound system and the promo.'

We walked into the building accompanied by the event organizer, who had been waiting for us. The grand staircase swept up in front of us, a mass of richly coloured marble at our feet and gold decoration above. Two great ormolu chandeliers hung over the staircase. My eyes were drawn upwards to a dome of gold decorated with a circle of female figures, each representing a different country. At the top of the staircase we walked past a sequence of the most extraordinary wall-sized murals.

One was called *Britannia Pacificatrix*. This showed the nations of the world as costumed figures who were paying homage to Britannia. Italy was depicted as a woman in white holding the *fasces*, Canada was a young man girdled with maple leaves, while Africa was a small naked boy with a basket of tropical fruits on his head! I looked more closely and saw that Portugal was depicted as a woman with a basket of grapes. Britannia, the peacemaker, was comforting a naked girl, Belgium, who was holding a broken sword aloft. We lingered in front of this mural for a few minutes.

'Quite extraordinary! It just oozes Imperial confidence, doesn't it? When was it painted?' Philip asked.

'Between 1914 and 1921 by the artist Sigismund Goetze,' the event organizer said.

'Great choice, Victoria. We should do a feature on this some time, Kathy.'

'Indeed,' I replied.

An uneasy peace had been restored between us but we were still at the chilly stage.

We entered the Grand Reception Room. A large plasma screen had been set up at the far end and a dais had been built in front of it with a table and two microphones for Philip and me. Two long tables covered in white linen cloths lined the side of the room and were being set up as bars. White-jacketed waiters were arranging trays of wineglasses in sequence down their length.

'I asked them to do interesting soft drinks as well wine and beer,' Victoria told us. 'Elderflower cordial and pomegranate juice. More and more people are swerving booze these days.'

'The hacks still like a drink,' said Philip.

One of the waiters came over and offered us a drink. I asked for mineral water. I was absurdly nervous and kept swallowing.

The event organizer said, 'We'd like to do a sound and picture check now. Mr Parr, Kathy, would you mind getting into your positions on the stage, please.'

Philip read through his speech. It was a good speech, quite funny in places, and he did acknowledge that the guide was my idea. He delivered it a bit too fast and I wondered if I should say anything. I decided not to. His closing words were the cue for a three-minute promo tape cut to music, which was made up of some of the best images and quotes from the guide. It was very well done and I was glad that they'd followed my advice and ended it with a freeze frame on Hector's shot of the Torre de Belem taken from the river. At this point the plan was to take questions from the guests and that was when I would be needed.

'Kathy, could you please say a few words into your mic so we can check the sound level?'

I said, 'The Torre de Belem in Lisbon, a UNESCO World Heritage Site . . .'

'That's fine. OK. Everything's ready.'

Philip and I got down from the dais.

'Great speech, Philip, maybe take it a bit slower,' Victoria said.

'You think?'

'Yeah, give the jokes time to sink in, it's very amusing. The photographer who did that last shot is coming tonight.'

'Kathy, make sure you introduce him to me. He's got something special . . .'

'Hector Agapito.'

'We should use him more.'

'I plan to,' I said.

I went to the Ladies and checked myself over. My stomach would not be stilled and I just wanted the evening to be over with.

Around five to seven the first guests started to arrive. Philip, Victoria and I positioned ourselves by the huge oak entrance door so we could greet people as they came in. It was such a large and magnificent room that the early guests looked a little awkward and they grouped together by the bar. I could hear the moan of the wind against the vast high windows and saw dead leaves being whipped up into the sky.

'Bloody awful night,' Philip hissed. 'May keep people away.'

'Don't worry,' said Victoria. 'People will want to see this amazing building.' She looked a bit anxious.

More guests started to arrive and slowly the room began to fill, the level of voices rose and it started to feel like a party. Markus came in and squeezed my arm. The organizer came over to Victoria.

'I think we'll start to circulate with some hot canapés now.'

'Fine; please make sure the food stops circulating as soon as he starts his speech.'

Then Hector was standing there in front of me. He was wearing a red brushed-cotton shirt and black trousers. His hair curled around his neck and he was smiling warmly at me.

'Kathy.' He kissed me on both cheeks. 'What a place! I'd love to photograph that staircase. Did you find it?' he asked.

'No, I didn't. Did you take a look at those murals?'

'I did; wonderful and quite absurd!'

'Portugal's in there – a woman with a basket of grapes, of course. Personally I far prefer the Mosteiro,' I said.

He looked at me, really looked at me. 'How are things?'

'I'll be glad when this is all over, to be honest. I'm happy to say that you are one of the stars of tonight's show. There are lots of your shots in the promo tape.'

Philip was standing next to me, talking to a female journalist from a Radio Four arts programme. He looked over at us.

'I want to introduce you to the publisher of our magazine,' I said. 'Philip Parr, this is Hector Agapito, who photographed the Portuguese sites'

Philip said how much he admired Hector's work. Hector thanked him and I remembered our conversation in the café and his description of Philip as a prick. Sensing this, Hector glanced over at me and winked. Victoria joined us then, introduced herself and said, 'You must be Hector. There's a journalist here from a photo magazine and he's seen some of your shots. Would you be willing to be interviewed?'

'Delighted . . .'

He looked over at me and said, 'We'll talk later.'

Victoria moved off with him into the scrum of guests and the media.

'Time to mingle,' Philip said.

The room was now full of people and there must have been over three hundred there. There was that excited clamour of voices you get at a good party. I found Markus standing by the great door that led out of the main room into a smaller room.

'Come here. I want to show you something,' he said. He led me through to the adjoining conference room.

'Look at the hinges on this door. See those acorns carved in brass above the hinges? What a superb detail to find on an oak door . . .'

He stroked the wood of the door and I loved him again at that moment for caring about the architectural detail and not caring about the loud, self-important people in the other room. I touched him on his back.

'I'm sick with nerves.'

'You look perfectly cool and calm.'

'Was Billy OK when you left?'

'He was as happy as could be.'

'Fran's good with him.'

We walked back into the reception room together. A waitress passed and offered her tray of miniature crispy duck pancakes. Markus took one.

'It is a bit of a circus. Go on, you'd better mix with the guests.'

This is the warmest conversation we've had for weeks and I was grateful that he'd come along to support me. I moved back into the noise and heat of the room.

Philip walked up onto the stage and it took him two minutes of calling for people's attention through the microphone before the voices were stilled and the room finally became quiet.

'Thank you, thank you. This won't take long. We are here to tell you about our World Heritage Sites guide. I'm Philip Parr, publisher of the guide, and this is Kathy Hartman, editor.'

Markus had moved close to the stage, at the side. Hector and Victoria were standing in the centre of the room. As Philip spoke I saw through the far window that the wind was getting ever fiercer. A plastic bag flew past the window and it ballooned and fluttered in an agony of movement.

Aisha was pushing though the guests from the door of the room as Philip was giving his speech. I wondered what she was doing. She was looking for someone. I tried to catch her eye but she did not look in my direction. She moved as quickly and as surreptitiously as she could through the crowd. Philip had finished speaking. He had got a few laughs with his speech. Then the lights in the room were dimmed as the plasma screen lit up with images of World Heritage Sites from across Europe.

I looked over to where Hector was standing, watching, and Victoria, who stood close to him, was looking very excited. There was a collective sigh of pleasure as the tape ended and then people started to clap enthusiastically.

Philip waited a moment and said, 'I'm glad you enjoyed that. We'd be delighted to take questions now. There are people with microphones in the room so if you could use the microphone to ask your questions, please.'

I noticed that Aisha had reached Markus. She touched his arm and whispered something in his ear. In that instant a profound change came over his face. I couldn't read it other than to say that it looked as if he had committed a terrible crime. He glanced at me for a split second, too quickly for me to acknowledge his look, then turned and started to walk out of the room, pushing through the crowd with real urgency. Aisha followed closely in his wake. My instant reaction was that something had happened to Billy. There was ice in my chest and in my stomach. People were talking in the distance. Their voices were muffled by the noise of my heart. There was a silence, a stretched-out silence. Then I heard Philip saying my name from a long way away.

'Kathy, that's one for you, I think.'

I looked at him. He was giving me a strange look.

'I'm sorry, would you, would you repeat the question, please?'

We got through the questions. Somehow I managed to get out the answers. Philip did most of the talking. Aisha had come back into the room and now she was standing where Markus had stood, to the side of the stage, and she was clearly very agitated. She could not keep her hands still; she was actually wringing them in her distress. And she would not meet my eye, although I kept looking in her direction. My mouth was dry and my mind was running through the catalogue of sudden infant death syndrome; of babies choking on their vomit; of fits and of accidents with boiling water.

Finally Philip said, 'Please enjoy the rest of the party.'

I got up and walked off the stage straight towards Aisha. Philip was saying something to me as I moved quickly away from him and Aisha looked at me at last.

'What is it?'

'Not here, Kathy. Let's go into the other room,' she pleaded.

'Tell me, tell me now! What's happened?'

'It's Billy. He's disappeared. Your nanny called reception and the security man found me.'

'I don't understand.'

'Your nanny went into his room and he was gone.'

The room started to turn on a strange axis. Philip must have been standing by me because he helped me on to a chair.

HEJA

OCTOBER

I crossed Oxford Street into North Audley Street and drove round Grosvenor Square. As I passed the Connaught Hotel I could see my father's face as he sliced into his chicken pie. His eyes were glittering with amusement as he looked over at me. I found myself smiling at the memory. I may not see him ever again. It is how I will remember him, his face lightened by pleasure. I turned left into Piccadilly and down to Trafalgar Square. The wind had grown stronger in the last few minutes and I saw pieces of paper and plastic debris being swept up into a frenzy in the centre of the square. A broken umbrella was caught by a gust. The bent spokes opened and twisted the black umbrella up into the sky, like a hideous broken-winged crow, up past the lion statue on the corner. The wind whistled against the windows of the car as we drove down Whitehall and turned on to Westminster Bridge. I felt the smack of the blast on the body of the car as we crossed the bridge. I tightened my grip on the steering wheel and wished, again, that I was in my low-slung convertible.

There was something alarming about the intensity of the wind. There had been no warning on the radio. I had listened to the forecast at six o'clock. I drove past Waterloo and on to the Elephant and Castle. Here the wind was whipping up grit and gravel into mini-cyclones. Several small stones hit my windscreen with a vicious crack that made my heart skid.

I had filled the car with petrol that morning. Now I wondered about pulling into a garage to take shelter. I decided to carry on. The storm would blow itself out. I wanted to put miles between me and London and reach Deal as fast as I could.

Markus and I were caught in a storm that summer of our holiday in Åland, the summer of our great row. He had made friends with a Swedish couple who had a small sailing boat. The four of us had taken her out for a day of sailing and diving. The day had started fine and we had sailed a good distance. Then by lunchtime the sky became overcast and the sea started to get choppy. We were planning to sail overnight to a mooring at Sottunga on the other side of the island. It started to rain and the waves grew to ten feet high, which the boat rode without difficulty. Then the bilge pump stopped working. The owners went below to bail out the cabin. Markus and I were left above to steer the boat.

The wind got up and the waves grew in front of us. Now they were fifteen feet high. We rode them down. As we rode them up again the moon pulled away from a cloud and shone down on us. It was nearly full. Markus shouted at me that the bloody moon was responsible for the turbulence. He looked so exhilarated, so alive. The owners came up and said we would have to do watches through the night. I went below to try to sleep for a few hours. Markus was up on deck with the boat owner's wife, Agneta, doing his watch.

Now we had reached the M20 and the wind was hitting the car at gale-force speed. It was taking all my strength and concentration to keep the car in a straight line. There were very few cars on the road, much fewer than usual. I saw a high-sided lorry in the slow lane in front of me. The driver was having difficulty keeping his lorry in the lane. The pressure on the side of the vehicle was making it swing over into the second lane. Then he would pull it back. I accelerated across into the third, fast lane, and passed him. Further on I saw five lorries parked on the hard shoulder. A driver was getting out of his cab and a gust of wind flung his cab door open. He leapt out of the way. I drove on, concentrating hard.

When we came off the motorway my arms were aching and my hands prickled. I could feel very little sensation in my fingers. Should I pull over and wait in the car for a bit? I longed to rest my head against the seat and let my arms recover. The wind showed no sign of weakening. If we pulled over the car might be struck by a falling branch, or worse. Now the tumult was coming from the trees on either side of the road as they were bent back and forth in a violent dance with the wind. There had been no sound from Billy on the back seat. He was sleeping through the noise and buffet of the wind.

I reached the A258 that leads down to Deal. There were pieces of ripped-off branches on the road. To my left was a stretch of farmland and I saw where a great tree had fallen on to a barn and its roof had caved in. Barn and tree had joined forces and become this strange hybrid, part brick, part dying sap. Now I felt the spray of the sea slap against the windscreen and the glass became sticky with salt and stuck leaves. The wipers fought against this onslaught. My arms were heavy, heavy but I was so nearly there. I turned into Cremers Drift, which led to the cottage. The road was choked with brambles and branches. I revved the Volvo to full capacity and drove over the branches. They cracked beneath the tyres.

Through the mess of the windscreen I saw that a tree had fallen right across the road in front of me. The road to the cottage was completely blocked. I would have to leave the car here and carry Billy and my stuff to the cottage. I turned the engine off.

Somewhere close by a house alarm was going off and there were lights in the sky as if searchlights were being used out at sea. I rested for a few moments then tried to open the door on my side. The force of the wind was tremendous. I pushed with all my strength and opened the door and climbed out. Now the wind was tearing at my clothes and my hair and the trees above my head were thrashing back and forth. I fought my way to the boot of the car and found the baby bottles, milk powder and nappies.

I pushed these into the holdall with my things and put the bag over my body. Then I inched my way round to the back door of the car by flattening myself against the body. Did I have the strength left to hold the door open and pick Billy up? At most I could make one journey from car to cottage. I laid my head against the roof and rested for a minute as the storm thrashed around me.

'Don't let this defeat you,' Arvo Talvela said to me at one of our last sessions. 'You have such strength of mind and character.'

I pulled the car door open and using my body as a door stop reached down and undid the seat belt straps on the back seat. Billy was still asleep but he woke up as I lifted him. He stirred against my body. I held him tight against me and wound the blanket more securely around his head and body. My arms were so weak and I had no strength in my wrists. He was heavy. I thought that I might drop him. I inched outwards until both our bodies were free. The wind caught the car door and slammed it shut with fury. I turned and walked the last few yards up the road. My legs were shuddering. Every step was an effort. Billy had woken up and was looking out of the cowl of his blanket at the rush and blackness of the night. He was making whimpering noises.

The fallen tree was my next obstacle. I lifted my left leg up as high as I could and straddled the tree. I had to sit there for a minute and rest. The smaller branches of the tree whipped against my legs. I could feel weals forming on my skin, under my trousers. I pulled my right leg over and continued up the road. Both my legs were now shaking so badly that I had to stagger the last few yards.

Billy had started to cry. I reached the gate of the cottage and pushed it open. The garden was a ruin of broken stems and branches and leaves. A terracotta pot had been flung over and smashed into pieces. Shards of pottery and earth spilled out over the path and crunched beneath my shoes. I reached the front door, found the key and let us in. I was completely exhausted. I slid down the door and sat on the floor with Billy in my lap. He was crying loudly now.

In a minute or two I will go to the kitchen and make him a bottle of milk. I may give him some Calpol. The woman in Boots told me that it helps babies sleep.

KATHY

OCTOBER

Philip and Aisha got me out of the room and into a taxi. The storm was raging and all I could think was, Where is Billy in this terrible wind and fury? How will my little boy support life in this great storm? Aisha came with me as far as the flat. She was squeezing my hand and I couldn't say a thing because my fear had made me mute.

When we got to the flat Aisha hugged me tightly and left. I took the lift up and Markus opened the door. The police were already there, two uniformed men, with Fran in the kitchen. Fran leapt to her feet the moment she saw me. Her face was swollen and her eyes puffy and streaked.

'Kathy, I was in the living room. He was fast asleep.'

She started to cry and shake.

'What happened? How *can* he be gone, Fran?'

'I don't know!'

'Did someone come to the flat?'

'No one . . .'

Markus said, 'They're sending a detective round. He's on his way.'

One of the uniformed men, the older one, was writing things down on a pad. I went into Billy's room. His cot was empty and his blanket was gone.

'She took his blanket,' I said.

She had left his blue teddy behind and it was on the floor.

I picked it up and smelled it. Markus was standing by the door.

'*She* took my baby, I know she did.'

He flinched and said, 'We're going to get him back.'

He started to walk over to me as if to touch me. I moved away from him and went back into the kitchen. Billy had just had his first birthday and there were greeting cards all over the kitchen, mocking me with their cutesy images of babies and bunnies and bears.

The men were still questioning Fran. She was slumped at the kitchen table and one of the policemen kept asking her what she had heard and she kept saying through her frightened tears that she hadn't heard a thing; she'd been watching television and Billy was asleep. The front door was shut. She didn't know how anyone could have got into the flat.

Markus said, 'That's right. I left after Fran got here and I closed the door behind me.'

'And you didn't open the door to anyone?' the policeman asked her again.

'Of course not. I already told you!' Fran wailed.

I said to the man who was questioning her, 'I know who took my baby.'

He said, 'Let's go in the other room for a minute.'

We went into the sitting room.

'A woman called Heja Vanheinen has taken Billy. She hates me and she's taken Billy.'

I could hear the storm outside as I was walking up and down the room. There was the sound of roof tiles falling as they gave in to the force of the wind, a whistle then a muted crash.

The policeman said, 'Can you spell that name?'

'He'll be so scared in this terrible storm. H-e-j-a V-a-n-h-e-i-n-e-n.'

I spelled it out for him.

He wrote it down and said, 'Why do you suspect her?'

'I don't suspect, I *know* she took him!' I said fiercely.

'OK, OK. Tell the detective when he arrives. For now we need to take your nanny down to the station for further questioning. She was here when it happened, whatever happened.'

I looked at him and realized he thought that Fran was somehow involved. 'It's not Fran. It's Heja!'

The doorbell was ringing and then Markus came into the room with another man in plain clothes who nodded at the policeman and said to me, 'Hello, I'm from Marylebone police station, Detective Inspector Nick Austin.'

He showed us his card.

I said to him, 'I know who did it. I know who took my baby.'

I couldn't look at Markus but I felt his presence, standing behind me as Nick Austin said, 'Let's sit down.'

'Her name is Heja Vanheinen. She's been stalking me for months . . .'

I looked behind me at Markus, challenging him to contradict me. He said nothing.

The uniformed man said, 'There was no forced entry. Someone must have had a key or been let in.'

Nick said, 'It's Kathy, isn't it? What do you mean by stalking?'

'She hates me. She came to my work and got a job there.'

'Why does she hate you?'

'She used to be with my husband. She hates it that we've got a baby.'

He looked over to where I sensed Markus was now standing, behind the sofa by the window. He'd said nothing all this time and I knew from his silence that he wanted to protect her.

'OK, let's go through this step by step. I need to know all the details. What makes you think she would take your baby?'

'She wants to destroy me!'

I knew I was sounding shrill and incoherent and might be losing the confidence of the detective. I tried to steady myself.

'She came to see me a few weeks ago and said she was resigning and going back to Finland, to Helsinki.'

'She's Finnish?'

'Yes.'

'What makes you think she's here?'

'Her boyfriend came to see me. It was odd, her going like that so suddenly . . . You can check it out, can't you?'

'Yes, we can. Where does she live?'

'In Blackfriars. She must have stayed here all this time and she waited and she took Billy tonight when she knew we'd be out and he's in the storm and she's going to kill him . . .'

'*No!* Don't even say that!'

Markus had found his voice at last. I could hardly breathe then, I was filled with such fury against him; he was trying to protect her.

'If you even think it, let alone say it, we'll both go mad.' He was hoarse as though he could barely get the words out.

'She's a monster,' I gasped.

Nick leaned forward, closer to me on the sofa.

'Kathy, we can put out all kinds of information to help us get Billy back. So I need you to stay calm and to tell me all the details you can so we can follow this up immediately. OK?'

He had an open face and a scar on his chin and I felt he wanted to help me.

'OK; but she's *not* normal.'

Nick looked over at the uniformed man and said, 'You've taken the nanny's details?'

'Yes, we're thinking she should come down to the station.'

'Agreed; we need to get details about the sequence of events,' Nick said. Fran looked at me piteously as they led her away. I had no room for compassion for her at that moment. I could believe anything of Heja. Was it possible she had prevailed on Fran to let her into the flat?

HEJA

OCTOBER

The storm had blown itself out. I was lying in the strange soft bed in the front bedroom. There was an old-fashioned eiderdown over the sheets and blankets, and I had spent a warm night there. I propped myself up against four large pillows. Billy slept on, next to me. Through the cottage window I could see a small square of washed-out blue sky, like a watercolour painting when too much water has been put on the brush and the colour is hardly there at all. I could hear birds singing. After last night's terror and tumult they were making the world anew. The house alarm was no longer ringing. There were footsteps on the road outside and other sounds of human activity.

Markus was very much in my thoughts. We fought that summer at Åland because I sensed that he was attracted to Agneta, the Swedish woman on the boat. We had made it through the night and had moored safely at Sottunga on a morning of intense freshness. Agneta suggested we do a longer trip together. She said we'd made the grade as sailors. If we could survive that storm without getting sick we could survive anything. She suggested we do a week-long trip around the smaller islands.

I felt sick at the very idea. Markus was excited and agreed at once, looking over at me with eager eyes. I said nothing. I got up and walked away from them all, along the jetty. He came after me. He grabbed my hand and shouted at me for being so rude as to walk away like that. What had got into me?

I screamed at him, 'I won't spend another minute with that bitch Agneta fawning all over you!'

'Your crazy jealousy again,' he shouted at me. 'You can't keep getting madly jealous every time a woman speaks to me!'

We fought, briefly and viciously. I kicked him on his bare leg with all my force and he gasped with pain. He lunged at me and ripped my white T-shirt, scratching my neck as he did so and drawing blood. I ran away from him back to our lodgings in the town.

He shouted after me, 'Your jealousy is driving me away, Heja!'

I packed my things in a fury and was wheeling my case up to the ferry station when he caught up with me. We made up. We went back to our room and went to bed and made love all afternoon. In the early evening a beam of sunlight came through a crack in the curtains and made a track of light across his naked body. I laid my head on his stomach and stroked the golden hairs above his penis. I rolled my face into these hairs and smelled him deeply. How foolish I was to be so jealous. Markus loved me, only me.

Billy had woken up and started to make a grizzling cry so I picked him up and took him down to the kitchen. My legs and wrists were very weak this morning. I noticed again how heavy he was and I rested him on my hip. I had to hold on to the banister tightly as the cottage stairs were steep and narrow. Then I laid him down on a towel on the kitchen floor while I made up a bottle of milk for him. He rolled over onto his stomach and started to crawl around the kitchen and out into the hall with surprising speed. I picked him up and brought him back into the kitchen and shut the door. This was going to be a difficult day. My body ached and I needed to rest but first I had to get the stuff out of the car. The car was down the road, blocked by that tree.

After he had his bottle I changed Billy and dressed him. It took a long time. He wriggled on the bed as I tried to pull on his trousers and there were all these buttons to do up while he kicked his legs. Then I got dressed.

It was a fine autumn day and I could smell the sea on the air. I walked down to the car. I had left Billy lying on the sitting-room floor with the door shut. I took the buggy and piled the rest of the stuff on to it. Then I left a note inside the windscreen saying, 'I am staying at Overstrand Cottage.'

Some time later I heard someone walking up the path. There was a loud knock on the door. My first instinct was to hide. Then I remembered the note I had left in the car. I left Billy on the sitting-room floor, shut that door and opened the front door. A big ginger-haired man in blue overalls and a neon jerkin stood there.

'Hello. That your Volvo down the road?'

'Yes.'

'We're going to cut up the tree and we need to bring our truck up to the tree. Could you reverse your car down the road? There's space to park down there.'

'Yes, of course.'

'So you were caught out in it last night.'

'Yes, I was.'

'Quite something eh?'

'It certainly was.'

'Well, I'll be getting on.'

He retreated up the road. And I saw all the activity. People were out in their gardens, clearing broken branches and fences and gates. I found a broom in the kitchen and swept the shards of terracotta and soil from the broken pot on the path. I cannot afford to fall over. Then I walked down to the car. There were three workmen standing by the fallen tree.

As I passed the tree, the big ginger man said, 'We'll be a few hours with this. She was a big 'un, lots of logs. I'll let you know when we're done.'

'Thank you.'

'My pleasure.' He grinned at me and looked over at the other men. There are always snooping eyes wherever you go. I reversed the car down the road, parked it and walked back to the cottage.

I put the radio on for the news and there was no mention of an abducted baby. All the stories were about last night's storm. It had caused a swathe of destruction across southern England and many ancient trees had been lost. A panel of experts was mourning the impact this would have on the countryside.

It was impossible to rest. I have had very little contact with babies or even children in my life. I have no nieces or nephews. So I had no idea how much attention a baby demanded. Every time I sat down on the sofa Billy would crawl around the room and knock things over. He would start to cry. You cannot ignore the cry of a baby. I had read somewhere that human adults are programmed to respond to the cry of a human infant. There is something in their cry that challenges you. I did not know what to do to stop the crying. I offered him a rusk but he didn't want it. His incessant crying was making me feel bad, as if it was triggering a deep unmet neediness in myself. I could feel pressure building in me. So I put him in the bedroom upstairs on the floor and shut the door and left him in there crying. I went downstairs, made myself some green tea and sat in the back garden. My arms and legs ached from the exertion of the night before and my right leg was bruised. I needed calm. I needed rest.

Finally I went upstairs again. He seemed to have cried himself out. He hiccoughed his last few sobs and fell asleep. I stretched out on the sofa.

It was a calm evening. The field that bordered the road was fringed with yellow wildflowers. Tall trees framed the field and the sun was setting behind them. These trees had withstood the storm. I grilled a plaice fillet and made a tomato salad. I put Billy into his buggy to feed him and he ate the fish without complaint. He seemed more interested in playing with the tomato than eating it. He rolled the pips between his fingers. I was ready for a bath and bed. I took him upstairs and laid him on the bed by the wall. I gave him two spoonfuls of Calpol and one bottle of milk. I put a wall of pillows along the middle so he could not roll off the bed, and closed the bedroom door. I ran myself a deep bath and rested my arms and legs in the warm water.

KATHY

OCTOBER

I heard more roof tiles falling last night, crashing on to the pavement and fragmenting into pieces. My sleep was filled with monstrous dreams, but sleep was better than the moment of waking and that first consciousness that my Billy was gone. The pain was actually physical, a cruel squeezing around my heart. Markus was not in the bed. I got up and went into the kitchen and the sky from the windows was palest blue and a deadly calm now prevailed.

Markus came in and said, 'I'm going to make you some breakfast.'

He got eggs and coffee out of the fridge. The phone rang and it was Philip. His voice was embarrassed and gentler than I've ever heard it before.

'Take all the time you need. We're all thinking of you.'

Markus put a cup of coffee and a plate of scrambled eggs on the table in front of me and then sat down opposite me.

'Eat something, Kathy.'

Then Nick called and I got to the phone before Markus. I had this feeling that Nick was on my side, perhaps because he has an open, kindly face and he has children of his own, as he told me last night.

'We've been round to her flat. She's gone away. I spoke to the caretaker. He saw her packing up the car yesterday; helped her carry her stuff to the car and said she had a lot

257

of stuff with her. She told him she was going to the Lake District.'

'The Lake District . . .?'

'Yeah, that's likely to be a cover story. We'll check the area.'

'I knew she was here.'

'You were right. We also know the car she's got, he was positive on that – a silver Volvo estate – though he didn't know the registration number, said it wasn't her usual car.'

'No, she's got a convertible, a dark green convertible.'

'She told him it was being serviced. We can trace the convertible. See what she did with it. Anyway, we're going to put out an all-ports warning at once.'

'What's that?'

'We alert all ports and airports to look out for her. She won't be able to leave the country. There's something I need to discuss with you and Markus. We're thinking of putting out an appeal for information. We'll need a picture of Billy and your permission to do it. Can I come over this morning?'

'Come over at once, please.'

I said to Markus, 'She was here all the time. Nick is coming over.'

He looked wretched, his face was grey and unshaven and I felt nothing towards him.

He said, 'Have you called your parents? And Jennie . . .? Perhaps she could come and stay here. You need your family around you.'

'I need Billy. People died last night in that terrible storm and she was out there with Billy. He must be so scared. What did you do to make her hate me so much?'

Finally he said, 'I left her.'

'How did you leave her?'

'I left her suddenly, without telling her where I was going. I had to, she was very possessive. She always wanted more from me.'

'Weren't you were supposed to be so happy?' I said, pressing my sore place.

'We were happy, at the beginning. It started to go wrong and finally I moved away. And she tracked me down. Heja never lets go.'

'So she's punishing you now by taking my baby.'

'He's my son too, my best boy.'

His voice broke then and I stared down at the table and would not look at him. He started to make another pot of coffee and he was fumbling with the pot and I wondered why because he was never clumsy. Was it possible that he was crying? You would think that this terrible fear and this awful hurt would have brought us together. It hasn't. An unbridgeable chasm has opened up between us and I find I cannot trust him or anything he says.

Nick arrived and the three of us sat at the kitchen table.

'She's put her flat on the market so it looks like she's not planning on coming back. I've got an officer going round to your magazine this morning, to talk to the boss . . .'

'She planned it carefully, didn't she?' I said.

'Looks like that.'

'It wasn't on impulse?'

Markus stood up and started to walk up and down the kitchen. 'Heja doesn't do things on impulse,' he said.

'You should know,' I snapped back.

Nick said quickly, 'She did plan it but we will catch up with her. We know the model of the car and she won't be able to leave the country. Could she have got a copy of your keys, Kathy?'

I looked at Nick. 'My keys? Yes, it's possible, I suppose. We worked together.'

'Did you ever leave your keys anywhere she could get them?'

I tried to think if I had ever left my keys on the desk.

'No, I don't think so. They were always in my bag; she would have had to go through my bag.'

Nick nodded. 'I think she got hold of them somehow and made copies. Our next step is to put out an appeal to the media. That's what I wanted to talk to you both about.'

Markus said, 'How does that work?'

'I'll need a recent photograph of Billy that we can give the media, and I need a picture of Heja Vanheinen too . . .'

'You'll name her?' he asked.

'Yes, we'll name her and say that we need to speak to this woman in connection with the disappearance of Billy.'

'Are you sure that's a good idea?' Markus said. 'It could tip her over the edge.'

Nick said nothing.

Markus went on, 'I just think it could make things worse, if she feels you are closing in on her . . .'

'Why are you still trying to protect her?' I burst out.

Nick said, 'We think it's worth doing. It's important to get her picture out there because someone somewhere will have seen her. She'll have to go out some time. I need you both to agree to this. Why don't you discuss it alone? I'll wait outside in my car.'

He walked out of the kitchen and closed the door behind him.

I've seen appeals like this for missing children on television and they have always made me shudder at the horror of a parent pleading for information about their lost child. And so often the child is already dead.

260

'It will be terrible, just terrible, but we have to do it,' I said.

Markus said angrily, 'You are so wrong to think for a minute that I would shield her. I'm just scared this might provoke her.'

'Nick is the expert and he said it would help us!'

'He doesn't know her.'

I said with great bitterness, 'And only you do.'

'Stop this, Kathy! You've been treating me like a criminal from the moment Billy was taken. My son is everything to me. I just want him back safe.'

'Why didn't you warn me she was mad? You said I was making a drama out of it!'

'I didn't think for a moment that—'

'That she'd take Billy . . .?' My voice was rising. 'But she did. We have to help the police.'

'Do you think they've thought this through at all? It's what they always do. Just do what they always do. Even if it tips her over the edge . . .'

'I trust Nick,' I said.

'You trust people too quickly.'

'What's that supposed to mean?'

'He may have got this wrong. I think it's too risky.'

'Of course it's risky. That monstrous woman has stolen my son. What is she doing to him at this very moment?' I screamed.

At first he said nothing, and then very quietly, 'If you insist, I will agree, with grave reservations.'

'Yes, go on, put all the responsibility on to me!'

'Then follow my advice and say no. If we have any doubts at all, we don't have to do this.'

'I'm with Nick on this because he has no secret agenda.'

'You can be a bitch sometimes, Kathy, a stupid bitch. Go and get your precious Nick.'

When Nick came back you could have cut the atmosphere with a knife. He asked me if I knew where we could find a recent picture of Heja.

'Maybe from Robert Mirzoeff,' I said.

'Who?'

'Her boyfriend. He might have a picture.'

'Have you got a number?'

'Yes, he's a psychoanalyst, he's got a practice here.' I got up wearily and found the card Robert had given me.

'Good, we'll follow that up at once. Robert Mirzoeff.'

Markus went into his workroom to get a picture of Billy and I followed him in there. Markus has taken hundreds of photos of Billy since he was born. He keeps them in albums and writes the date and place under every picture. He lifted the most recent album onto his drawing table and started to leaf through it.

He said in a low voice, 'Do you want to help me pick one?'

I said, 'You choose.'

I looked at the pictures of my baby and Markus pointed at one and I nodded. He took the photograph out carefully and handed it to Nick.

'Thank you both. I'll be in touch again soon.'

He left the flat then. I felt quite overcome and had to go and lie down on the bed in our room.

Some time later Markus came into the room and said, 'We must tell Jennie and your parents now. We can't let them find out about this on TV.'

'Will you call Jennie? I can't do it. Not my parents, not yet . . .'

'Shall I ask her to come up?'

'No, I . . . I can't be around anyone at the moment.'

'She'll want to talk to you. She'll want to help.'

'Not now.'

Later, I left the flat and walked to St James's Church in Spanish Place. Billy had been gone one whole day, twenty-four hours, and the world was a completely different place. The debris of the storm had been swept away. Everywhere there were signs of damage and two shops had had to board up their windows. I have known these streets for years and St James's is the church my mother uses when she stays with me. I can't phone my parents because it will become too real when I tell them. When I was a teenager my mum said she used to dread phone calls when I was out because phone calls only ever meant bad news.

Mum's a true believer and she wanted me brought up a Catholic. Dad let her take me to church because he respected her faith. I stopped going to church when I reached adulthood, except for Christmas and Easter, but it means so much to Mum. She wanted me to have Billy christened; she asked me to do it several times and I did nothing. I pushed the door of the church open and there was that familiar smell of incense and candle wax. I have always liked the Golden Lady statue on the side aisle and I walked up to her. She and the baby are both covered in gold leaf, except for her shoes, which are red. They both wear crowns and Mary is holding a sceptre and the baby is holding an orb and he's a lovely chubby baby.

I sat down in a pew and I thought about Heja having the keys to my flat. She must have come to my flat and been around my things; maybe gone through my things. I had this intense revelation that for these last few months she's been digging tunnels under every aspect of my life. There was that photograph of Eddie left where Markus would find it. Then I remembered my lost presentation notes and my bungled appearance before the board. She must have taken my notes. I shivered. That was months ago. She has caused real trouble between Philip and me and she has driven a wedge between Markus and me, and because of her actions I have been feeling shaky for months. Now the killer blow; she came to our flat when she knew we would be out at the launch and she took Billy. Her malevolence towards me is boundless.

I am no believer but I got up and knelt on the prayer stool in front of the Golden Lady and I prayed that I had made the right decision about the photographs and had not endangered my Billy.

HEJA

OCTOBER

I woke early. Billy was asleep on the other side of the bed. I bent over him and listened to his breathing. It was calm and regular. His breath is pure. His skin is new. I thought of my dead brother Tomas then and of my mother, when she woke from the nursery floor after falling asleep that night he was ill. She would have got to her knees and looked into his cot. He was pale, still breathing, and unresponsive. She knew at that moment just how ill he was. Then there was the panic and the rush to the hospital. He died suddenly. He did not have a slow death, like Tanya's.

My death will creep up on me day after day, month after month, year after year, as it crept up on Tanya. I may have ten more years of dying ahead of me. First my legs will go. I will need a wheelchair. My arms will become weaker and weaker until I will not be able to turn the wheels. I will need a full-time nurse to wash me and dress me and feed me. Then my neck and my throat muscles will start to waste until I cannot swallow or breathe. Difficult to be noble when your body walls you in.

Solange did not want them to bury Tomas. When they told her he was dead she demanded to be left alone with him in the hospital room. They left her sitting there, holding her dead baby in her arms. Hours passed and she would not come out of the room, or let Tomas go. Rigor mortis had started to set in. There were purple livid patches on his body and he was cold and stiff. My father tried to take Tomas away from her. She clung to her son, screaming at him.

'He just needs to be kept warm.'

Still she rocked him and whispered to him. In the end three nurses had to hold on to her while my father took the baby's body from her frantic, clawlike fingers.

On the day of Tomas's funeral she was in the secure unit of a mental hospital. She did not see the small coffin being lowered into the earth. How do I know this? My father did not tell me. He would feel it was a betrayal of Solange. I was a journalist and I found out the truth. I discovered that Solange Vanheinen, my mother, suffered an acute psychotic reaction to the death of her son. Billy is almost exactly the same age as Tomas was when he died. I looked at him and thought how different a living baby is from a dead one.

When he woke up I gave him a bath. It was difficult because he was slippery and wriggly and splashed his hands up and down. If it is your own child maybe you have reserves of patience that I did not have. Maybe you are hardwired to cope with the baby's constant demands. I dried him and dressed him. The only way to do it is not to hurry. If you take time and let him roll and kick on the bed, it is easier. Suddenly there was a knock on the door. I moved to the front window. I looked down onto the path. Wayne was standing there. His car was parked in the road. He stood there for a minute. I knew he would look up so I drew back. When I looked again his head was bent. He was writing something. He pushed something through the letterbox and walked away. I heard his car reverse and drive off up Cremers Drift.

I waited until my heart had settled. Then I went down

the stairs carrying Billy. Wayne had left a piece of folded paper on the mat. I read his rather childish handwriting.

Just checking you arrived safely and everything OK after big storm. Call me if you need anything. Best Regards, Wayne'

All my life men have paid unwanted attention to me. Arvo Talvela said I should look on it as a sort of tribute. I do not see it that way. I do not want these unknown men to intrude into my life.

During breakfast I listened to the news. There was no mention of Billy. The police will be involved by now and she will be demented. She will have named and accused me of course. They will have spoken to the caretaker at my flat and probably to Philip Parr and to Robert too. One thing I do regret is the pain this will cause my father when they track him down. He will be so shocked, and so worried about me.

I have to be careful yet I would like to get out of the house for a few hours at least. I cannot tolerate another day cooped up inside with the incessant crying. I tied a scarf around my hair, put Billy in the buggy and locked the cottage up. It was another calm, clear day. As I pushed Billy along the path he stopped crying and kicked his legs up and down.

We reached Deal. I pushed him along the paved path that runs parallel with the beach. How I would like to be able to run over those pebbles and sit at the water's edge as I did as a child. We got to the lifeboat station. There were seagulls circling the water's edge and their raucous cries filled the air. A profound and mournful weariness was creeping over me.

I will never forget the last time I saw Tanya alive. It was the holidays and we had gone to grandfather's house in the country, as we always did. These holidays were very adult affairs. I was the only child in the house. There were lengthy family dinners with talk about books and music. My mother would go on long walks with her two dogs. Sometimes I went with her. She made it clear that she preferred to go on her own. She said she could walk further and faster without me. I had packed my new pink satin ballet shoes, which were my pride and joy. I practised my dances in Grandfather's large sitting room.

My father liked to go fishing and would always ask me if I wanted to go with him. He said he liked to have me along. I sat by his side on the riverbank while he cast his fishing line and it plopped into the water, making concentric circles that moved outwards. He would hunch forward, as if entranced by the sight of the water's surface, and I would play with my glazed pottery mouse. They were peaceful afternoons.

On this particular day I was skipping through the hall. Aunt Tanya had been moved into a ground-floor room that looked out over the garden. I had already been in the house a week and had not seen her once. Usually I spent some time with Tanya. She was patient with me and would teach me songs or read to me. This time I was told she was too ill to have visitors to her room. It was lunchtime and the door to her room was open. I looked in as I reached it. Tanya was in her wheelchair. She was thinner than the last time I had seen her. A nurse was bending over her. The nurse held Tanya's head back against the headrest of the chair with one hand and with the other she was feeding Tanya with a spoon, like a baby is fed. Tanya looked over the nurse's shoulder and our eyes met. She did not acknowledge me or smile at me, as she usually did. She just looked at me and her eyes were the saddest eyes I ever saw. Then the nurse became aware of my presence in the hall and she closed the door. I could never be like Tanya. I could never be their gentle suffering angel.

It has been such a long lonely journey since I first heard I was ill. I have spoken to no one about my illness since Arvo died. The time has come to tell Markus. He needs to know that I am dying. And he needs to know about our baby. I *must* see Markus so that I can die in peace.

I pushed the buggy towards the parade of shops until I found a phone box that worked.

KATHY

OCTOBER

I lay in bed, waiting for Nick to call. He said he'd ring and let me know when the appeal was being broadcast. Markus had gone out and I can't understand how he can function normally when my Billy may be dead already. The pain was overwhelming. I could see no point in getting out of bed to get washed and dressed yet bed was a place of torment too.

My breasts were so painful, swollen and hard with the milk Billy would have drunk over the last two days. I ran a hot bath and squeezed the bath sponge over my breasts again and again then squeezed at them till the milk came out, and it eased the physical pain a bit.

After my bath I sat at the kitchen table draped in towels with no energy to dry or dress myself. It was a very old table. I traced the lines on the wood. My aunt Jennie had it for years and so many dramas had been played out around that table. I've seen a few since I've lived here. I remembered the morning we confirmed my pregnancy and Markus and I sat at this table, stunned at the news and, in my case, filled with a tremulous happiness.

And I thought that what was happening now was the most profound drama of all, because if anything happened to Billy I would never be the same person again. Would I even be able to go on living? I'm not the same person I was just two days ago. I thought that I was suffering then because things were so tense and unhappy between Markus and me. That was nothing, nothing at all; how could I have made such a fuss about that? I could have got over him not telling me about his relationship with Heja.

I should have known that Heja would not be satisfied with just making me wretched. She wants to destroy me. There must be something else behind this monstrous hatred of hers. It is abnormal and it must come from some deep disturbance. It can't just be because Markus left her. Could something else have happened to her; could she have had a miscarriage?

It suddenly occurred to me that Robert might know something. I helped him once so perhaps he might help me now. I rang his practice immediately and a woman said he was with a patient and would be out in twenty minutes. I said it was urgent that I speak to him as soon as possible and I gave her my name and number. She said she'd get him to call me as soon as he was free. I got dressed and I waited. My phone rang and it was Robert, and I asked if I could come and see him straight away. He said he was so sorry, he had a patient waiting for him and he couldn't cancel. He would be free in an hour and a quarter. He was very precise about that, pedantic almost, and he gave me the address. His practice is at Belsize Park.

Robert's consulting rooms were in a white stucco, double-fronted house. There were a number of practices there with a shared waiting room on the first floor. The receptionist told me to go straight in and buzzed open a door on the left. I looked into his room and saw the couch, where all his patients must lie down. He led me into the room, closing the door behind us.

'Can I get you some water or tea?'

'No, thanks.'

'How can I help you?'

'Have the police been in touch?'

'Yes, a detective called Nick Austin. Please, sit down, Kathy.'

I perched on the edge of a chair.

'Heja has taken my son Billy,' I said.

'He didn't quite say that . . .'

'She has. And I know she'll hurt him.'

The unshed tears were pushing up my throat and behind my nose. Then they started from my eyes as if they had a life of their own. I rubbed hard at my eyes.

'Don't push the tears back in. Let them come out,' he said.

I let the tears out and it was a relief to sit there and sob. He handed me a box of Kleenex.

'I don't think she will harm Billy. I really don't . . .'

'How can you say that when she's taken my baby?'

'Why do you think she took Billy?'

'Because of Markus.'

'Markus . . .'

'Because I'm with him now; because we have a son; because of Markus! I know you recognized him when you came to my office.'

'Yes I did recognize him. I met Markus, just the once, at Heja's flat.'

'When was this?'

'In July. I guessed they had been lovers once.'

Another stab of pain; Markus told me he had seen her when I was in Lisbon, and that was in June.

'They were together for nine years. Markus left her suddenly, about seven years ago.'

'I picked up there was something powerful between them.'

I discovered that the pain of jealousy, however sharp, was as nothing compared to the pain of losing Billy.

'Markus told her he wouldn't see her again. She resigned and told me she's going back to Finland. She didn't go. She stayed here all the time because she wanted to take Billy and destroy me. And you don't think she'll hurt him!'

'I'm sure of it.'

'And I'm sure you've lost your professional detachment!' I said it angrily. How could he still believe in her? My angry comment stung him, I could tell.

'I came here because I hoped you'd try to help me. She didn't love you, you know. She's only ever loved Markus!'

'That is possible,' he replied calmly.

'Then help me; please help me. Tell me what's going on in her head.'

He stood up then and walked up and down his room and it was as if he had moved into analyst mode.

'I'm sure Heja has been through some kind of trauma. And I'm certain she was in analysis for a long time, though she flatly denied it. She also has a difficult relationship with her mother. I was struck by how she called her mother by her first name. And her mother is cold towards her too.'

'She is very cold.'

'She is a profoundly reserved person. Whatever trouble she has had, she keeps it locked within herself. Can I ask you a question, Kathy?'

I nodded and he sat down now, opposite me.

'How long have you been with Markus?'

'Just over two years . . .'

'So Billy came along quickly.'

'Yes, we'd only been together six months when I got pregnant.'

'That is fast; a new relationship and a baby. You are rather different people, aren't you? You seem a very open and direct person, Kathy.'

'And Markus isn't? I know, but Billy is everything to us.'

'Of course he is. Perhaps it has been difficult for you both though?'

I was starting to feel uncomfortable now.

'Yes,' I said shortly. 'It's not been easy.'

He looked at me silently, waiting for more.

'It's not been easy. We both want it to work, though, and it was OK, it was good, until she came into our lives.'

'You said just now that Heja has only ever loved Markus.'

'Yes.'

'Do you also believe that Markus only ever loved Heja?'

I looked down at my hands in my lap and at my scrunched wet Kleenex and I felt vulnerable and shaky. I hadn't expected this, that he would make me feel so exposed.

'I don't know,' I said finally.

'Well, I think that Heja is very possessive in her attachments,' he said.

'Intensely possessive; Markus said that she never let go.'

'She will think Markus still belongs to her. She hoped she could get back with him. Then she finds he has a son he adores. She thinks if she takes his son he will come to her. So the last thing she would do is hurt Billy.'

I sat and thought about what he'd said and it sounded almost reasonable. Then I remembered that we were dealing with Heja and she did not behave like other people did. And I remembered Markus's fears about provoking her, and he was the person who knew her best of all.

'It's deranged, what she's done. Markus is beside himself. He can't forgive her for this.'

'It *is* deranged behaviour, and I think that's because Heja is afraid.'

'*She*'s afraid? What's she afraid of?'

'I suspect she may be ill.'

'How ill?'

'Very ill, I think; possibly terminally ill . . .'

It was a shocking moment. My terror, which I had thought could not be any greater, exploded.

'You're saying she's dying?'

'I think she is very ill.'

'Then don't you see? She has nothing to lose. Oh, God, she is going to kill Billy!'

'No, Kathy. It doesn't work like that. Heja is someone who has to be in control of her life. This will be her cry for help.'

'Cry for help! The clock's ticking on my son's life and you sit there defending his kidnapper . . .'

'Kathy . . .'

'You're like the rest of them,' I shrieked, 'always trying to protect her. Never once seeing her for the monster she is.'

He just looked at me.

'What *is* it about her?'

I slammed out of his room.

HEJA

OCTOBER

The phone box worked and a woman put me through to him.

'Thank God you called. You've got Billy?'

'I've got Billy. He's safe.'

'What the fuck are you doing, taking my son?'

'Don't shout at me, Markus.'

'Where's Billy? Where are you?'

'Stop shouting or I'll hang up.'

'I'm going out of my mind. Is Billy OK?'

'Billy is fine, just fine. I need you, Markus.'

'Tell me where you are.'

'I need you. I'm dying.'

'What . . .?'

'I am dying. I have what Tanya had and I will be dead soon and I had to tell you and I'm going now . . .'

'*No!* Wait, Heja. *Wait!* Are you still there?'

'Yes.'

'How *can* you be dying?'

'My muscles are wasting away.'

'But you were OK when I saw you.'

'I wasn't. I've got a terminal muscle-wasting disease. It's in my genes, Markus, the precious Vanheinen genes . . .'

'How long have you known this?'

'I found out just after you left me.'

276

'No . . .'

'Yes . . . And no one else knows.'

He was silent for a moment.

'That's why you came to London?'

'Yes. I needed to see you again before I died, and while I could still move.'

Then there was silence again and I think he was crying.

'Where are you? I'll come at once. The police are after you.'

'I know they are. I can't tell you Markus. You told me you couldn't see me again . . .'

'I didn't mean it. Tell me, Heja. Please . . .'

'You will just tell the police and—'

'*No!* I give you my word. I'll come at once and I'll help you. Please, Heja, it has only ever been you.'

'You're just saying that because you want Billy.'

'I want Billy, and you too. I have been so lonely in this marriage. Tell me where you are, Heja. I won't betray you. You know I won't. You have my word.'

I wondered then if Tanya had had a great love in her life. I never knew of anyone. I hope she did. It is the most important thing to have loved someone deeply.

'If you are lying to me, I will kill myself and Billy,' I said.

I told him where we were because Markus does not lie. He was the truest man I ever knew. I told him to come to the lifeboat station on Deal seafront and I would meet him there. He said it would take him at least two hours to reach Deal. I drove back to the cottage.

The world was receding. The world mattered to me once. Markus was right when he said that I cared about my job and my celebrity and that the way I embraced the world of the media had come between us. I talked about this with Arvo Talvela, after Markus had left me and I knew I was ill. I told him that my work had been an issue between us. He asked me if I felt that Markus had resented my success. No, I told him, I didn't think so because Markus never valued material success in that way. It was more that he made me feel shallow for being a successful media star. Arvo said that must have felt like a rejection. And it did because I liked my work. Then he asked me what it was I liked about the job and I remember our exchange so well.

'I like feeling at the centre of things. Working in a news-room, you get to know what is happening before other people do. And, yes, I do like the recognition too. The adulation, as Markus once described it!'

He said, 'Like it? Or need it? Perhaps television is like the light in a mother's eyes.'

I was puzzled and he repeated the phrase.

'You are drawn to television because it is like the light in a mother's eyes.' I thought about that for a few minutes. He knew that my mother's eyes never lit up when she looked at me.

KATHY

OCTOBER

When I got out on to the street I was dizzy with panic. I saw a taxi and hailed it, knowing that I had to see Nick straight away and tell him what Robert had said. Was he right and could Heja be dying? I told the driver to take me to Marylebone police station. So Markus had been right about the photographs all along and we had to stop them at once. She was mad and she was ill and she had my baby and if she saw her picture and heard her name on television it could tip her over the edge.

And yet Robert continued to defend her. Cry for help! They are all fascinated by her – Markus, Robert, Philip Parr.

We arrived at the police station and I called Nick from my mobile, saying I was in Reception and needed to see him at once. His assistant came down and led me up to his office. I was trembling, on the edge of hysteria.

As soon as his door opened and Nick was greeting me I said frantically, 'We can't put the photographs out! We mustn't! I've just seen Robert. He thinks Heja is dying.'

There was a flash of concern in Nick's eyes. 'Slowly now; what exactly did Robert say?'

'Have the photos gone out?'

'Not yet.'

'Thank God!' I shuddered with relief.

'Sit down, Kathy. Calm yourself. Tell me what Robert said.'

I repeated everything he had said to me.

'He didn't share *any* of this with me when I spoke to him,' he said crossly.

Nick picked up his phone and he spoke to someone and he told them to hold the photographs of Heja Vanheinen and Billy Hartman until they had explicit instructions from him.

I was still trembling, unable to calm myself.

'If it's true, I know she's going to hurt him,' I said.

'You've got to keep it together, Kathy. We won't do anything with the photos for now. And I plan to visit Robert Mirzoeff again. He should have told me his suspicions since they are clearly relevant.'

'And you know she's got Billy?'

'We think she has Billy. We've been on to the police in Helsinki and they've spoken to her parents. She hasn't been back there since last year. And no one has heard from her for weeks. Now, go home and update Markus and I'll keep in close touch with you both.'

HEJA

OCTOBER

He was standing outside the lifeboat station, as we had agreed. He had parked his Saab where I could see it. I told him I needed him and he had come.

I had left Billy with Wayne. My next conversation with Markus had to be just the two of us. I told Wayne I was visiting an old friend. She had shingles and I couldn't risk the baby being near her. I told him I would be an hour at most. Billy was asleep in his buggy and would probably sleep the whole time I was away. Would Wayne do me the biggest favour and look after him? Wayne looked nonplussed. The woman who sat next to him was helpful. She wheeled Billy's buggy next to her desk and told me not to worry. She had three kids and Billy would be fine with her.

I drove past Markus and I know he saw me. I did not stop. I drove around the streets of Deal looking for any signs that the police had come with him. I did not think he would betray me. Then I drove back and parked next to his car. He walked over and his face was full of fear. Before he could say a word I put my hand up.

'Billy is safe. You'll see him in twenty minutes. He's with a friend. I need to tell you something now, Markus, something I should have told you years ago.'

He got into the Volvo and I drove us to a quiet back street and parked. I turned to face him.

'Promise me Billy is safe,' he said.

'Safe and well; I would never hurt him. He is your son.'

And then, and I could not stop it, my eyes filled with tears. I did not cry – ever. He reached for my hand.

'I'm dying, Markus. I feel weaker every day. I have to tell you this now.'

I stopped and wiped my tears away with my hands.

'Seven years ago, very soon after you left so suddenly, I started to feel sick and my period was late.'

He swallowed hard.

'I saw my doctor and he confirmed that I was pregnant with our child.' His face registered shock, or was it disbelief?

'That last time, after that dreadful row, I conceived our child.'

We were both remembering that night. We always fought and then we always had passionate sex afterwards to make up. That time something had been different and he had left me a few days later.

'Markus, I wanted our baby so much. You were gone but I was sure you would come back. For a few weeks I was truly happy. Then I started to feel very ill, dizzy and sick all the time. My doctor ran these tests and he told me I was carrying the gene that killed Tanya.'

Markus looked stricken.

'He said our baby could not survive. Was "not viable"; those were the words he used: "not viable".'

'Oh, Heja . . .'

'It was the most terrible moment of my life. I found out I would die a dreadful death at the very time I thought I was carrying new life.'

Tears were rolling down my face, tears that I had never been able to cry before. He held me close then and he cried

282

too. It had started to rain and the rain knocked on the car roof as if it was mocking us as we sat there in that embrace. Finally it was me who pulled away.

'Promise me you'll never leave me again, Markus.'

'I promise.'

'I need your help.'

'I promise.'

'We'll get Billy now. Can you drive? I feel too shaky.'

We swapped seats and I directed him back into Deal and to the parade of shops and the estate agent's. I walked into the office. The woman had Billy on her knee.

'He's a great little lad,' she said.

'Thank you so much for looking after him.'

I put Billy into his buggy. He didn't really want to go back into it. Then I shook the woman's hand and Wayne's hand. He held the door open for me. I pushed Billy towards Markus and he knelt down on the pavement. When Billy saw his father he gave a huge beaming smile, put his arms up and said, 'Dada.'

Markus lifted him up and hugged him tight and looked at him and hugged him again. Then he said to me, 'The police know you've got a Volvo. We need to park it somewhere out of the way and then use my car.'

I agreed. He drove the Volvo to Deal train station. There was a long-stay car park at the back of the station and he parked the car there. He said he would put money in for a week of parking. Then we sat and waited in the Volvo until the rain had stopped. We took everything out from the boot and put Billy back into the buggy. I was exhausted now, almost too tired to walk back to his car. I clung to his arm as he slowly pushed the buggy back to the lifeboat station. We got into his Saab. Then I directed him to the cottage.

We went into the house and I sat down on the sofa and said, 'I have to rest now, Markus. I am exhausted.'

'Lie down,' he said, and I stretched out and he sat at my feet and took my shoes off. Billy was wriggling on his lap so he put him down on the carpet. It was the most incredible relief to have Markus there with me.

He took my hand.

'Always such cold hands; now I understand. This is what we have to do, darling. We'll go to the north of England. We'll find somewhere to live. First I have to take Billy back to Kathy.'

'*No!*' I pulled my hand away abruptly.

'Yes, darling. Think about it. They're about to issue a photo of you and Billy to the media. As long as we have Billy with us the whole country will be on the lookout. You have *me*. Let Kathy have Billy.'

He took my hand back and started to stroke it. I said nothing.

'My love,' he said. 'I'm going to look after you now.'

'You never guessed that I was ill?'

'No. You looked very white the last time I saw you. You said you'd had flu.'

'Not flu; I was having a bad gravity day. I have good days and bad days, Markus. Though I seem to be having more bad days recently . . . Will you make me some green tea? There are teabags in the kitchen.'

He came back with the tea for me.

'I'm going to change Billy's nappy' he said.

'Everything is upstairs in the bathroom,' I said.

He left the room with Billy and I thought about what he had said. They would be looking for us and as I had found out over the last few days, having a baby with you changes everything. There is no time for anything else but the baby's needs.

When he came back downstairs I agreed that he should take Billy back to her. Markus said he would drive back at once. He had to. Time was running out. I insisted on going in the car with him. I did not want to be on my own. So he carried Billy to the car and then he helped me into the passenger seat and we set off.

KATHY

OCTOBER

When I got home I found a letter from Hector lying on the hall table with the rest of our mail, so he must have heard about Billy being kidnapped. I stood in the hall and opened his letter right away and read it through. It was so sensitively written and offered no false reassurances. He wrote that he was thinking of me a lot, that I should call him any time if I needed someone to talk to, and he signed it *From your friend and fellow veteran*, which I found touching. He was referring back to our lunch, of course, and I remembered how easy I always found him to talk to. He was a genuinely kind man: that was clear from the day he helped the old man on the boat and now he had taken the time to write to me and offer support.

I took the lift to our floor and opened the door into our silent flat. Markus was still out and I felt the absence of my Billy so acutely. I cannot bear to go into his room at the moment because his empty cot feels like a reproach to me, a reproach that I did not protect him. I had to tell Markus that the photographs of Billy and Heja are not being used today. He will be relieved to hear that. I called his mobile again and it went straight to voice-mail, as it had done all day. He does not want to talk to me. So I left a message about the latest developments and asked him to please come back to the flat. I told him I was scared and I needed him to be there.

When he gets here I will have to tell him what Robert said about her. I can't tell him that Heja is dying over the phone. It has to be face to face for that.

I called Jennie and told her what was happening too. She said, 'Let me come up and be with you, darling.'

And I said, 'Yes, please come, I'm so afraid she'll hurt him.'

And then at last I called my mum and dad and told them everything. It was an awful, painful phone call and my mum was crying so hard and my dad was being calm and strong. He said they would get the next flight over.

I lay on my side in our bedroom and stared at the digital clock, watching the numbers change, working out exactly how the numbers changed one into the other. Each number was made up of straight lines. Number one was made up of two short lines. The zero was made up of six, two on either side, one at the top and one at the bottom. The number eight had the most lines. It was made up of seven lines, like the zero, with a line across the middle. How many more minutes and hours did I have to live through without Billy? I was freezing and too exhausted to even get under the covers.

After many hours, I don't know how many, I heard a key in the door. That will be Markus, I thought. I couldn't make myself move. I felt so cold and without an ounce of energy.

'Kathy!' he called out.

I got up wearily and opened the bedroom door and Markus was standing there in front of me with Billy. He held Billy out to me. Billy was in my arms again and it was the most joyful moment of my life, an even greater joy than the moment of his birth.

I hugged him, smelled him and kissed him. I was crying and laughing and kissing my baby again and again.

'Thank you, thank you, thank you . . . Where did you find him? How did you find him?'

We walked into the kitchen together.

'I was able to track Heja down. And I know why she did it too.'

He looked at me and said quietly, 'She's very ill. She's dying.'

So he knows. I said nothing. I had Billy and I was just kissing him and smelling his head and his smell was like a wonderful drug I couldn't get enough of.

'Tell me everything, first I have to change him.'

I went into Billy's room and took off his Babygro and kissed his fat little stomach and he laughed in delight. What a joy it was to be changing his nappy again.

'Jennie's on her way here,' I called out.

Markus had gone into our bedroom and I heard him opening some drawers. I got Billy changed into a new nappy and a Babygro. I couldn't stop kissing him. I wanted to feast on his skin and on his presence.

'I'll never leave you again, my darling boy,' I said to him, picking him up and resting him on my hip. He seemed unharmed, just happy to be with his mum. Markus had gone into the bathroom now.

'I must call Mum and Dad at once. They're on their way here. And Nick, of course . . .'

'No, Kathy.'

He came out of the bathroom with his wash bag.

'What do you mean?'

'Don't call Nick just yet, please.'

'Why not? What's happening?'

He went back into our bedroom and I followed him in there with Billy. I saw him put his wash bag into a holdall and then his drawing pad.

'What's in that bag?'

'I have to go away.'

'You're going?'

He zipped his holdall closed and it dawned on me. 'You're going to her, aren't you?'

'I have to go now.'

'You're going to Heja. She stole our baby and you're going to her now.'

He picked up his holdall and walked towards me. I wanted to hit him, scratch him, hurt him. I was holding Billy so I just screamed at him.

'How *can* you? She's a monster!'

'Look after Billy. He's safe and that's all that matters,' he said.

He moved forward and tried to kiss Billy then. I pulled away from him.

'Get away from us. You're not fit to go near Billy.'

He gave me the saddest look and he left the flat with his bag.

HEJA

OCTOBER

I sat in the car and waited for him. I could have worried that he would stay with her and call the police, yet I had no fear at all that he would not return to me. The streetlamps were on and the road was quiet, with the odd swish of a car passing. I rested my head against the car window. I felt spent.

He came out of the apartment block, his face set. He slung his bag on the back seat, got in next to me and turned the engine on.

'You're angry with me,' I said.

He did not reply. He just looked straight ahead as he drove us out of London. Finally, after he turned onto the motorway and was in the fast lane, he said, 'How long did you rent the house for?'

'For October and November.'

'Did you intend to stay there?'

'I wasn't sure what I was going to do. I needed you to come back to me, Markus.'

'We have to move fast. They'll be on our trail once Nick has my car registration number.'

'Who is Nick?'

'He's the detective on the case. You committed a crime, Heja, and they're after you.'

Then he told me that the police had tracked down the number plate of the hired Volvo. It would not be long before they found the Volvo sitting in that car park in Deal station. They would assume we were in Kent then and would start asking around. It would not take them long to track us down, he thought. Someone would have spotted me over the last few days. He was angry with me, but I also knew that he was thinking hard about what we should do next. I knew he would do everything in his power to stop the police arresting me. He has always had a deep antipathy to the police.

Finally we turned into the rutted road that led to the cottage.

'You certainly chose a secluded spot,' he said.

Then we were in the cottage and it was just the two of us alone together at last. We stood there in the small hall and looked at each other, and I said, 'Thank you.'

I went to turn the heating up. Markus looked in the fridge and took out some eggs. He looked in the cupboard.

'No pepper and no coffee! I'll have to get us some proper supplies tomorrow.'

He beat the eggs and cooked us an omelette. It was as if we had reverted to an earlier way of being together. Few words were spoken. After we had eaten we went into the little sitting room and he pulled the curtains closed and sat down. I went over to him and sat on his lap and put my arms around his neck.

'I'm going to have to fatten you up. You weigh nothing,' he said.

'I was so frightened that first time you saw me again. I thought you would see that I was ill.'

'You looked good to me.'

'I've spent years presenting myself to the world as if I was fine.'

'And no one knows? You didn't tell your father or Robert?'

'I would never tell Robert and my father has suffered enough.'

'He would want to help you, Heja.'

'He's not well, Markus. He has a heart condition.'

'I always liked your father very much. He said to me once that you hadn't had it easy and I was to look after you.'

We kissed then and I said I wanted to go to bed. I wanted him again after all the wasted years.

We lay in our naked embrace. His body has thickened a bit. His smell is the same. He said nothing although I know he noticed how thin I have become. As he stroked my back slowly it was as if he was counting the bones of my spine one by one. When I turned round to face him my hip bones jutted against his groin. He seemed scared that he would hurt me if he penetrated me. I wanted him inside me again. Afterwards I rested with my head on his shoulder.

'If only I could have had our baby,' I said.

'If only . . .'

'Sorry I let you down.'

'You didn't let me down!' He said it vehemently. 'You had no choice.'

'No choice at all. I'm the last of the Vanheinens. It ends with me.'

The next morning when I woke up a sea mist lay thickly over everything. I saw Markus standing at the cottage window and you could hardly see the trees at the edge of the field. I felt weak and shivery and didn't feel like getting out of bed.

'We can't travel anywhere today, Markus, I feel too shaky. I need to rest.'

'I'll make you some tea.'

I heard him use his phone once to call his work and explain that he had to be away for a while. His voice was tense and it seemed that someone on the other end was pushing for more information as Markus said, 'I will call again when I can, I have to go now.' Then he came back into the bedroom, bringing me a cup of green tea.

'Do you have your mobile with you?'

'No, I left it at the flat.'

'Good.'

He turned his mobile off and took the battery out.

'I won't be long. I'm going to walk down to Deal to get some food for us and a newspaper. I need some coffee.'

'Won't you take your car?'

'Best I leave it here.'

I heard him leave the cottage. I got up and found my handbag. In the inner pocket was a small tin. It was one of those tins that used to hold gramophone needles. It was a gift Markus had given me years before, when we were students. He said he found it in a junk shop. On the lid was a picture of the His Master's Voice dog. He will do it for me, I know he will. He has come this far.

It was about two hours later when I heard Markus unlocking the front door. I was in the sitting room, wrapped in a blanket, and as he walked into the room he brought a blast of sea air in with him. He looked so healthy and so vital.

'I got us four beautiful fresh mackerel. A fisherman was selling from a kiosk on the beach. He wasn't doing much business today,' he said.

We spent a quiet afternoon together. The mist did not lift all day. We did not talk much about what we were going to do next. Markus had been thinking about options and wanted to discuss them, I said tomorrow, it can wait till tomorrow. We talked about the years we had been apart. I told him about Arvo Talvela and how in my greatest trouble he had helped me. And then Arvo had died suddenly and I knew that I had to find Markus again. Arvo had always said that I had to tell Markus about our baby. I was sorry I had taken so long to tell him. We did not mention her or Billy once.

Later he ran a bath for me and I lay in the warm water for ages, hoping it would bring more feeling back into my legs. I had not dressed all day. That is the kind of thing an invalid does, stays in their night things all day. Tomorrow I will get dressed. No matter how weak I feel, I will get dressed. I went downstairs to the kitchen, carrying my little tin with me.

Markus had the news on and I just looked at him and he knew what I was thinking and said, 'No mention of us. I'm going to cook us those mackerel, with lots of lemon and pepper.'

I put my little tin onto the kitchen table.

'You've still got that tin I gave you.'

'Yes, and this little tin is a great comfort to me.'

I opened it and showed him the small white pills it contained.

'There are enough strong painkillers in here to finish me off.'

'Oh, Heja . . .' He hugged me tightly.

The next morning dawned mild and golden, the kind of day you long for in the dark days of winter. The sun had burned off the sea mist. The trees at the edge of the field were a palette of russet, amber and ochre. Markus made green tea for me and coffee for himself and brought it up to the bedroom. I sat up against the pillows.

'I'm going to make us a picnic and take you to Dungeness today,' he said.

'Is that one of your frontier places?'

'Yes, a particular favourite of mine. Put on two jumpers. It's milder today and I want us to sit on the beach.'

He drove us along the coast road and we reached Dungeness and a great expanse of shingle opened up in front of us. I had not been there before. The distinctive bulk of Dungeness A and Dungeness B stood to our left, bunker style with no windows.

'Only you could find beauty in a place that has two nuclear power stations!' I said.

'That's not fair; it's an amazing place. Look at those houses.'

He had slowed right down and he pointed to some small wooden houses on the shingle. He said they were converted railway carriages. They looked like houses until you looked at the windows and then you could tell that once they had indeed run along railway tracks. Now they were moored on the beach. He said they belonged to the local fishermen. There were a few small boats pulled up on the beach nearby. I saw a sign in front of one of the railway houses that said *Brown Shrimps for Sale*. He parked the car right by the beach.

'How I wish I could run over that shingle and down to the sea. My legs are bad again today. I can hardly feel them.'

'I'll carry you,' he said.

He'd brought a thick blanket with him and he wrapped me in a cocoon of wool and carried me down to the water's edge. Then he walked back to get our picnic. We sat hunched together on the pebbles and I rested my head on his shoulder as we listened to the surge and the suck of the waves. It was so peaceful there, all sea and sky and just the two of us with some gulls wheeling on the up-drift of the gentle breeze. I sat up and started to look at the pebbles around me.

'I'd like to find a completely round pebble,' I said.

'Ever the purist . . .'

'This is such a Markus place. Did you ever come here with Kathy?'

'No, never . . .'

'You weren't suited, Markus.' I said it gently, without malice. 'She doesn't have your amazing clarity.'

'I've never met anyone except you who had my love of clarity! Some people might call it obsessive.'

'It *can* be a bit of a curse.'

'Yes.'

I continued looking for a perfect pebble among the grey, brown and white stones. There were small pieces of green glass among the stones that had been rubbed to a smooth opaqueness by the motion of sea against sand. Markus picked up a piece of driftwood that was lying on the shingle. He looked at it closely with his architect's eye, tracing how the water and the weather had rotted the wood. There were pieces of driftwood all over the beach and some lumps of rusted scrap metal. A few hardy salt-loving beach plants held their place among the pebbles.

'I'm so frightened of losing it, though,' I said after a while.

'Losing your clarity?'

'Losing control of my body. Tanya died at forty-seven. She was in a wheelchair for ten years and gradually every muscle wasted away until she could do nothing.' I shuddered 'Not even swallow.'

He hugged me closer to him then.

'You wouldn't let a dog suffer like that, would you? You'd put the dog out of his misery.'

'You would,' he said, stroking my face.

'It would have been such a kindness to help Tanya out of her misery. No one had the courage to help her die. No one loved her enough to do that.'

I looked at him as I said this. He kissed my lips.

We sat on the shore in silence then and later he unpacked our picnic. He had made cheese sandwiches and brought apples and nuts and raisins. I ate a little. Then a group of three birdwatchers came into view. They had binoculars with them. They seemed to be very excited about a bird they had spotted at the water's edge. We watched them watching the bird.

'It is beautiful here,' I said. 'Bleak but beautiful . . .'

We sat for a while longer. We didn't want to leave until the light had faded from the sky. I felt so calm as I looked at the bowl of the sea and the darkening sky with Markus at my side. Arvo Talvela had been right. My body was weak and my mind had never felt clearer. Nothing would stop me from being true to how I had lived my whole life.

He carried me in his arms back to the car. On the way home we passed one of those small convenience stores that is part of a garage.

'Can you get some milk and a jar of honey, please?'

'You don't often drink milk.'

'I like it warm with honey and some cinnamon sprinkled on top. I don't think you will find cinnamon in there.'

'No chance.'

It was dark as we turned into the road that led to our cottage. Everything I had looked at on our journey back that evening was charged with beauty and meaning in a way I had never felt before. Even the most mundane sights moved me. I noticed the lighted windows of the houses on our road, squares of warm light, the rooms ready for the evening ahead.

When we got out of the car I asked Markus to wait a minute and we stood in the garden together and looked up at the sky. I was so glad it was a cloud-free night and that I could see the stars clearly. Then I walked with difficulty into the kitchen. I found my little tin of pills and pressed the tin into his hands.

'Help me get into bed now, please. I'd like some warm milk and honey. Please grind them fine so they dissolve.'

'Heja, no!'

'You said you would help me.'

'Look after you in your illness, yes.'

'I won't get better, Markus.'

'I know.'

'I cannot bear a slow lingering death.'

'Don't ask me to do this.'

'It's been a perfect day. Perfect. Please, help me. Don't make me argue.'

He carried me up the stairs and undressed me like a child. I wanted to wear the white T-shirt he had been wearing that day so he took it off and put it on me. It swamped me and I could smell a trace of him. He helped me into bed and then he went down to the kitchen.

He seemed to be a long time down there. He won't let me down. I was sitting propped up in bed as he carried the glass to me. His face was pale and I think he might have been crying.

'Heja . . .'

I looked at him.

'I am sure, my love. It is what I want.'

I took the glass and he plumped up my pillows and put his arm around me. I drank the milk slowly, carefully, and drained the glass. Then I lay back against the pillows. He got under the covers next to me and we both lay there, looking at each other. He stroked my hair and my face, knowing how I love that and remembering, I am sure, how I longed for my mother to do that when I was a child. We didn't speak. There was nothing to say. I felt no fear, only the blessing of Markus being there with me.

Later I started to feel waves of deep nausea, one after the other, like very bad seasickness. It brought me to the brink of vomiting. I would not be sick. Somehow I would hold it down. I closed my eyes and made myself breathe slowly and deeply and brought to mind the image of a waterfall, a great rush of clean water splashing into a pool. The nausea went on for ages but I held the sick down. It was my last battle with my body. Then at last the sickness subsided and I felt myself getting drowsy.

'Love you always, Heja,' he said.

I pulled my eyelids open, they were so heavy now. 'Love you always, Markus. Thank you.'

'Rest softly, darling . . .'

What peace to know that nothing else is ever going to happen to me. So many images, such colours: the sun-splashed strawberries in grandfather's garden; my pale pink ballet shoes when I was nine; my father's fishing rod lying on the wet grass; a bowl of oranges and lemons; the light on the river

KATHY

OCTOBER

After Markus left the flat to join her I just stood there in the hall, holding Billy. My heart was unbearably full at that moment. I had my precious boy back and I also knew that Markus and I could never be together again. We were finished. These two extremes of emotion were colliding inside me and I slid down the wall and sat on the floor and sobbed while I held Billy tightly against me.

Jennie arrived several hours later and the next morning my parents joined us. We were joyful to be reunited as a family and I don't think Billy was put down once over the next few days; we all needed to hug him and kiss him and hold him close. I gave my parents the master bedroom and made up a bed for myself on the floor in Billy's room. I kept waking up those first few nights to check he was there, lying safely in his cot. I wondered if he would have any memory of the events of the last week. He had been taken out in that great storm by a stranger. What had she done to him? I scanned his sleeping face and he looked peaceful and unchanged.

The next morning I told my father that Heja must have gone through my bag to steal my keys. That was how she had got into the flat. And she came to the flat while we were out, more than once, I was sure of that.

'That thought chills me so much, Dad; her walking around the flat; going through my things.'

'I'm going to change the locks,' he said.

He was as good as his word. He went out straight away to a locksmith's shop in Marylebone and bought replacement locks for me. When he got back he asked me for a screwdriver and some pliers. I went into Markus's workroom to get his toolbox. It was a large metal box and, as you would expect, every tool sat in its allotted place, ready for use.

As I bent to pick it up I suddenly felt a tremendous sense of loss. Markus would never work in this room again; he would never sit with the light shining on to the plane of his drawing desk while I sat in the armchair, watching him. He would come and take away all his books, his plan chest and his table. The room had become so much his domain that I could not imagine what I would do with it. Heja had wanted to break us up and she did break us up. I couldn't stop the tears that welled up then. I carried the toolbox to my father and he got to work.

'She won't get in again,' he said when he had finished.

I hugged him tightly.

'Why the tears, darling? You're safe now.'

There was joy but there was also anger and incomprehension that Markus could have left me to go to Heja after all she'd done to us. My mother in particular was very angry. Jennie and my father tried to rein her in but she had to give voice to her feelings; she has always had to do that.

The second night Mum was in the kitchen, making chicken with black olive sauce for us. I was in there with her, ironing some of Billy's little T-shirts. She asked me about Heja. I was reluctant to talk about her because I knew it would make Mum agitated. She pressed me for details so I told her some of the things that had been going on and I saw how angry it was making her. I watched her tearing hard to pull the skin off the chicken breasts.

'Don't you need a knife for that?'

'No, it's OK.'

She dropped the skinned chicken breasts into hot oil and started to brown them, moving them around the pan with a wooden spoon. She said she couldn't understand it. Markus was my husband and he owed it to Billy and me to stay with us. She reached for the onions and was slicing them ferociously on the chopping board as she said that Markus should renounce that evil woman! I imagined my mother confronting Heja – what a scene that would be.

Finally I had to say, 'Mum, we can't *ever* be together again. Surely you can see that?'

Mum believes that marriage is for life and I know that all she has ever wanted for me deep down is to have a good marriage and a family. I am not my mother and her manifest anger and disappointment wasn't helpful. I didn't want to stay the angry bitter woman I've been ever since finding that photograph in Botallack. I was sad and hurt yet my overpowering feeling was one of gratitude that Billy was safe.

Jennie had gone back to Cornwall. My parents were with me when Nick came to the flat the next day. I opened the door to him and he asked me how Billy was and I said just wonderful. Then he came in and I introduced him to Mum and Dad and offered him coffee. He said, no, thanks, could we all go into the sitting room as he wanted to update us on developments. I noticed that he was being quite formal with us.

We all sat down in the sitting room and Nick leaned forward and, looking directly at me, said that Heja was dead. I was stunned. I had started to believe that Heja was invincible, that she was capable of anything. She was such a strong, powerful presence so how could she be dead? She had got what she wanted – she had got Markus back. So how could she be dead so quickly?

'How can she be dead?' I finally said.

Nick said that Heja and Markus had been staying at a house in Kent. Markus had contacted the police. She had not died from natural causes.

'What do you mean?' I asked.

'It's an unexplained death. It's not exactly clear what happened. We know she drank a lethal drink.'

'So it was suicide?'

'We can't be sure of that. As I said, it's an unexplained death and we need to investigate it,' he said.

My parents looked worried then.

'You're not saying that Markus had anything to do with it?'

'I'm not saying that, Kathy. We don't have the full picture yet. There is evidence that he was there when it happened.'

'Is he in trouble?'

'We have to carry out a detailed investigation into how Heja died.'

'But he won't be charged with anything?'

He looked at me almost sternly then.

'I can't tell you any more, Kathy. It would be wrong for me to say anything else. I just wanted to update you before it reached the news.'

So Markus was in trouble and the nightmare wasn't over. I should have known that even when she died Heja would not leave us in peace.

KATHY

ONE YEAR LATER

Last night Heja appeared before me. It was as if she was standing in my bedroom at the foot of my bed. I saw her face so clearly: her blonde hair scraped back into a severe French plait; the fine bones of her face that the cameras had loved; and that inscrutable expression when she looked at me across the office. I struggled into wakefulness and felt afraid. I tried to piece together the dream before it melted into the shadows. What had she been doing to me? The details had fled and I was left with an angry heart and a dry mouth.

Why could I never understand that expression in her eyes? There were so many clues I missed. The way she looked at my pregnant bump the very first time we met, on the afternoon Philip and I interviewed her for the job. There was her profound reticence whenever I tried to talk to her. I was an open book then and she was a mystery. I do know that she made me feel inadequate and lacking in finesse and in those early weeks of meeting her I often felt the need to apologize or to appease her.

And then I remembered that today is the actual day in October that she died one year ago. What funny tricks our minds play on us.

The last time I saw her alive was that day she came into my office to resign. She looked so in control and so elegant in her black suit. She walked out of my office but not out of our lives; with her death has come a mountain of trouble.

The police carried out their investigation and they found Markus's fingerprints as well as Heja's on the glass that held the lethal drink. It is illegal to assist in a suicide and Markus is currently standing trial for assisting in Heja's death. We are living apart and I've been attending his trial every day to give him some support during his awful ordeal.

I work from home now because after Billy was kidnapped I gave up my editorship of the magazine. I did it without a second thought or even a pang of regret as I was never again going to leave Billy in the care of another person. Rather to my surprise, Philip Parr and I came to an understanding and he agreed that I could edit the World Heritage guides from home.

I did ask Fran to look after Billy just for the duration of the trial and she's been coming to the flat every day. She'll be here soon so I need to get up. I swing my legs out of bed and put the kettle on. Then I get washed and dressed quickly. Billy's still asleep so I'll let him sleep on. I wait for the bell and I buzz Fran in, make her a cup of tea and then hurry out of the flat to get to the court in time.

The last three days in court have been difficult enough for me to sit through so how must Markus be feeling? He sits in the dock and looks impassive, unperturbed almost. I cannot believe he is not in turmoil. No one has come from his family to support him. No one. Heja's mother and father are here; they have been all week. Her father has looked very emotional at times and has cried more than once during the proceedings. Her mother has kept her composure throughout. She looks a bit of an ice queen, like her daughter. Robert Mirzoeff is here too, sitting next to them.

The trial is getting a lot of press attention, particularly

from the Finnish media. Heja was such a big name there, the face of Finnish TV news, and now she is mysteriously dead. I've been watching the international news every night on the internet and something of a myth is growing up in Finland around Heja and Markus – the beautiful blonde presenter dead at thirty-five and her left-wing lover in the dock. Their angle seems to be that Markus is an honourable man who helped her die out of love and who is being hounded by a vindictive legal system. A Finnish camera crew has been outside every day and the judge got irritated at one point by the 'media circus', as he called it.

Today the testimony is focusing on Heja's illness. Her father cried a lot while the doctor described the symptoms and trajectory of her dreadful disease. I started to feel hopeful for Markus, though, because the medical evidence gives such a clear motive for her suicide. She was suffering from a catastrophic muscle-wasting disease and it had taken a strong hold of her at the point at which she killed herself. Heja was, of course, *capable* of killing herself. We all knew by then how much she needed to control her life; so why not also the time and manner of her death? And she could have done it so easily on her own. Why did she make Markus play his part?

It's been another long and upsetting day. At the end of proceedings the solicitor takes me to the small conference room in the court as Markus has agreed to meet with me. The verdict will be given tomorrow and what a very difficult night Markus has ahead of him. I feel no animosity towards him any more; I just want to strip away the secrets and the lies that have built up between us.

Markus comes in and sits at the table opposite me and the solicitor leaves us on our own. It is, finally, an honest conversation between us. He starts by saying that if he's found guilty then on no account am I to visit him or ever to bring Billy to the prison.

'You can't go to jail! It would be too unfair!'

He smiles at my vehemence.

'One of the things I've always liked about you, Kathy, is your optimism and your belief that things will turn out for the best. It isn't going to be like that. I think there is every chance that they'll find me guilty.'

Then he tells me everything. How he'd left Heja suddenly after yet another fight. It was only a few weeks later that she found out she had the terrible illness and would die prematurely. I said then that he did not know that she was ill, so he mustn't blame himself for leaving her when he did. I know he does. He said she had been helped by Arvo Talvela, a famous Finnish analyst. Then he died suddenly while Heja was still under his care. It was this that had triggered her move to London. She must have decided then that she needed him to help her die, he said.

'She was dealt some devastating blows. But why did she make you help her, Markus? She could have done it on her own,' I said.

'I've been thinking about that too. It was a test, I think, a test to show how much I loved her. I've been feeling tremendous rage against her these last few days. I've recognized an old feeling from our relationship; Heja drawing me in step by step into doing what she wanted me to do.'

And I think to myself, yes, she did that to him – love, guilt and reparation. Of course, he did love her deeply. There was the deepest connection between them.

I hardly slept last night. Fran arrives early and I get to court and sit down and I'm feeling sick with nerves because it's the day of sentencing and what happens today will impact on all our lives. The media are here in force again. There is a strong feeling of anticipation in the court as we are all assembled to hear Markus's fate and the last act is about to be played out.

During the summing-up I can see that two things may go against him. Firstly, there was no evidence that Heja had persistently expressed the wish to die or had shown a 'clear, settled and informed decision to take her own life', as they put it. She was ill, but she was coping with her illness, they claim. There was ample evidence that she lived well, held a good job and had a beautiful home.

The second and most damaging fact that has come out is that Markus stands to gain by Heja's death. She left everything to him, her large flat by the river and a lot of money. Her will was in a box at her flat together with photographs of Markus and every letter and card he'd sent her over the course of their nine-year relationship. Markus has said very little throughout the trial, but he did say that he had no idea that Heja had left him her estate. And crucially Pieter Vanheinen, her father, spoke up for him on this point, saying he believed Markus was wholly motivated by compassion. He said that anyone who knew Markus would know that financial considerations would play no part in anything he did.

I also wonder if Markus's very reserve, his refusal to plead or even to open up at all under questioning, is also hurting him. He has stood in the dock every day, proud and silent and giving the impression that he does not recognize the authority of the court to judge his actions. He has such contempt for these institutions of authority. I'm afraid this will go against him.

They are about to announce the verdict. I clench my hands

so tightly on the wooden bench in front of me, willing them to let him off, to let him have his life back. Markus is a man who needs his freedom so much and prison would be the most terrible ordeal for him.

Markus is pronounced guilty of assisting Heja in her suicide. His face is so pale and set when the judge announces the verdict. He is given a fifteen-month prison sentence.

At the end of the trial I see Pieter Vanheinen and Robert standing together. Her father says, 'It's a travesty of justice. I don't blame her and I don't blame Markus. My poor little girl must have been so frightened.'

Robert replies in a solemn voice, 'She was the brightest star, Pieter, and the brightest stars shine for the shortest time.'

Pieter shakes his hand warmly. I look at them standing there, united in their loss and their high-minded feelings, and I'm furious at how they are rewriting history. They're forgetting what Heja did in the last months of her life; how she caused us so much fear and misery. She stole Billy from his home and now Markus is going to prison. Yet somehow the tragedy of a beautiful woman dying young seems to have absolved her of any criticism. That is the power of a beautiful face.

I hurry over to Markus's solicitor and ask if he really has to go to prison. Can't he appeal the sentence? He says Markus has told him he doesn't want to appeal. He won't serve the full fifteen months; he will be out in under a year. Under a year. Billy will have no contact with his father for all those months and that is a long time in the life of an infant. And one day we'll have to tell Billy that Heja kidnapped him; one day we'll have to tell him that his father went to prison. Markus will never build his arts centre and cinema in Durham now. It was his most cherished project. He will come out of prison but he'll never really be free because he is implicated for ever in her death. She made sure of that. How cruel and perverse that her legacy to him has helped put him into prison. I'm worried that he will withdraw even more from contact with people after his term in prison. He's always had a tendency to shut out the world.

I think about her more often than I would like and perhaps more often than is good for me. Is it because I have unfinished business with her? Is it because I never got the opportunity to tell her what I thought of her actions? Looking back, I can see that I was open and optimistic then. I was also a bit careless and unprotected. Now I find myself questioning other people's motives much more than I used to and I am more guarded in my relationships.

A few weeks later I'm on my way home from one of my occasional work meetings with Philip Parr and I decide to walk back to the flat up Primrose Hill and through the park. As I reach the brow of the hill I stop to admire the view of London laid out below me. There is my city with all its many lives and all its many possibilities. I suddenly feel wistful, as if I'm missing out on those possibilities. That evening I email Hector and tell him that Billy and I are coming to Lisbon for Christmas and I need a friend. I hope he understands. I'm not ready to trust again or get involved, but I need a friend.

Could Markus and I have built something lasting? We came together when we were both feeling lonely and troubled and looking for new beginnings. There were those weeks during my pregnancy when we achieved a precarious happiness. It was a fragile thing and Heja arrived in our lives shortly afterwards.

Heja is dead but the dead do not lie down. She fought so

hard against her illness. What extraordinary willpower she possessed to track Markus down, to torment me, to steal Billy and to get Markus back. We get on with our lives, we are productive, but you don't forget someone like Heja Vanheinen.

ACKNOWLEDGEMENTS

My warmest thanks to the fantastic team at Head of Zeus whose love of books is inspiring; and especially to Laura Palmer for her very smart suggestions that made this novel better and to Becci Sharpe for her support.

I am lucky indeed to have so committed a champion as Gaia Banks, my agent, and thanks too to Lucy Fawcett for her encouragement – both of Sheil Land.

They say you write with an ideal reader in mind. Well I had four: my daughter Amelia Trevette, Roomana Mahmud, Karolyn Shindler and Jan Thompson. Thank you all for reading and discussing earlier drafts with me.

Jessie Price created the stunning film noir cover of the paperback which feels perfect. Ros Jesson was responsible for the meticulous copy-editing and Nick Trevette gave me expert guidance on police and legal procedure. Thank you all.

Most of all my special thanks to Barry Purchese for his masterly feedback and loving support.

QUESTIONS FOR YOUR BOOKCLUB

- The story is told from the perspectives of two female characters, Kathy and Heja. Who do you think is most important to the plot? Do you feel sympathetic towards them?

- Kathy is 'embarrassed and ashamed' of her body at times Heja feels that she is 'carrying her death' around with her. Does self-image affect the way that other people treat them? Is the difference between image and reality important in this novel?

- Kathy finds Heja 'coolly immaculate' and 'inscrutable' and seems to find these traits both enviable and unnerving. Do you admire Heja's self-control?

- Sea bream, salt cod, rye bread, spaghetti vongole, garlic... Meals carry a lot of significance for these characters. Why do you think that is, and how does the author convey this?

- Should Heja's illness absolve her of judgement?

- We only meet Markus through the eyes of Kathy and Heja. How does that affect the way we feel about him?

- Mothers and children are an important theme in this

novel. How do you think the two mothers of the main characters, Luisa and Solange, have affected their daughter's lives?

- In persecuting Kathy, what do you think Heja was trying to achieve? Do you think she was successful?

- 'Kathy thinks she has everything: the job; the baby; the friends and him. But she does not have my will.' From the very first line, we are inside the heads of the characters. How does this affect the way you feel about them? Do you always trust their versions of events?